IN NOT-TOO-DISTANT FUTURE...

ROBERT LEAL. Clever, playful, sly. A New York 'game master', he sells decadent fantasies to the rich and the bored...and the sensual scenarios he runs help him ignore his own fragile mortality. Then he hears the voice of an old friend, a voice from beyond the grave.

CHRISTOPHER KANE. Robert's long-dead friend, alive in the realm of Capricorn. Charismatic, talented, and feisty, he is the leader of the transdimensional rock group known as The Feral Cell and foremost in Capricorn's fierce battle against The Undying Cabal.

CAPRICORN. An alternate world neither dead nor alive, ravaged by forces of malice. Here lies the key to what could either be Robert's salvation—or the total destruction of both of his worlds.

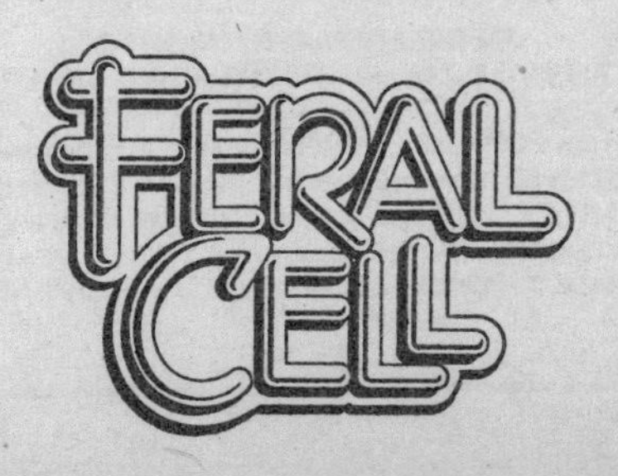

Also by
RICHARD BOWES

Warchild

Published by
POPULAR LIBRARY

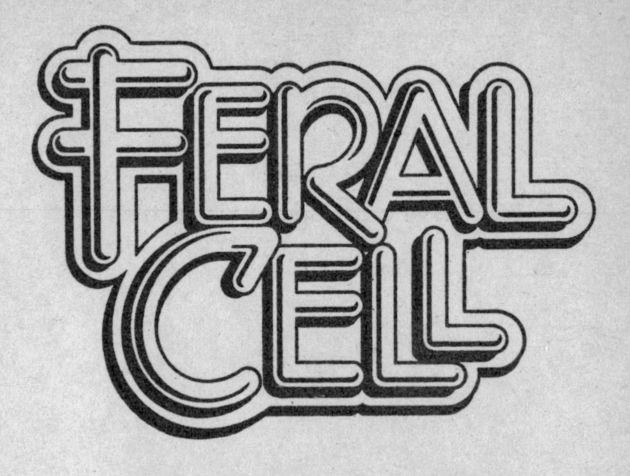

RICHARD BOWES

POPULAR LIBRARY

An Imprint of Warner Books, Inc.

A Warner Communications Company

For Gerry with deepest affection

POPULAR LIBRARY EDITION

Cover illustration by Stephen Gervais

Popular Library books are published by
Warner Books, Inc.
666 Fifth Avenue
New York, N.Y. 10103

 A Warner Communications Company

Printed in the United States of America

First Printing: May, 1987

10 9 8 7 6 5 4 3 2 1

PROLOGUE

The events of which I am going to tell you began a week before the winter solstice, more than a year before the third millennium. Downtown in Manhattan everyone on the scene knew that the era of Andy Warhol, the silver prince, was ending. Nobody knew what was going to happen next, although the rumor was that New York was going to join the long list of places that had gone bad.

My name is Robert Leal, and at the time my story begins, I was a game master. That is, I was one who for a fee concocted mystery and memorable events for clients whose lives seemed dull compared to those they saw on television.

Some might think that at that time everybody in New York was selling dreams and illusions, whether in the form of art or drugs or financial speculation. But in fact the city contained the whole spectrum of humanity, the hard working and the damned, the righteous and the unemployable, the honest and the police. And all were about to witness the coming of the Beast.

CHAPTER

One

My first hints of Capricorn started one night with me in a black cape, slouch hat, and fake nose sitting in the back seat of a rented Bentley between two half-naked Swedish twins. Up front my assistant, Bridge and Tunnel, was dressed as a chauffeur. Crouched next to him, a kid from Vain Video Co-op, sprouting minicameras, taped and recorded everything. Following us down lower Broadway that December Thursday night were four dentists in a van.

"So, my children," I hissed as the cameras ground, "you understand what will happen to you!" I was giving an overripe performance as a character of my own invention: Dr. Cobalt. The twins, Erik and Erika, young and not quite sure of themselves, nodded.

A team of my dentists, following clues I had planted, had found the twins arriving at Kennedy Airport, "captured" them, and taken everything but their overcoats. Making them vulnerable was a turn-on for the dentists and maybe for potential video viewers. If it made them happy it was good for my business as a game master. The kids' bodies didn't do much for me. Nothing did. I was dying fast and not facing it.

Followed by the van, we turned onto my block. The club

called Toys stood on the north corner. Peroxide-haired kids hustling in their neo-Carnaby clothes paused to watch us pass. We rolled down to the front of my building, a two-story job opposite a gas station at the Lafayette end of the street. Bridge and Tunnel stopped and got out. I dropped the Cobalt hiss and spoke to the twins in my own voice for a moment.

"You understand the releases you signed? You'll be with us until Saturday, at which point Phil Armbruster will pick you up. Right now you are going to be turned over to my clients with nothing but the code of ethics of the American Dental Association to protect you."

People approached the car. My clients were insurance brokers, computer programmers, lawyers, but I called them dentists because I felt they had the souls of dentists. They had names but I won't bore you with them. They opened the rear door and cold air hit us. The twins shivered.

"Shift them," barked B&T, and the dentists began hauling the Swedes to my house. He came around and ostentatiously helped me out. "Let me give you a hand, Dad," he said, forgetting the Albanian accent he was supposed to have.

"Shut up, Danello," I breathed, exhausted but remembering to call B&T by the name that I had given him as the chauffeur. Then the cold cut through me, and I was glad to have B&T's arm. At the Broadway end of the block, the kid hustlers stood still in their Regency overcoats and watched. The moon shone that night on New York, the Dream Crusher, the Empire City where you could get everything from a Keith Haring original to a case of AIDS, often from the same person.

Out of nowhere came a puff of warmth, and I was aware of a piercing smell of grass in summer and of the memory of a lost friend. Then I saw someone striding toward me. Joan had opened the front door of the building. My clients were herding the twins. The striding figure was among us. I had an impression of a blond-haired youth with oriental eyes. One hand held a gun.

"Watch it!" I said out of character. The dentists and B&T

looked but couldn't see. I could see but wasn't going to be able to move fast enough.

The gun was a foot in front of my face. The eyes that looked into mine shimmered. But the gun, in the unending second I stared at it, gleamed bone white and solid. Seeing the way I stared, thinking I was going to faint, Joan moved to help me and smacked right into the kid. His arm in its regency sleeve flew up, his blond hair came off, and his gun hit the pavement. Suddenly everyone could see him. "I had him all the way," Joan said.

"Why didn't you say something, Danello?" I hissed at B&T.

"Joan had him all the way."

"Get them inside," I told him. Swedes and clients alike were gaping at this newest manifestation of my art. Bridge and Tunnel herded them through my front door. Joan tried to grab the assailant. He was going for the gun, but I bent, fumbled once or twice, and picked it up. My fingers felt clumsy. But the gun was warm in my hand. It was a beautiful thing with a carved bone handle. Thongs activated a sort of cross-bow mechanism. The filigreed ivory barrel had several chambers loaded with what I guessed must be cylinders of paint. I was still thinking in terms of games.

"Get the glimmer twins ready in the garage," I told Joan. "I'll take care of this one." She looked doubtful. But the thongs on the gun were taut, and when I stuck it in the kid's face, he went rigid. I shoved him into the alley beside my building. So she nodded and went inside.

I looked at the face in front of me. The features were Chinese, and young; the eyes, as alive as a cornered animal's; the face, so pale it seemed to flicker in the alley light. "Answer a couple of questions very nicely and I don't empty paint all over your hair and clothes," I said in my back-of-the-throat voice. "What's your name?"

"Bloodsucker!" he said. I tapped the bow strings with one of my fingers and felt them hum. The kid felt it too. "Billy Gee," he said.

The name was phoney. The idea was to get him started answering questions. "Who sent you to do this?"

"Some fucking bloodsuckers," he answered.

"And we all look alike, right? But somehow you managed to pick me out. You don't know me. I don't remember ever having met you. You were waiting here. I came along and you jumped out. Who put you up to it?"

He looked away from the gun into my eyes. "The Undying Cabal is gonna drink your blood." The words meant nothing to me. But the kid's eyes held mine for a second. They were burning and dying at the same time.

"Hey, you disappoint me. The first Chinese punk who didn't say his big brother in the Shadow Warriors was going to come and get me."

"Shadow Warriors are all dead or in jail. It's the Cabal now. They'll use you as Chase bait. I've seen you floating like a ghost in Capricorn." There was wonder as well as contempt in his voice.

Which made no sense. But from his eyes I guessed he was gone on something heavy. One of the new synthetics, like Salvation or Dawn, probably. "Where can I find out more?" He looked at me, shaking his head in pity at my stupidity. I stuck the gun in his face.

He jerked his head in the direction of Toys. "Under the goat's head, man," said this street kid who was never going to see twenty-one. "They don't need to send me. You won't last. I saw you in Capricorn tonight, you were clearer than you are now." As he said that I realized he was working something around in his mouth. He bit down on it.

I had hold of his coat front with one hand. Suddenly he stepped free of it and backed down the alley. I aimed the gun at him, and he turned and fled. Billy Gee seemed to become part of the shadows or to pass through a wall. Nothing was left but a pile of hustler threads lying on the ground.

I turned the gun to a wall a few feet away and aimed at the poster of an already forgotten candidate from the '98 elections. My pressing the trigger released a hook that held the sinews. The twang of those bow strings seemed to come from the middle distance. The filigreed barrel ejected a capsule.

I expected bright yellow paint, a little prank by my friendly, rival game masters. Instead, the face, the poster, the paint on the wall disappeared. Acid bubbled and spat as my guts turned over.

That could have been my face, my eyes. I would have been writhing blind on the street right then, the clients and the Swedes marveling at my game mastery, B&T and Joan calling an ambulance and preparing for the arrival of the cops. As I visualized that, the night seemed warm and the gun felt alive.

My first instinct was to throw it away. My second was to examine it carefully. A crab was engraved on one side of the bone hand grip, a goat on the other: the astrological symbols of Cancer and Capricorn. It was light and so small and flat that after snapping the trigger guard back on, I put it in my cloak pocket and went inside. It was well after midnight, and I wanted to wrap up the evening's entertainment.

Inside, Joan was coming out the door to what had been a stable and then a garage and which was now refitted as an extra special rumpus room. She was dressed in leather leotards and platform boots—a jailer costume. Even wearing a Tina Turner wig, she still stood only five foot four, and her face looked small and concerned when she glanced at me.

"Is nothing, Natasha, darling," I hissed loudly. Upstairs in my loft I could hear the clients' voices raised in stoned argument. I stepped into the garage, which tonight had been turned into the secret chambers of a sadistic planetary security chief. The main furnishings were Erik and Erika, tied to tables, naked, stoned out of their minds.

"Ah, my little Swedish meatballs," I said in my Dr. Cobalt voice loudly enough for any client listening to have heard. Then, quietly and out of character, I said, "The hoards will be down here in a few minutes. Fourteen warped American dentists will try to extract secrets from you. The ones you are to give them are the ones I asked on the phone that you memorize. You remember them?"

"Our uncle is a tall dark man with a limp," said Erika.

"He owned a stone necklace, which—" began Erik.

I cut him off. "Fine. All I ask is that you play them along for half an hour or so. Give out the secrets little by little. Joan will be here to make sure there's no permanent damage. Understand?"

They nodded, looking curious and apprehensive. This was the first day of their North American vacation. It would be bizarre and disorienting, at moments dangerous, at times disgusting. But it would be free, and when it was over they could go back to Sweden and start game mastering on their own. They were twenty-one and out to make their fortune before Stockholm went bad.

I had gotten use of them free in return for favors rendered to Phil Armbruster, who ran games up in Connecticut. I closed the door on them, and Joan handed me a mirror with three thick lines of my private coke. I got that free in return for all the dentists' business I threw the dealer's way. "My life is an endless promotional consideration," I told Joan as I inhaled deeply three times.

"Another week with this bunch, and we can take a Christmas break," she told me. "Better straighten your wig," she added.

I tilted the mirror up, saw myself: black slouch hat, flowing white hair, powerful nose, eyes sunken and exhausted. Only the eyes were mine. I adjusted the hat and wig, unfurled my cape. "Any idea who sent the kid to see me?" I asked.

"Someone who wanted to see you all covered with paint." She had made the same mistake I had. "A business rival? Things are getting scary, Rob." She said that as flatly as if she were telling me there was a leak in the cellar.

I was going to mention the acid but thought better of it. Paint was an embarrassment. Acid was real. Instead I started up the stairs hissing under my breath. "Dentists of America, here I come."

My loft was the whole top floor of the building. The front half was a rolling plain of rugs, couches, entertainments electronic and organic. Lounging on my furniture, dressed in everything from medieval leather-wear to Star Trek uniforms, fourteen clients abused my opiated hash.

"So, Dr. Cobalt, I guessed correctly," a client said in a dull and outlandish accent of his own devising. "I beat you and your 'son' to the airport."

"Yes, kind sir, very astutely." With sufficient hints and clues he had guessed when and where the Swedes would get off the plane. "The prince and princess are downstairs awaiting your questions."

"How many answers will we be able to get out of them?" someone asked.

"Answers come in threes, I believe."

"Why only threes?"

Because, I thought to myself, that's all I bothered to invent. Now hurry up and find them, so you can get back to Montclair and drill teeth. Aloud, I said, "It is as it is," and shrugged at the cosmic mystery of it all. "Now, hasten to question them. Then depart. There will be messages on all your answering machines tomorrow morning."

They all got up and shambled to the door, yuppies with lots of money and unfulfilled childhoods. "They looked very arrogant when we caught them, demanded that we address them as Your Highness," a woman giggled. "But we made them undress under their coats, and it took the fight out of them." I hoped making a Swede take off his underpants was worth two and a half grand to her.

One lingered for a moment. "I liked the hash."

"Glad to hear it," I said out of character, turning away.

"And I wondered about getting some."

"B&T will give you the connection," I said, walking to the door of my loft. "Show's over," I added.

My sleeping area was a big room with high ceilings and a skylight. In there, alone for the first time since morning, I shed the hat and the wig. The nose came off with a little pop. Sitting at a makeup table in front of a mirror, I removed from a drawer a little wooden box that I'd had for years. Only when I'd calculated my ups and downs for the day, opened the box, rolled a small opium ball, and swallowed it, was I ready to confront the mirror.

Off came the antique evening clothes that I used for my Dr. Cobalt character. I dismantled the face, removing the white spider eyebrows, the contact lenses that glittered in the right light, the teeth that half resembled fangs. When I was finished, I looked in the glass.

There sat Robert Leal, game master, designer—for a fee —of fantasies for those too dull or too lazy to have any of their own. The face I saw was almost as alien as Cobalt's. Who was this gaunt forty-eight-year-old man with gray-flecked hair? An actor with a gimmick, a guy who had known good times and was waiting for the opium to come on so that he could catch a distant memory of them.

Below me the clients made merry with the Swedes. One thing remained to do before I could fall out. Maybe the accumulation of drugs and fantasy over the last years had kept me from understanding that this last task of the night was real.

Standing up, I felt myself float for a moment as I dressed in black jeans and shirt. Putting on a foreign-correspondent trench coat, I slipped the gun I'd found into an outside pocket. For an instant I heard a horn call, looked up at the skylight over my bed, at the windows and back door. As I listened, the sound faded.

Downstairs I found B&T and Joan waiting in their back apartment for the party to break, like minor players standing in the wings for the last scene and the curtain calls. "Bridge and Tunnel, my boy," I said quietly, "will you please stop calling me Dad in every goddamn scenario we do. Now I have to put in some kind of crap about Danello the chauffeur being Cobalt's son."

B&T, six-feet-two inches of gym muscles, smiled his crooked smile. He was called Bridge and Tunnel because he came from the outer boroughs. The eyes beneath the brim of his cap were a foot apart. "Right you are, Pops," he said giving a little salute.

Joan had brought him into my life when she started working for me ten years before. I had known her since she was an underage kid in peroxide hair hanging around the clubs looking for a touch of fame. You could say the three of us were a kind of ménage. "Where are you off to?" she asked.

"Toys." I touched the gun in the overcoat. "I just want to talk to someone." Muffled screams and laughter came from the garage.

"I left stuff, salad and chicken, in your refrigerator. Your phone messages are on your desk." Joan's last name had been Arque when I first knew her. Her last name changed a lot till she settled on a simple Jones. I'd met her mother, a gabby Italian lady from Jersey City, and I couldn't get Joan's real last name even from her. But the Joan was constant and authentic.

Now Joan wore her hair short and dark and didn't go out an awful lot. She and B&T were twenty years younger than I, too young to look as worried about me as they did. I resented it. If we were a triangle, then my side was badly warped out of shape.

"Good night," I said. A hysterical shriek burst from the garage. "Better check on the dentists," I added on my way down the hall and out the front door.

The crowd of kids in front of Toys had thinned out. Either they had found patrons to take them inside or they had only been waiting before to see the show put on at my place. Toys' front door was right on the corner.

As I approached Broadway a blond-headed figure stepped up and asked, "Take me inside?" Remembering Billy Gee, I shied for a second. "It won't cost you nothing," the hustler said seeing my reaction. "I need an escort. My brother's in there and I gotta find him."

Any tired line would do. It was the law of the city that a kid could go into a place that served liquor only in the company of an adult relative. Nightly, the front stairs of Toys saw uncles and aunts united with nieces and nephews they had never met before. Stepping around the kid I continued walking.

"Mister. I need to get in there right away." The voice had

an edge to it. I looked and saw the face of a girl, maybe fourteen, under bangs so straight they looked ironed. She was Spanish, thin, tired and grubby. A boy just as blond and no older waited, ready to try the moment she failed. Unable to think of a reason for not bringing her, I nodded, and she followed me.

Toys had started out as a bank building at the turn of the century. CHEMICAL EXCHANGE TRUST was still engraved among gargoyles and goddesses over the door. Just one doorman remained on duty. It was Otis, never one of my favorites but not an enemy either, someone who had been letting me into clubs for the past twenty years.

"How's it going, Otis?" I asked. He looked right through me, focused on the girl. "I think my, uh niece, and I are on the list."

As I said that, he saw me, and I caught something between fear and uncertainty in his eyes. He touched the brim of his high silk hat. "Mr. Leal. There's a new owner and a new door policy starting tonight." Otis was black and stood a head or two over me. He gave the doorman smile, all teeth and dead eyes.

I rocked back on my heels. "If there's been some kind of misunderstanding just between us." I reached into my pocket for a tip, felt the gun, saw figures move under tall trees. Fear triumphed over uncertainty in Otis's eyes.

"Hey, I got money, too," the hustler said, digging into the pockets of her coat. "I need to get in before it closes." She sounded very anxious. Half a dozen other hustlers watched us. Behind them, some kids on skates paused to look on. A woman in her forties with a nephew in his late teens, a kid with earrings and full makeup, stumbled as she walked up the stairs but got waved right in.

Just to test Otis' reaction, I said, "Billy Gee told me to ask here about the Undying Cabal."

"I have to go talk to someone," he said backing away.

"Otis, darling, let him in. I can assure you Benjy will say it's OK." Standing in the doorway, his thin face somewhere between an aesthetic's and a clown's, was Jason Beautemps.

We had started out not much liking each other, but over thirty or so years on guest lists, we had become fellow veterans of the circuit. "If he doesn't, just say you never saw him."

Some kind of calculation took place behind the doorman's eyes, and he nodded me through. The kid followed, unnoticed. "What have you been up to, Robert?" Jason asked as we crossed the lobby. "How have you been? And your assistants." There was an instant's pause here while he remembered. "Little Joan and B&T?"

More people were hanging around the lobby than I had expected. Some were gossip writers like Jason himself.

"What the hell was that about at the door?" I asked loudly. "Any time in the last five years I could walk in here." As I complained, Jason guided me through the lobby to where a double flight of marble stairs flanked a pair of bronze doors that led to what had once been the business floor of the bank. We stopped at the foot of the stairs.

"What brings you here?" he asked.

"A kid named Billy Gee."

"Billy Gee went with the Cabal," said the girl beside me.

I wanted to hear more but Jason glanced up the stairs and said, "There's your brother." A Spanish kid in a leather jacket who looked like her stood at the top. Without hesitating, she ran up the stairs, and they disappeared together.

To get my attention back, Jason asked, "And you are what? Smitten by Mr. Gee? Anxious to meet his sister? About to go into business with him?" His manner was as piss elegant as his name. He had watched it all, seen Pop Art and the Velvet Underground come and go, seen New York become obsessed with late-night television comedians, restaurants, painters, rejuvenation, fugitive foreign millionaires. "I don't hang out here myself," he said. "Just dropped by to see the place before Mangin has his way with it."

"Billy Gee tried to blind me just now."

"And you came looking for him here?" Jason gave me the same kind of look that the doorman had: an eye-flash inventory. "It's those silly games that you play, Robby. Reality erosion."

"No doubt." I touched the weapon in my pocket and felt like I was going to faint. Would I use it on someone? No. So what was I doing here? I would have to either do coke or sleep soon. It seemed that I could hear hunting horns. "Maybe it was just something the kid told me so he could escape. I don't think so, though."

"You think this is one of your games. Maybe at your end of the block it is. Down here it's your friend Mangin's game." Jason stared at me as he said the name.

"Why do you keep mentioning him?"

"Because Benjy Mangin is running the place now, sugar cake. His trust fund owned the property all along. The Chemical Exchange was granddaddy Mangin's bank. The old management went bust, and he took over just this week. It's supposed to be a big secret."

"This is the same one who was around when I first came to New York?" I tried to remember him.

"Right. He looked like he had never been young." Jason looked around and said, "I mean a serious troll."

"Not good looking," I agreed. "On the other hand he had a lousy personality." I remembered a heavy, sullen face, a slow boring voice. We made fun of him but only behind his back, said he was a creature from another dimension. He had a way of making us uneasy.

"But he had more money than he could count."

"Meaning he was very wealthy or very stupid. Or both."

"He's not stupid." Jason sounded sure of that. "And he's richer than ever. They said his grandfather could pick people's pockets from all the way across a room. Thirty years ago we weren't supposed to care about money. Only about youth and happiness and freedom. Stuff young Benjy couldn't understand." Jason Beautemps turned and lead me to the bronze doors. "Now, being rich and dull is where it's at." The doors to the main playpen opened, washing us with light and sound.

The music was Gerry and the Pacemakers singing "Don't

Let the Sun Catch You Crying." The last great turn that music, fashion, nostalgia had taken centered around the years 1964–1966, when the Boomers had first found themselves.

That was why the kid who had picked me up wore an imitation Carnaby Street miniskirt and a blond mod wig. From a distance, in the right light, when the customer was in the right mood, she might evoke a moment a third of a century ago when she was unthought of and Boomers were young.

The floor of the main room at Toys slipped under my feet. The walls changed from orange to purple and pulsed in and out. It had been called the Trip Room back when the club had opened five years before. The idea was that it evoked the acid experience without necessarily subjecting middle-aged bodies and minds to the muss and fuss of heart attack and memory loss.

Now it was a dying club; most nights a few April–September couples moved in the flashing lights, slid on the pulsing floor. The panel I stood on fell a few inches while Jason's moved up.

"I've seen this several times before. What's the point?"

"The point is that New York's going bad," said Mr. Beautemps. My mind recoiled automatically as it did whenever certain subjects came up. As Jason ran on about the plight of the city, I looked around. There were more people here than I had thought. And some of them weren't with companions forty-three percent their age. A Japanese fashion designer and his black boyfriend were at the bar. Looking through the lights I saw well-preserved faces from the club-and-party circuit, eyes hooded and intent as they rode the undulating floor.

Following my gaze Jason said, "There's a lot of nervous money in New York right now, honey buns. If New York goes, where do these people go next? What if someone had the ultimate escape hatch?"

I was beginning to fall out. The opium had turned off a few pains I had forgotten I had. Toys was a dream. "You mean they all come to this place that topped out four summers ago and wait for the waters to rise?"

"Why does Mangin come back to New York after all these years and want to operate a club in granddad's old bank? Both his grandfather and father died mysteriously, you know."

"I guess Benjy's just a sentimental fool. Jason, it's been like old times, but I must go home." I tried to turn, but the panel I was standing on suddenly slid the other way. The floor began dancing to a different rhythm. The lights went to a pulsing blue, and a gray fog rose up.

"Don't leave just now, cookie. You may find out something that could save your life."

At that moment my breath got short; the hair on my neck stood up. Instinctively I grasped the gun in my pocket. The door of the VIP lounge across the floor had opened, but I was seeing through the wall. Figures holding torches wavered under trees, watching as a burly man strode toward the floor of Toys.

Everyone on the floor and at the bar squinted, fascinated by what they had obviously come to see. As the man moved toward us his stride turned into a sort of slogging step. That was familiar. So was the blob of a face when I made that out. Benjy Mangin lurched among us dressed in a black-leather outfit with a hood, looking like a very kinky member of the Inquisition.

He rode on a puff of summer air, a rustling of trees, and somehow in that bizarre costume in that disorienting room he seemed less foolish and more awesome than I had ever seen him before. He looked right at me, and as he did a kid who had been dead for twenty-seven years sang, "It's a marvelous night for a moon dance."

At first I assumed it was Van Morrison, then I realized the voice was more familiar. It belonged to Chris Kane, as close a friend as I'd ever had. I knew every song he ever recorded, had taken a hand in winding up his estate, helped produce the memorial album. "Moon Dance" had been one of Chris's turntable hits. He played Van Morrison's recording a lot. As far as I knew he'd never even done a basement tape of it.

"A little sabotage, I think," said the voice at my side. I realized that Jason was watching my reactions very closely. "Is that Kane or not? Mangin certainly seems to think it is."

The crowd had began to buzz when the music started. Mangin was staring at the deejay booth up near the ceiling, looking shocked and outraged, the lights and floor making him seem to undulate. Benjamin Mangin III had been away from New York for some years. He had left at the center of a scandal. Afterward, the usual rumors abounded: illness, madness, satan cults.

Mangin's face was the same gray blob; his gestures, spastic. But his eyes darted, the lips were tight with fury, and I remembered what I had realized once many years before: this was one dork who could kill.

The ones who stood behind him watching were even more interesting to me. Some wore the same kind of black doublet and pants as Mangin. Others were brightly dressed in reds and yellows. It was hard for me to bring them into focus. They seemed to elongate and waver like flames in a wind.

Mangin gave an order. Someone ran to the disc jockey's booth obviously to kill the music. "Moon Dance" played a little longer. I concentrated on trying to pick out the place where it became just an impersonation of Chris. I couldn't find any seams. The voice had the high rasp with just the hint of sweetness; the singer took the song slowly. "To make sure you are never alone . . ."

Suddenly it was gone. In the silence I realized that Mangin was staring right at me.

I stared back. "Where did that track come from?" I asked Jason. No reply. I looked where he had been, and found I stood alone. Very unobtrusively a man and woman, both in blazers, appeared beside me. The club security people gestured for me to approach the presence. I took one step forward and stopped.

"Dr. Cobalt, I presume." Without appearing to shift a muscle, Mangin suddenly stood right before me. A smile sliced his face like a knife through butter. The voice was just as silly as I remembered, soft and slurred, sounding like an unknown Loony Tunes character, a relative of Elmer Fudd and Sylvester the cat. And he had the trace of an accent.

"Only during working hours, Benjamin. I'm plain Bobby Leal right now, an ordinary guy just like you."

"It's your game I want to talk about, Leal."

"Kind of you to be interested." For some reason the ridiculous voice made the hair on my neck bristle.

"I think you challenged me just now." He indicated the sound system, the deejay booth. "I challenge you. I want your Swedes."

"I guess if I'd just bought a nice place where lonely chicken hawks could meet third-world kids, I'd want to upgrade it . . ." I trailed off. Without music my voice carried over the dance floor.

"It's a pity you are such a fool, Leal." Mangin's voice sounded angry. "But I have a foolish proposal. I'm told you play a variety of Keep the Flag as part of your game. I have played something similar with your friend Phil Armbruster at my place in Westchester. We'll call it Keep the Swedes. If I win that's what I do. If you win, there's ten thousand dollars in it."

All the time he was speaking I tried to focus my eyes on the place Mangin had come from. He seemed to know a lot about me, but I was egocentric enough to think that was only natural. "Fuck you and your money," I said smiling, the idea for a promotional scheme taking shape as I spoke. "I challenge you. I'll bring my Swedes and a video crew. If you win you keep them and expose the tapes. If I win I own the films." I was angry. It felt good.

Mangin was tall enough to be able to sneer down at me easily. But at that moment the floor carried him down and me up. I could see it made Mangin mad to have me at eye level. He said something I couldn't understand to the party beyond the walls.

Then he said to me, "Done. But not only will the Swedes

come with me, you will provide the entertainment for the Chase on the killing floor in Capricorn."

"The last one who talked like that left me something." I had my hand on the weapon in my pocket. Before anyone could move, I drew it halfway out and wondered if I would actually be able to fire it. I started backing up toward the door. Mangin and the people behind him came into sudden focus. They were a hunting party standing in the night, looking more than half-afraid of the gun. The air felt summer soft. My legs were water; my spine felt a thousand knives. Without turning I moved toward where I thought the door was.

Suddenly, a new track had begun to play: "Concrete & Clay" by the Unit Four + 2. The mood broke, and Mangin's hunting party faded. Then I felt the door with my free hand. "Great place you have, Benjy," I said. Half the onlookers broke into applause.

Out in the lobby, under a Peter Max chandelier, a girl about fifteen was having a drug-crying jag while her john tried to make up his mind about ditching her. Figures dashed down a flight of stairs and out the door: the kid I had let in and her brother.

They were being chased, and I realized they must have been the ones who had put the "Moon Dance" track on the sound system. At the front door they dodged Otis and took off down Broadway. Hustlers and skate boarders tried to block the pursuit. As they mixed it up, I got out the door without anyone trying to stop me and headed home.

My head spun; my heart pounded. It reminded me of being very young and alive and in the Village on Friday night with Chris Kane. I almost felt him walking with me. On a wall near my house I noticed some graffiti. It was a sketch of two crabs, facing each other, their front claws crossed and touching the claws of the crab opposite. *FERAL CELL RULES!* was written under that. Something I didn't want to think about stirred inside me.

My place was quiet, the dentists gone, no sound from Joan and B&T's place nor from the rec room where the twins slept. It was an old building, dating from early in the nineteenth century. My high-ceiling loft had been a counting house and storeroom. On my bedroom door was a message from Joan: *Dr. Thoreau and Sandy Burrell called*. I tore it down, locked the door, fell on my bed and into deep, chaotic sleep.

CHAPTER Two

That night I floated over a landscape where the moon shone on trees with awestruck faces, where blue lamps flickered and horns called. Then I awoke Friday with sun at the windows, lights on, a radio and a TV playing, the signal on my phone flashing, and Joan banging on the door, yelling, "Robbie, are you all right? Please answer." The landscape faded but never again entirely disappeared from my awareness.

"A Sun Bum day," a TV voice said. "Bring on the suntan lotion." I located the controls near my head and struggled to turn the thing off. "I've located a nice car hood to stretch out on—" It died. I couldn't reach the radio, which played on softly. My guts ached; my head spun. I tried to answer Joan, but the words got lost somewhere between my flattened brain and the sticky mess that was my mouth.

"Robbie, that's Sandra Burrell on the phone. You missed a court appearance, and she is real upset." Joan paused, and I heard her say to B&T. "We may have to break the door down. And we should call Dr. Thoreau."

That was a stagey ploy, but it worked. What I tried to do was shout no! What came out was a strangled cry. I slid across the bed. The loft was overheated, smothering me. A sheet caught my foot and got dragged along as I staggered off the bed and headed for the door. A chair appeared, cracked my shins, then fell away.

At the door, I jammed two of my fingers trying to get the lock open. My hands shook so badly that I had to hold on to the knob with both of them. Joan and B&T half-caught me as I pulled the door open. At some point during the night my clothes had come off. B&T found a full-length robe and put it on me. He led me to the kitchen area and began making tea. Joan got on the phone with my lawyer. This wasn't the first time a day had begun that way.

"Sandra, I'm afraid he can't make it." There was a pause. Joan and B&T exchanged glances. "I see," she said. "A subpoena." I shivered and sat down. "He's awfully sick, Sandra." I shrank into the robe. My arms and legs ached; my stomach was hot lead. "Can't you, as his attorney..."

"What is to be wishing," B&T asked. "Russian caravan tea?"

"Is this just to protect Jackie Fast?" I watched B&T measure loose tea with his huge hands, heard Joan tense as she fought for me. My inlaid wooden box lay on the table. I opened it and took out four number 4 codeine tablets. "Jesus, Sandra. I don't see that you're giving him much protection."

"Is very strong," B&T said in his lousy Russian accent, pouring water into a tea kettle. "What do you think. Can I play a KGB operative next time?" I ignored him.

Joan hung up and walked over in front of me. "Sandra Burrell, Esquire, says court is recessed until one. If you're not there and ready to give expert testimony, the D.A. is going to subpoena you. The judge is very pissed. Sandy thinks it's important for you because the cops want to move against the whole games scene. She says the D.A. would have called you as an unfriendly witness if she hadn't pulled this."

Joan looked at me angrily and asked, "Why didn't you tell me it was this morning, Rob?" I shook my head, put the hand with the pills to my mouth, got all of them in. "It's just after twelve now. We can get you there on time."

The phone flashed again, and Joan went to answer it. B&T poured tea into a mug and placed it in front of me. They faded to the background as my attention was caught by the radio where Chris Kane was singing. It took me a couple of takes to realize why the song was familiar. It was "Lonely Is the Wind," originally recorded by a group called Circus Maximus too many years before.

My fingers fumbled for the volume. The song was jazzy, dreamy, a New York hit by a local group that never made it. Chris and I had heard it played in a club on Bleecker Street one night when we had driven in from Long Island and music and freedom were new.

The voice faded into the background when I listened to it real hard. The accompaniment was a guitar and some kind of soft percussion. And a horn or horns. *Who Knows the Wind?* Chris's voice wailed softly, and a horn swooped in and almost drowned him out. All very evocative, but I knew Chris hadn't recorded it during his lifetime.

"I'm afraid he'll be busy this afternoon, Mr. Beautemps," Joan said, trying to catch my eye as I dealt with the pills, which had turned to acid powder in my mouth and the tea, which scorched my lips and tongue. B&T had the shower on. Joan hung up, then answered the phone again. "You're calling for Benjamin Mangin? To set up a game with Mr. Leal for tomorrow?"

I nodded for her to make the date and tried to concentrate on the song. I choked down the powder and scalding tea. Other horns joined the first. Chris's voice came in over them. I strained to hear, not believing but wanting to. "Shower's ready, Dad," said B&T.

"If you call later we can arrange the details." said Joan.

"Shut up! Let me listen." I wanted to dive into the radio, to get closer to my feeling on a night over thirty years before. I wanted to catch the thrill that came from being in the city when I was supposed to be home, nervous, alive on four beers, high in all the senses. "I'll tell you when I need you to run my life!"

"Robbie . . ." Joan began. But I threw her a look, right in

the eye. "We'll be downstairs. You're meeting Sandra in forty-seven minutes," she added, leaving with B&T, the two closest to me in the world.

The music died as the door closed. "Now let's evaluate," a dry-voiced deejay said. "The category is cult songs by forgotten groups sung in new arrangements by deceased minor celebrities. Think about it and listen to this." Then he played "Up in the World," the song by Chris that people would be most likely to remember. It was the better-known, live version.

Maybe it was the pills and tea coming on all of a sudden. My eyes misted. I hadn't even liked the live version of "Up in the World." Because it had been Chris's biggest hit, I'd put it on the commemorative album. Hearing it always reminded me that the song was the start of the end.

And that reminded me of Chris the last time I had seen him. He floated before me—the skeleton face, the huge inhuman eyes, the cap shoved down to hide the bare skull. Leukemia: Dachau in Manhattan.

Getting to my feet, I staggered into the steam of the bathroom, soaked in water and soap, stood toweling myself. My breakfast swept into my stomach, producing a burning pain that continued down to my bowels. I sat on the john. When I was through I was careful not to look at the amount of blood I'd left.

The electric razor weighed heavy in my hand. "Up in the World," ended as I tried to assemble what I saw in the mirror into my memories of my face. Guitars reverberated the last chord after ten minutes and forty seconds of 1970s' concert rock. The studio version had been shorter, quieter, more haunting.

Up in the world where no one can tell
Who it was that cheated and lied.

"Chris Kane in the second song, maybe in the first. A couple of people have called to say they think it's an impersonation. Let's analyze that. Would anyone go to that much trouble to pretend to be Chris Kane?" The mood that had touched me earlier was gone. I snapped off the radio.

Clothes had been laid out; a gray three-piece suit, blue shirt, brown loafers, rep tie—the very image of respectability. I had some trouble with buttons and belt buckles, and I told myself it was the numbing effect of the pills. Dressed, I turned around a couple of times in the mirror, an actor assessing his costume.

Twice I started for the door and came back: once to put a small selection of drugs into a vial and slip it into my pocket; then I remembered it was December and went back for an overcoat. Seeing the one I'd had the night before, I picked it up, felt a slight trembling in one pocket as I threw it over my arm.

Downstairs, the twins were talking in Swedish in the playroom. B&T was at the front door, jacket on. Joan stood at the door of their apartment. "Is that Mangin appointment for real?" she asked, very businesslike.

"Yeah." I felt myself slipping into a role: the one I called my life. "Phil Armbruster has played up in Westchester; ask him about it. If he says it's OK, tell the dentists to be here before noon tomorrow. And Vain Video. We're going to film." B&T pulled out the car keys. "I can go to court by myself. The Swedes have to be at the Café Ciao at three. There's a fashion lunch there and a photo opportunity afterward. Make sure they get at least into the background. Moira at channel 5, Seti at Art Net are the ones to see. If they need any details, they are the prince and princess. Got that?"

"OK, Daddy."

"You have thirteen minutes to get to court," said Joan.

Outside, the sun hadn't worked its way down to street level. It shone on the upper floors of Toys, bounced off the windows. In the shadows some of the night's coldness remained. Walking toward Broadway looking for a taxi, I noticed that the kids in front of Toys were dressed as Sun Bums in shorts and thongs. A couple were stretched out on the roofs of cars. None of them turned their heads to watch me pass. Later I realized that none of them were Sun Bums and that all of them were aware of me as I hailed a cab.

Vaguely I noticed the cabbie. He was black. He had news on the radio. "Centre Street. Criminal Court." We pulled away from the curb and began to inch our way downtown through lunchtime traffic. It was then that the heat hit me. It felt like an early September afternoon. I remember regretting the overcoat.

"On a day like this, December fifteenth, temperature a balmy and needless-to-say record-shattering seventy-two degrees, people are talking about the weather," a woman's voice said from the radio. "A thirty-eight-degree turnaround from this time yesterday. We have a spokesman for the National Weather Service on the line. Al Yando. Well, Al, what is happening? Twenty record days so far this year."

"She's going to give him hell about that," the driver said shaking his head. His name, I saw from the plastic I.D. above the dashboard, was Desmond Dupree. He looked to be around thirty. We had stopped at a light. The windows were open, but no air was moving. Sweat formed under my collar. My scalp began to itch.

"All of this, Brenda, lies well within the parameters of possibilities. Remember we have been keeping records only for the last hundred and twenty years."

"That's what you said when it snowed on Labor Day."

"A few flakes. And I believe that was the week after Labor Day. Again not unprecedented." Traffic crept down Broadway toward Canal. On a wall, in blood-red paint were the words *FERAL CELL RULES*. Under that was a stenciled form. I knew what it was; two crabs with their front claws crossed and touching. There, half-stalled in traffic, with people on the radio arguing about the weather, I realized that I was paralyzed with worry.

The court date, which I hadn't even thought about, seemed sinister. Mangin last night hadn't been acting. Dr. Thoreau wanted to cut out my liver and lights. I had fourteen bored dentists whom I was going to have to keep occupied Saturday afternoon. The pills hadn't dulled the pain in my abdomen. But none of those was my big worry. I searched my pockets for the drug vial and found the gun.

It felt alive. My hand jumped away. Someone had tried to blind me the night before. I had put that out in the distant place where I kept all the other things I hadn't wanted to think about.

Car horns blared. The cabbie said, "Nothing is moving." Looking ahead, I saw Sun Bums: kids in bathing suits, smeared with suntan lotion, most of them still nicely tanned. They were street surfing, threading through traffic on their skateboards. Some carried spray-paint cans. I watched as one of them wrote *CANCER SUCKS!* on the back of a bus.

That was a sentiment with which I agreed, but seeing it there in blood-red disturbed me. The fact that a Sun Bum had done it bothered me too. At least in the popular mind the Bums were middle-class kids who couldn't cope, who found no place for their skills in society, and took advantage of erratic weather to cultivate year-round tans. "I need to make a court appearance real bad," I told the cabbie. He nodded and crept to the left.

"The greenhouse effect has not yet been observed," the man from the Weather Service was saying. I watched more Sun Bums, the ones on roller skates, thread their way through the traffic behind the cab as the weatherman told us, "Global temperatures as a whole have barely risen."

The Sun Bums behind us looked harder, tougher than the goofy prototype. They scanned all the cabs they passed. I understood that they were the ones I had seen in front of Toys and that they were following us.

"Trying to shake this traffic," the driver said turning down a side street. When we turned, the group on skates peeled after us.

There was a folded bill in my pocket. "A C-note if we get to court in about two minutes."

"Mister, I can't take a chance of hurting one of those kids." I looked behind and saw two of the roller skaters hanging onto the back of the cab. One of them began working his way around to the open window on my side. He had a spray can.

"It's two hundred if you kill one of them," I told the driver. Remembering, I grabbed the gun from my overcoat. It seemed to spring to my hand. When it did, I caught a glimpse of a blazing landscape and heard horns. The cab squeezed through a Chinatown street, ran a red light.

The skater at the window had a thug's face. He raised his spray can. I leveled the gun, fingered the trigger. The kid recognized it and let go of the cab. I gestured with the gun. He and the others fell back. They stared hard, and a couple of them spat. They followed at a distance as we bled another light and turned onto Centre Street. Looking back I saw other Sun Bums riding skateboards, trailing the ones who trailed us.

"Isn't it true," the radio lady was asking the weatherman, "that this is part of what people mean when they talk about a place going bad?" On Centre Street lined with court buildings a demonstration was going on.

The cabbie called Desmond Dupree snapped his radio off. "You knew those guys," he said. "I never saw Sun Bums like them. They recognized that piece you got there." I nodded and handed him the bill, stuck the gun back in the overcoat. The blinding sun, the distant horns disappeared.

On the sidewalk, a man carrying an attaché case and wearing a pinstripe jacket with Yale tie, but with no pants on, screamed, "ONLY A D.A. KNOWS HOW YOU SHOULD HAVE FUN." A drag queen in high-fashion evening dress but with short hair and a mustache was telling him, "KEEP THEATER WHERE IT BELONGS: ON THE STAGE."

A man with a noose around his neck, some kids dressed in fantasy-game costumes, a woman dressed in leather cracking a whip, a guy on stilts disguised as the mayor—all circled on the pavement awaiting their turns. The Fast Action Street Theater company was performing their own version of their founder Jackie Fast's trial.

"Robbie!" Sandra Burrell stood in the crowd on the court steps. She carried the attaché case and wore the gray suit of the lawyer's guild, but there was a blue scarf around her neck that mirrored her eyes to uncanny effect. "So glad you could make it, Mr. Leal. The judge was steamed this morning." For a moment I saw a compassionate woman, beleaguered and harassed by erratic clients. She gave me an appraising look: what kind of shape was I in?

Sandy, when I first knew her, was a serious student who hung around the artists at college. It got her invited to wilder parties, and later when she set up her practice, it got her more interesting cases. We walked up the stairs and into the building. Looking back I saw the Sun Bums following my cab.

An actor dressed as a judge ran down the stairs and past us. His robes were covered with oversized headlines: "GAMES MISTRESS UNDER ARREST. 'NEVER SAW BLOOD,' CLAIMS FAST AS FANTASY-GAME TRIAL STARTS. LAST MOMENTS OF VAMPIRE VICTIM DESCRIBED."

"This kind of publicity is bad for the case. And some of it makes me look bad professionally," said Sandy. I told myself that retaining lawyers is like keeping pets: sooner or later you begin attributing human motivations to them. "WE'LL TRY YOU TO DEATH!" the actor playing the judge was screaming.

"From what I've heard this seems pretty much the way the D.A.'s office is running things."

"Yes, and I've brought that in. They can't prove that Jackie or any of her clients killed Drew. But they're pursuing a vendetta against her. They've indicted Jackie for criminal negligence and ten other counts: everything from running a sex club to selling narcotics. If they hang any of that on her, my advice as your lawyer will be to get out of the gamemastery business."

We walked down marble halls, and she added, "So it's in your interest as well as hers to appear as professional as possible. You remember our going over what your expert testimony is supposed to be?"

"Certainly. Certainly." I vaguely remembered a conversation on the phone. "What game masters do is a form of performance art with a certain quotient of audience participation." That came rattling out of some corner of my brain. "As for whether members of the audience indulge in drugs and sex . . ."

The sight of Jackie Fast waiting at the elevators shut me up. She looked bad; she had been elegant and ermine haired, now she was tense, glassy eyed, frowzy. That wasn't what stopped me, though. A guy stood with her, someone from Sandy's office. And someone else, a misty gray figure.

"Two minutes to one," said Sandy's assistant. I nodded to Jackie. She looked at the secret one standing beside her. An elevator door opened, and we got on: Sandy and flunky, Jackie and myself, a gray-haired lawyer in pinstripes talking to a tough Spanish man in his twenties, three West Indian secretaries, and a retarded delivery man in shorts, a baseball cap, and a T-shirt that said SIT ON MY FACE. That made ten of us, not counting one other who stood just behind me and to my left; a woman with long silver hair whom I couldn't quite focus on or touch.

The doors opened. The secretaries got off. "They say Princess Di will soon have her face lifted," said one looking in the paper. The others sighed sympathetically. The paper headlines read: "A GREEN CHRISTMAS?" A detective with his badge pinned to the lapel of his jacket got on. That was eight people. I turned suddenly trying to catch sight of the secret one. "So far, no surprises," the gray-haired man was telling his client.

The elevator doors opened again. Sandy motioned me off. The detective got out just behind us. Sandy stopped and he walked past. "I had wanted to get together with you sometime before your actual appearance." We stopped outside the open door of a courtroom. The judge wasn't on the bench yet. A clerk and a bailiff chatted.

A tall man with a discrete mustache walked past us into the courtroom, saying, "Judge wants to see us, counselor," to Sandy.

He stared at me for a moment, and I wondered why he looked familiar. "Who's that?" I asked.

"The assistant district attorney. He's their courtroom hotshot, and he's trying to eat us alive," said my lawyer. "They're acting like the case is real important. It might be good if you and Jackie did the same. I'll only be a few minutes." She hurried after the A.D.A.

A few spectators sat in the courtroom. A couple of reporters stood at the back talking. A cameraman and correspondent from channel 4 hung around. I noticed a couple, a grey-haired guy about my age and a Spanish-looking woman in her twenties, standing across the hall watching silently.

"Let me use the bathroom," I said wanting to be alone with my drugs. Sandy's man looked like he was going to object. But Jackie drew me down the hall. I hadn't seen her for a while. She was thin, seemed to be burning up inside. Her fingers were like talons. Her eyes were glazed with fear. She indicated the one who secretely followed her, worked her mouth for a moment.

"Let Morgan see the gun," she whispered. I tried not to show my surprise that Jackie knew about it. "The men's room is down the hall," she added.

The municipal corridors were warm and close. I hurried into a stall, and my shaky hands got steady for as long as it took to medicate myself. As far as I could tell I was alone. A moment later standing in front of the mirror and splashing water on my wrists and face, I noticed my neck was too small for my collar.

Something moved behind me in the mirror: Jackie's friend Morgan. A couple of lights were out, and in shadows she appeared more clearly, though still wavering before my eyes. Morgan wasn't blond and pale so much as translucent, dressed in what looked like soft gray leather. She gestured at the overcoat, which I'd placed on a sink. She said what sounded like "Bow gun."

I felt it had saved me a couple of times. And now it even had a name. I put my hand on the bone butt and was blinded by the sunlight behind the woman.

She pointed to herself. "Morgan." She breathed the word while looking very hard as if she was in danger of losing sight of me. "The Feral Cell will stand by you." That was said like a password.

"This doesn't make much sense," I told Morgan. Her eyes flickered toward the door. Someone was coming. "But since I obviously am not in a rational state." I held out the gun. Jackie's game, if that's what I was playing, was obviously superior to any I had ever devised.

Her hand snapped forward to grasp the bow gun as if it were a fish in water or a bird in the air. In a single gesture she stuck it in the belt she wore at her waist.

"The thing about him as supervisor is he always has his foot on the back of your neck," one off-duty cop entering the bathroom said to another.

Morgan spun toward the door, somehow passed right between them without the cops really seeing her. They felt something though and gave me their hardest stares. Picking up my coat, I walked into the corridor. Morgan wasn't there. But it didn't bother me. Opium and coke were coming on. I followed the logic of a dream. Sandy Burrell's assistant rushed up. "You're wanted in court," he said out of another dream.

"More media were here this morning," he told me as Channel 4 and a couple of photographers shot me walking into the courtroom. I gave a professionally cool look, but I didn't feel at my best. The couple lounging outside the court watched me closely. The Spanish woman, I was sure, had noticed something different about me.

Sandy and the assistant D.A. were standing at their respective tables while the judge talked to them.

When he saw me, he asked, "Is this your witness at last, counselor?"

"Yes, Your Honor."

"Then I suggest that he be sworn in."

I stood in the witness box while a clerk wrote down my name and address, and a bailiff swore me in. Jackie Fast sat beside Sandy. She was dressed in a blue suit, little makeup, and no jewelry. This was supposed to make her look demure, a contrast to the pictures in the papers just after Drew Whitley's death. Then they had shots of her wearing metal-mesh bras and spiked wrist bracelets. She looked at me questioningly.

"DoyouswearsohelpyouGod?" the baliff asked. The jury stared at me, empty faced. Jackie looked at me questioningly, wondering what had become of her friend Morgan.

"I do," I said and sat down.

They asked me simple questions: my name, age, address. The idea, I guess, was that if I'd lie about those I'd lie about anything. I had always expected that this little game-mastering racket, which Jackie and myself and a few others had going, would come to an end. Only I had thought that would happen because everyone would be tired of it and there wouldn't be any more dentists willing to pay money to play games.

Instead Drew Whitley, a sound engineer and a close friend of Jackie's, managed to die at a little soirée she had held in a haunted mansion on Staten Island. Apparently he had done it in a closet while Jackie and her clients were cavorting all around without noticing.

The media said they had been dressed in rubber cowboy suits and that almost all the blood in Drew's body was missing and couldn't be accounted for. And because of that—the sort of stupid household accident that could happen to anyone—the heavens fell down on her in particular and the science of game mastering in general.

Sandy came forward and said, "Mr. Leal, you are what is called a game master?"

"That's what people, especially the media, call us. We call ourselves interactive theater directors," a term I had never before heard anyone else use. But I was still groping for an interpretation. Testimony is performance, too.

"Your background is the theater?"

"Yes." And off we went, covering the college years I sat through while waiting for the draft to end. We covered my career: the small parts in movies and big parts in obscure plays. The assistant D.A. watched me and waited as we showed how the whole tradition of western theater led to game mastering.

"*New York* magazine, November 23, 1998, described you as 'the top fantasy master'," Sandy said as I felt the coke fade and the downs come on. Jackie Fast looked at me, gave a little nod. The room was warm, uncomfortable. The door at the rear was ajar. Morgan came through it and walked down the aisle. One juror, a middle-aged Chinese man, started for just a second and shook his head. A clerk looked up, then looked away as Morgan walked to a place near the windows from which she could see the whole room.

"Would you," Sandy had raised her voice to call me back to the testimony, "say that the improvisational games that Ms. Fast and her clients played that evening were in any way unusual?"

"Not at all," I said slowly, judiciously. I had found the interpretation I was looking for, the character I would play: a trusted family doctor, the kind that never existed and everybody recognized. "Tragedies like this are why interactive theater directors buy insurance. But companies will sell us insurance." I let a deep professional concern for what had happened to Drew radiate to the jury.

"Objection," said the assistant D.A. He and the judge had words. Jackie Fast's face had come alive. She was staring fixedly at the spot where Morgan stood.

"Proceed, counselor," said the judge.

"How would you describe what you do?" Sandy asked, watching me with fascination. "As an art? An entertainment?"

"And as a business, a profession. We render a service, providing something that is unique to this city." I was sorry I hadn't thought the part through a little more carefully. I could have worn horn-rim glasses and a tweed jacket, tried to look like a scholar. "We are part of the history of innovation in the arts that brings tourists here. Those who want to experience it, learn it, have to come here." I thought of the

Swedish twins the night before, tied up and assaulted by my dentists.

The assistant D.A. objected again. Jackie watched Morgan, who stood almost invisible in the light, watching the courtroom doors. The one to the hall was propped open. The ones behind the judge and the jury box were closed.

"Would you say there was any real danger in what Ms. Fast was attempting on the night of the accident?" Sandy was hushed, respectful in the presence of my expertise.

"Of course not," I said gravely. We hammered home the point that people die all the time. We glossed over the fact that seldom do they do it next to a room full of people in rubber cowboy suits nor do they drain themselves of their blood. As the assistant D.A. objected steadily, we brought out the fact that no one could prove that the death had anything to do with the game.

Until the night before, I had accepted all of this as just the kind of mistake that happens when a bunch of kinky dentists have a little fun. That afternoon, I watched Jackie watching Morgan and thought differently.

Sandy said, "That's all, Your Honor," and the assistant district attorney stood up, approached me. He stood so that to watch him I had to look away from the jury and the spectators. He also blocked my view of Morgan, but I think that was inadvertent. Then I realized why he looked familiar. I had seen him in the crowd at Toys the night before.

"Mr. Leal, you've received a lot of media coverage in your career. Ms. Burrell just read us some, what do actors call them, notices?" The words "actor" and "notices" were in subtle quotes as he said them. "I have a notice from the magazine *Shrapnel*, which I would like the court's permission to read to this witness."

Sandy objected and was overruled. My abdomen ached; I felt sweaty and gritty. The judge beside me cocked his ear suddenly, gestured the bailiff toward the jury room door.

"It's from the September 1997 issue. Do you recall this, Mr. Leal?"

"Not precisely. It's a semi-amateur thing, run by kids. I didn't pay it much attention."

"Well, you gave them an interview, quite a long one, and you are quoted as saying, 'To make the game effects real, the drugs have to be real, the sex has to be real, the danger has to be real.' Is that a correct quote, Mr. Leal?"

"Objection, Your Honor."

"What grounds, counselor?" I saw Jackie's expression change, her eyes widen. She turned to stare toward the jury room. I looked and saw the bailiff open the door and look inside. A form slipped around her, moved toward Jackie. It was the kid who had called himself Billy Gee the night before. "Continue," the judge told the assistant D.A. I realized that neither he nor the bailiff had seen Billy. I had an impression of grass and trees. A blade in his hand caught the light of another sun.

"Mr. Leal, is the term *snuff film* familiar to you?" the D.A. asked courteously. Sandy was on her feet immediately.

Then the court stirred. People were aware of something. Jackie leaped up from the defense table, knocking over her chair, and let out a strangled moan. The assistant D.A. turned, and I saw Morgan aim the bow gun at Billy. He saw her. His eyes widened.

She aimed and fired. The barrel turned, the bow snapped, Billy was hit. His shirt dissolved, and his mouth opened in a silent scream. He wheeled and ducked through the arms of the bailiff who looked like she was grabbing smoke. Morgan went after him.

Jackie was screaming, "They can't even protect me in the goddamn courtroom. The fucking Cabal is going to kill everyone."

"Counselor, control your client. Bailiff, what was that?" Spectators were standing. Jury members were looking at the open door through which the two ghosts had passed. "Recess for half an hour," the judge said banging his gavel. Sandy and her flunky were trying to control Jackie, who was hysterical. No one noticed as I left the witness box and walked out the door.

CHAPTER Three

My memory of the rest of that Friday is of an afternoon so warm I was surprised the sun set early. Lots of things remained to be arranged for the contest with Mangin the next day, but I took a slow walk home in the gold light, stopping once or twice in bars, turning things over in my mind, listening for the sound of Chris Kane's voice.

At a lawyer's bar near Centre Street, TV news showed shots of December silly season, Christmas shoppers and Santas sweating in the heat. They also showed the performance outside the court, actors from FAST Company disrupting traffic. The camera dwelled on the lawyer with no pants.

That segment ended with shots of Sun Bums sunning themselves on car hoods. "Not all Sun Bums took things lying down," a voice said. "Police report several instances of violence by young people described as Sun Bums."

"Sun Bums?" the bartender asked a red-faced patron. In the popular mind the bums were figures of good-natured fun, kids who had devoted themselves to the perfect tan.

"Street actors playing pantless lawyers?" was the reply of the patron who looked like a lawyer. Actors, too, were hard to take seriously.

"Sounds," said the drunken lawyer, "as if New York is

going bad." It occurred to me for some reason that a clown costume was the perfect disguise for an assassin.

Later, on Broadway and Canal, amid crowds Christmas shopping in shirt sleeves, I heard Chris. He was singing something new or at least new to me. Looking for the source, I saw a group of Sun Bums carrying radios. For a moment I flinched, then recognized them as the kind of Sun Bums we all knew and loved.

Paint-splattered cutoffs identified a couple of them as artists without galleries. Others were probably moviemakers without cameras, unpublished writers, a surplus population produced by the great, art-school boom, a new urban mob.

"This is that dead Boomer," said one boy. I flinched at the casual way he said it but realized that against all odds Chris was hot again.

Some of them carried compact sound boxes. They turned them up. For a couple of blocks I walked a foot or two behind trying to hear as the noise of the street ate up the sound of Chris. "The Feral Cell," said one girl and gave a stagey shudder. I remembered Morgan using that name also as I caught a fragment of the song:

Where the Chase goes on all night
Got to fear with all your might.

The voice seemed to be whispering. It sounded like Chris, but it also reminded me of the way Morgan had spoken. All this meant I was going crazy; I accepted that. The kids turned and went into a building. It had never occurred to me to wonder where Sun Bums lived. Before the door closed behind them, I caught that voice singing:

And can't understand what we have to learn
Before death makes slaves of us all.

The dark was falling when I got home. Flags hung outside Toys, silver on black. The emblem was two goats facing head-to-head, their horns intertwined. I couldn't focus on that. All I really wanted to do was slip in the door of my own house and fall out.

Joan was the only one home. "B&T is showing the twins the sights," she said. "I saw you on the news." I nodded. "I've got it on tape if you want." I slid onto a chair arm. "There are a lot of calls waiting for you. Sandra Burrell is frantic. Seems the judge wanted you on the stand again after you left. What happened? Jackie flipped out in court? You want a brandy?" I nodded.

She rewound the tape, and figures flew backward across the screen. Joan handed me a glass. Perched on the chair, I sipped Cavallos and watched a collage of images, actors and Sun Bums, Sandra escorting Jackie down the stairs of criminal court—all with the sound turned off. At one point I saw myself scuttle across the screen.

"Did they have anything to say about me?"

"No. Did you have anything good to say?" Joan put the TV back on without the sound. Weather maps and satellite pictures appeared on the screen as she talked to me. "A whole bunch of calls. Clients."

"Have them here before noon, prepared to skirmish. We'll go in convoy up to Westchester. Make sure B&T knows where Mangin's place is."

"I called the video people, explained it was a Capture the Swedes game out at Mangin's place. They weren't real interested. They seem to think they have enough footage of the Swedes after last night."

"Explain that it's for keeps. The kids belong to Mangin if he wins." I wondered how that would sound in court. "He's not going to, of course, but tell them I guarantee there will be material they can sell for videos. I want at least a dozen of them. And offer all of them a little money to serve as observers. Keep Mangin's judges honest." As I spoke the next day's events fell into place.

"Call Phil Armbruster and tell him he'll be picking the twins up at Mangin's. It's closer for him and he can work it into his story line. Make sure from him that Mangin actually knows how to run a Take the Flag contest. Did B&T get the twins on screen?"

"Briefly on Art Net. The reporter got it all confused about who they were supposed to be. There's going to be some footage on cable later." She looked at a pad. "Jason Beautemps called. Also the doctor."

"Did Jason leave a number?"

Joan handed me a slip of paper. "What about Dr. Thoreau?" She asked it casually, but I knew that everything else —the brandy, the tape, the conversation—led up to that question.

"Dr. Thorax? The man is a bore. I'm going to take a nap."

"He says you had an appointment with him this morning. Said this was your third no-show."

I nodded vaguely, asked her "Could you round up some material, pictures, books, on Mangin's grandfather and the estate?" and walked out. I'd left the overcoat somewhere, but the clothes I was wearing seemed to weigh me to the ground. Everything inside me from my throat on down ached. Every stair was an effort, and I climbed one step at a time like an old man.

In the loft, I didn't so much get undressed as walk out of my suit. I fell on the bed and lay there for quite a while. Usually my mind worked by itself, setting up a game schedule for days in advance. At that moment nothing was on the agenda beyond Mangin's challenge tomorrow. I had no idea what I was going to do up there. After that was a void, one that scared me so much I didn't think about it.

After some time I worked my way over to the edge of the bed, got hold of the phone, located Jason's number. On the third ring his answering machine clicked on. "This is Jason Beautemps. Since you're calling we can assume that you've heard of me. Tell me who you are and why that should interest me."

I said, "Mr. Beautemps, you've never heard of me. I just came to New York and someone told me to look you up. I want to be an actor."

"Give it up, cupcake. You don't have what it takes. You

gotta have brains and not just a body." Jason was on the line. "What was your impression of last night?"

"That I was set up."

"Well, I admit that the kid showing up with you in tow smacked of Divine Providence. But at first I thought you knew what was going on."

"You called me just now," I reminded him.

"I wanted your opinion, as the other Chris Kane specialist besides me."

That, I realized, was one of the things about Jason. He had known Chris and still remembered his music. "Of the tape? I've heard some stuff from it." I kept my voice as neutral as possible. I had no information and didn't want Jason to know that. Chris had been my closest friend.

"It's him you know, Robbie. We thought it might be you doing an imitation. But after last night when I saw the look on your face as the tape played, I knew it wasn't. They've done all kinds of voice-wave testing. There are some weird things about the range and the way it was recorded but nothing to prove it isn't Chris's voice."

"I want to listen to the whole tape." I wanted that more than anything in years. That got through to Jason.

"You two were such bosom buddies, I thought you'd be involved."

"I'm not convinced it's real. Who put it out? Who's distributing."

"You really don't know anything?" Jason sounded surprised and disappointed. "A little company in Jersey is supposed to be distributing it, a bunch of kids. I just volunteered to do promotion. I'll get a tape to you tomorrow."

"As soon as possible." I didn't care how anxious I sounded.

"I'll do my best. I'm amazed you're not in on this, Rob." I could tell that Jason thought I was holding something back.

The phone had lighted up with another call. My answering machine clicked on as Jason hung up. I listened in. There was a long pause as if the caller couldn't decide whether to talk or couldn't remember the message. It was from a phone on the street somewhere. A siren sounded in the background. A moment later I heard the siren myself, a bit uptown, heading west. Someone was breathing, short and frightened.

"Yes?" I said quietly.

"Rob? Don't say my name." It was Jackie Fast. She was disguising her voice, but we went back too far for that to fool me. "I have to talk to someone."

"Honey, be my guest."

"Not like this. Remember a few years ago after I just got involved with Gallia? We met you on the street one night and went to a little place?"

"Yes."

"Meet me there at nine. Make sure you don't bring anyone else."

She hung up before I could tell her about being too tired. I turned over on my back and realized I wanted very much to talk to someone myself. I won't tantalize you any further with the details of my chemical preparations. It's enough to say that they took me a while, and I was running late when I put on a sweater and jacket and was ready to leave. Joan buzzed me on the phone.

"Dr. Thoreau is on the line and insists on talking to you."

"I'm trying to get out of here."

"Rob, you have to at least talk to him."

My mouth went dry. My hands were numb. Joan clicked off and Thoreau said, "Robert?"

"Dr. Thorax! This is Dr. Cobalt, here." I slipped into the oily professional voice he had once found amusing. "You wish to consult with me? Split a fee?"

"Robert, I thought you were smarter than this. You were supposed to go into Cedars this afternoon for tests. Where were you?"

"In court." I answered without the accent. I hardly recognized my real voice.

"You didn't even tell your people about this. I have to talk to you."

"So talk."

"In my office. Robert, you are a very sick man." He sounded baffled even a little hurt, as if I wouldn't play his favorite fantasy. "I want to see you tomorrow. Say at two?"

"OK." I put the sound of reluctance in my voice as if he was dragging an agreement out of me.

"Two P.M., then," he said, and I hung up knowing I was going to be up in Westchester at that hour. Then I had to hurry. B&T still had the twins out. I didn't stop to talk to Joan, just bolted out the door, escaping from my own house. Remembering what Jackie had said, I looked to make sure I wasn't being followed. My arm when I raised it to hail a cab felt light, unattached to my body.

The place Jackie had mentioned was in the East Village. I looked out the back window a couple of times and couldn't see anyone trailing me. My destination was a coffee house on a quiet block. It had a small brick interior, cozy enough on a cold night. But the garden was the place's gimmick, a shady grotto set behind renovated tenements, cooled in summer by a fountain, closed during the cold weather.

Scanning the house from the door, I couldn't see Jackie. Had she left because I was late? Had she not shown up because she was so haywire? Windows looked out on the garden. Something gray moved in the darkness.

I stepped out the door and a voice whispered, "Rob." A couple of tables and a few chairs were scattered around in the dark. The lamps that hung in the trees were gone; the fountain turned off. Through a gate at the end of the garden headlights on the street gave scattered seconds of light.

Jackie sat leaning against a bare tree still dressed as she had been in court. In a flash of light I looked at her tight emaciated face. Struggling to pull a chair near her, I wondered if I looked any better. "What the hell was that today?"

"Morgan protected me. You, too. Saved our asses from the Cabal," Jackie sounded impatient, as if anyone should have known that.

"Who is she, Jackie?"

"Morgan? She's Feral Cell," Jackie whispered, but even that seemed to exhaust her. She was dying, I could see her fading into the dark. "I'm being recruited. It's like AIDS; each recruit gives it to the next."

"Can I get you something?"

Jackie squinted at me. "You don't know about any of this. Oh, you poor baby. You don't even know how sick you are. I thought because of Chris, you were in on it. Oh, poor baby. In Capricorn they call us the Cancii, the Crabs. They call this place Cancer."

At that word I felt pain. "Recruit? Sick? What are you talking about, Jackie?"

"Drew Whitley, the guy who died?" In a moment of illumination I saw that her eyes were closed. She spoke in a fast whisper. "He was the recruit before me. You know the tape of Chris Kane everyone is listening to? Drew mastered that. He tried to make it sound like Capricorn. He and Chris did it in Berlin and Manila, places that were going bad. You know how he died?"

"The police say he was hanged." The case was one of the many things I hadn't wanted to hear or think about. "They seem to think it's your fault."

"The Undying Cabal killed him. I had rented that haunted house for an alien sex scenario. Drew had been working with me for a long while doing special sound effects. Early in the evening he disappeared. I wondered if the Cabal had gotten him. But there were all these clients to take care of. Three A.M. one of them wanders into a closet, starts screaming. Mangin got Blood of the Crab from him and used his body to set me up."

Most of it made no sense, but a name stood out. "Mangin?" I had thought just the two of us sat in the garden, but I was aware of a third. Jackie was crazy and so was I.

"And the Cabal. That D.A. on the case is one of them. The police are on their side."

"Mangin is just a rich dork. What does he have to do with

it, Jackie?" Like any good paranoia this one had started tying together very neatly.

"He's old and bloody. He's the Undying Cabal." She shook her head slightly. "Drew tried to tell me. The first time I was just like you. Maybe that's part of it." She opened her eyes and saw the way I looked at her. "Rob, this place, doesn't it feel like we're out in the middle of the woods in summertime?"

"Sort of."

"We are. We've both got one foot in Capricorn. Look and you can see the trees. I can't stay here any more, Rob. You're dying, you know, or you wouldn't have been able to hold that gun. Cell diseases, like cancer, are what allow us to go to Capricorn. The Feral Cell call it crossing the Transept. We've been good friends for a long time, and I thought you must have known about this from Chris."

"He died in '72. It was twenty-seven years ago in March." In a flash of light I strained to see Jackie. Something moved behind her, passed through a brick tenement wall. I could make out trees in full leaf. Blue lanterns shone in a woods. Traffic noises, conversation from inside the coffee house were no louder than a distant horn playing one long note.

"You ever seen him dead?"

"His mother had moved to Canada. They sent the body up there. She didn't want to have anything to do with anyone from New York."

"Convenient. My leaving's going to cause a lot more trouble." The horn grew louder; what had been a lonely note sounded menacing. "The Chase is riding in Capricorn tonight. Those are the people who follow Mangin and the Undying Cabal. Nothing's left for me here. There's danger in Capricorn, but you can live until the net falls. Morgan will talk to you."

She stood up, almost seeming to float out of her seat. Her clothes fell on the ground as her head turned toward the sound of the horn. I saw she wore a tunic and pants, close-fitting suede like Morgan's. Her chest heaved in short breaths.

Thinking that it was silent sobbing, I tried to go to her. My legs wouldn't support the weight of my body. My own breath was short. My heart turned over. I sat down. Morgan stood with Jackie, who seemed to be drinking something. I heard the rustle of leaves and a distant roaring.

Morgan reached down and placed something on the table with moves as deliberate as if she were under water. Words floated from her in a whispered rush. "I return the bow gun to you. Its chambers are filled. The Feral Cell can guard you in Capricorn if you stay in the city."

Before I could reply, the horns whooped. Both women turned and were gone. I reached out and picked up the gun, and I sat for a long while listening to the sound of leaves, smelling summer. Then I got up and walked back through the coffee house. Some people looked up; most didn't seem to see me.

On a garage wall across the street someone had painted a silver crab with crossed claws. Under it, black letters read *CANCER OVER CAPRICORN*. I stared, trying to make sense of it.

Sleep came to me at some point after I had gotten back home and drugged myself into a stupor. My only memories that might be from that night are of a panel discussion about global weather. Animations of wind patterns and satellite photos of disappearing forests on the equator made a nice lulling display.

Sometime very late I woke up with only the light of a TV shining. It showed a music video. One shot before my eyes glued themselves shut was of a bunch of kids playing guitars on a street corner in a tropical city. On the wall behind them were words in Spanish and two goats' heads with horns crossed and touching.

It took the buzzer on my phone, a clock radio, and B&T banging on my door shouting, "The dentists are coming!" to wake me up. Without being fully aware of why, I knew I wanted to get away from my house fast that Saturday.

"Sunny at 11:27 and the temperature is going down," said a lady deejay, and played something that tried to synthesize an early sixties innocence. As I went to let B&T in and start water boiling, I saw the gun lying on the table. I hid it quickly, deftly, not even thinking about it.

"Vain Video has a crew coming over. A couple of independent videoteers Joan contacted yesterday are waiting outside." B&T started to lay out the Dr. Cobalt costume while I medicated myself.

Wondering when it was that I started needing someone to help me get dressed, I told him, "Cobalt is more than I can take today. Let me go as Rosko." That was a minor character I hadn't used for a long time, a small-time smuggler and thief with some vague psychic powers. The best part was that being Rosko meant wearing a cap pulled down over my face, and an old leather jacket. It was about all I could handle at that moment.

"You going to wear those bug-eye contact lenses?"

"I'll wear dark glasses. You and me and the Swedes will go in the Bentley." I fell into the Rosko voice. "One of the video kids should ride with us. Get the one we had Thursday night. He knows how to be quiet. How are the twins doing?"

"A little pissed that you don't pay more attention to them." B&T was happy to fall into the Rosko mode. It was close to the way he really talked.

"They should consider themselves lucky." Turning so he couldn't see, I slipped the gun into my pocket and headed for the stairs. My steps seemed light. I attributed that to drugs. Things I didn't want to consider waited for me. The hairs on the back of my head tingled. Joan met us at the bottom of the stairs.

"You come too, lady," I said, not wanting her around to talk to Dr. Thorax.

Joan shook her head in a way that made me not press. She told us, "It's set for Armbruster to pick up the twins at Mangin's Roost. He has nothing but admiration for Mangin." Joan thought Armbruster was an idiot. I just thought he was a fellow game master.

Erik and Erika dressed in ornamental robes with warm clothes underneath. This was for the benefit of Armbruster and his crew, who were looking for the lost heirs of the unicorn throne.

"Nothing's going to happen to them with Mangin?" Joan looked worried. So did the twins a little.

"It's in the bag. Any calls from Jackie?"

"No, but Jason called saying to listen to WLUV from twelve to one this afternoon." She handed me some papers. "This is some of the information you asked for yesterday." I looked at her blankly and shoved them in my pocket. "Rob, take it easy, please?" She kissed me, tried to look through the dark glasses and find my eyes.

I nodded and went out the door and into the Bentley. The Vain Video Co-op van was there and another van with half a dozen dentists. Some more cars started their motors when the drivers saw us. B&T signaled for the videoteer. I put him in back with the Swedes and sat up front. B&T went to talk to the others.

My dentists all noted my Rosko outfit. As they did I became aware of someone observing them and me. Down the street, the windows of Toys were empty. "You get any shots of that kid who attacked me Thursday night?" I asked the videoteer.

"He came out underexposed. I wasn't ready for him. You should have given us some warning that was going to happen." The video people were looking for exotic footage to use in rock videos. The games were perfect for that. "We didn't get much Thursday." Joan had decided against letting them shoot the dentists and Swedes cavorting in the garage. Jackie's trial had that effect on the business.

Erika leaned forward. "This is a war game we are going to?"

The idea of having them alone in the car had been that I

could relax, stay out of character. But that meant I had no distance and was actually going to have to make conversation. I nodded and fiddled with the radio. WLUV was the sixties retro station and wasn't a strong band. B&T slid in, looked in the rearview mirror to make sure the motorcade was set and off we went.

"These games are illegal in Sweden. They are called militaristic."

"Yes. Well that might make it more fun. A little whiff of illegality is part of what the people are paying for." Remembering Drew Whitley hanged and Jackie chased out of this world, I dropped that line of conversation.

Then the music distracted me: Hardin's "Reason to Believe." Chris and I and two girls who wanted to be folk singers had seen Hardin so many years before in a little club on Bleecker. He had been backed by a flute player and a jazz combo. It wasn't Hardin this time, though. As we turned onto the FDR Drive, I realized that with a jazz flute ornamenting a line behind him, Chris, gone twenty-seven years, was still pulling my wires.

"In this contest, we are the trophy." Erik was leaning forward. "If we loose, we are to go with Mr. Mangin?"

"We met Armbruster in Munich last year," Erika added. "He was demonstrating mystery-game technique. We came here because of him, and he has recommended you. Mangin, we have only just heard of yesterday. And his reputation . . .," she trailed off in uncertainty.

"Mangin would only concern you if he won, and he's not going to win." On the radio, Chris had gone into "Stagger Lee." Piano backed him up on this, dirty, crude, electric. This sounded more real, more present, somehow. The Chris Kane voice sounded like it had a lot of wear and tear on it. The other songs had been haunting, removed, the voice almost in the background. This sounded more of this world.

"You will understand that we wish to have a similar organization in Stockholm," Erik was saying. "That is why I asked."

"Asked what?"

"He want's to know why you're dressed as Rosko today," B&T prompted me. The video kid started to shoot again.

"I wanted to give Dr. Cobalt a rest."

"Have your clients seen you as Rosko before? Do they understand that is who you are?"

"I change everything when I do a different character: costume, voice, face, walk. They've seen Rosko before in situations like this. It may be that, for the finale of the game, clues and hints will be placed to indicate that Rosko and Dr. Cobalt are the same person. Or it may be that someone else will dress up in one or another of the costumes and be seen with me."

"You do not know how this is going to turn out?"

"Only in outline." I had no idea what was going to happen the next day. I didn't even know what was going to happen at Mangin's place. Traffic was light heading out of the city. B&T kept track of the cavalcade behind us. The music faded slightly as "Stagger Lee" played. I adjusted the station finder, but WLUV was at the end of the dial.

"What do you think is most appropriate that we learn?" The twins were both looking at me intently, beautiful in the winter light, uneasy about being so helpless. All that interested me was the voice coming out of the radio. The sound fuzzed as the song ended. B&T fiddled with the adjuster.

"Magic," I told them as we rolled up the highway.

The sun went behind clouds. A woman deejay said, "Some oldies from the 'new' Chris Kane album. We will talk with the critic Jason Beautemps in just a moment. But first let's listen to a song I at least have never heard before. It's called 'Death Drops in for Tea.' The album is called *Feral Cell*."

"You said magic? Could you explain?" asked one of the beautiful twins.

"Theater magic. That's my background . . ." Then Chris began to sing again, something new. I strained for the words. The voice was a whispering echo, the kind they use on sound tracks to indicate that someone is thinking.

I saw him in a crowd once,
Brushing by me in a hall, . . .

"Is it him?" asked B&T. I said nothing. "This is by an old friend of his who's supposed to have died," he told the twins.

Among gents in suits, dudes in do's,
Women advertising VPs . . .

We were on a bridge, gray river below, co-op towers in the distance. For a moment I saw another landscape, green fields, a summer afternoon with the sun suddenly gone behind a cloud. Everything was distorted, elongated. People looking up to the sky, saw something that amazed them: me sailing overhead. They shivered and disappeared. On the radio Chris sang:

I thought I had the rap beat
He'd never notice me,
But when he's least expected
Death drops in for tea.

At the other end of the bridge, the station fuzzed out again. I moved to fiddle with the dials aware that the twins were staring at me intently. The twins exchanged a few words in Swedish. Erika asked me in English, "How did you do that, the shimmering effect just now?"

I wanted to brush them off. They were the dream. The fields and people under the bridge, the dead voice out of the radio were real. "There are certain secrets that I'm afraid I can't share." The song disappeared into a mush of static.

"You think it's him don't you," B&T said.

That's when I realized that I did. Knowing that somehow made it less important to hear the radio. "See if Joan can set up a meeting for tonight with Jason," I told B&T. "What did you think?"

"Fire and ice. Whoever he is." That was high praise indeed.

"Tell us, if you will, what is intended for us this afternoon," Erika said. The videoteer was straining at the leash. I knew it was time for the performance to begin. I had palmed a ball of opium into my mouth a short while before, and that rush was coming on. I understood the form of what I wanted shown on camera.

On the radio, the song had ended. An occasional phrase or two from Jason drifted through. ". . . so it seems to kids that rock is for adults. That we've stolen it from them."

I drew a deep breath, gave the camera my best angle, and started talking. As we drove into the hills of Westchester, the afternoon grew darker. I found my Rosko voice as I talked: soft, a little slurred as if the tongue worked its way around some damage to teeth and brain. "We're going out here, prince and princess, to turn you over to some individuals who call themselves the Black Flag."

That was their friend Armbruster and his dentists. I explained for the video in a Damon Runyon voice how the twins were supposed to be the rightful heirs of the Black Flag's native land. "The Black Flag is a bunch of magic revolutionaries, OK?" I heard myself saying. "It seems they got enemies who are trying to steal the prince and princess." That was Mangin and his people. Armbruster had told Joan that Mangin had played the game a lot. Thinking that made me shudder.

"The strange weather is tied in with it somehow," Jason said. "And all those other places that went bad."

"And this has something to do with the tape?" the deejay asked, trying to bring him back to the subject as they were both lost in aural snow.

"Why have you decided to abandon your Dr. Cobalt for this performance?" Erik wanted to know.

I gave a short nod and a sneer. "Cobalt is an old fraud. Rosko is tough and cold." I slipped in and out of characters like someone deciding what to wear. Rosko had seemed like an arbitrary choice that morning. Now I knew he was no accident. We were heading toward danger, not a fantasy but reality. As Cobalt I would be weighed down with the costume and the need to act old. Rosko was a survivor.

Only then, flying through Westchester in front of a cold wind, did I think about what had to be done that afternoon. The deal with Mangin had begun as my way of defying a rich dilettante. It had turned into business as usual, a chance for time on the tube, usable footage that could be sold, an addition to my legend. I now understood that Mangin was a link to Capricorn. And accepting Chris Kane's being alive meant trying to understand Capricorn.

"The question on a lot of minds," the deejay said from the radio, "is why Kane?"

"Oh, but he was there at the cusp in the late sixties and early seventies: Max's Kansas City and the Weathermen, Sam Shepard . . ." Jason faded into a buzz. It was true; Chris had known every scene in the city. The ones he introduced me to had been my livelihood ever since. Apparently there were ones he hadn't shown me. I turned off the radio.

Capricorn: the word made my neck tingle. Somehow it was life and death. "We are to understand that you made a bet with Mangin for us. Are we to be considered his guests if you lose?"

"You get treated real well no matter what," I answered in the voice of Rosko while wondering if that was so.

"Rosko's got it all taken care of," B&T said as Danello. We performed well together. Turning to look at the twins, I caught sight of the other cars following me. A videoteer was hanging out one of the van windows for a shot. The camera in our car caught me smiling Rosko's cold little smile as I wondered what in hell I was going to do.

"Nothing has been left to chance?" Erik wanted to know. B&T assured them the whole thing was a set up. As he did, I took the information Joan had given me about Mangin and the estate out of my pocket and tried to focus on it.

Then B&T said, "There it is," and following his gaze I caught sight of a gray tower on top of a hill.

Mangin called his estate Capriole. His enemies called it

Mangin's Roost; we lost sight of it behind some houses and pines. In the middle of expensive Westchester lay twenty acres of nearly empty hilltop. I glanced at two pictures; a before and an after shot. First was the estate as he had built it—all imported stone, flying marble staircases, and curling turrets. The after was stark. Nothing was left but something people called the Tower, a huge pile of stones built from the rubble left after the fire of 1928.

Scott and Zelda had danced at Mangin's Roost. Mangin had married his last wife, the dancer Antonia Ferrar, there and been burned to death along with her shortly afterward. I had a picture of the two of them. She was wasted looking but beautiful, eyes haunted as a Poe heroine, and I felt that I knew her. Our way uphill led through houses set in landscapes. They blocked sight of the Roost until we turned onto a dead-end street to find the Roost above, and a stone gatehouse and iron gates before us.

The parking lot was a dirt strip outside those gates. Just one car was parked: a blue Buick that looked like company property. A man and a woman waited at the gates. They were dressed in down vests and jeans: Suburban clothes. On a single glance I would have described them as stocky and stolid, anonymous gray people whom it would be hard to identify. Then one of them moved, and the careful lumbering motion was very familiar. We drove up and parked in formation. My dentists piled out as the couple sized them up; and video cameras caught it all.

A neighborhood woman stood in front of a house down the street, waiting for her husband to back the car out of the garage. She looked up at us, shook her head, and looked away quickly. As Rosko I sort of slouched out of the car. B&T fetched the twins.

My dentists wore a uniform of black vests and caps to protect clothes and hair from flying dye capsules. Some of them took out binoculars and were studying the terrain. A few of them were examining the gates. The ironwork was in the form of two goats, heads down, horns crossed and touching. Only at that moment did I remember Morgan telling me to stay in the city.

The couple approached us. "We will explain the ground rules. Act as judges," said the woman speaking slowly, her words coming out pre-chewed. That was familiar, as were their eyes. I glanced again at my photo of Benjamin Mangin the First. His eyes were small and piercing like those of a power-crazed pig. I realized that his grandson looked more than a lot like him.

The two who greeted us had the same eyes without the intensity. The gatehouse was obviously inhabited. I wondered for a moment if they were illegitimate descendants of the old man. "I'm Risa. This is Brad," she said as he carefully unlocked the gates. They both wore smiles that looked as if they'd been rehearsed in front of mirrors.

I wiped them off their faces by looking at the gates and saying, "From Cancer into Capricorn." Maybe that gave too much away, but cameras were running, and the bow gun tingling in my pocket made me brave.

CHAPTER

Four

"These are the rules that were worked out on the phone." Risa, who I thought was a few yards away, suddenly handed me a sheet of paper. "Briefly, they state that you must get up the hill with your flag." Here she nodded at the Swedes. "You must then be on the marble floor under the tower at the end of two hours. If you succeed you keep the twins and any film footage. If you fail, you lose the film and the twins. And you must stay and entertain your opponents."

When I listened carefully, what seemed like a speech defect was a kind of accent. "The two hours start when you pass through these gates. You are permitted fifteen combatants. Your opponents have taken as a nickname 'the Chase.'" She looked at me carefully. "Their team will also have fifteen people."

"Maybe the trick is the word people," I said.

The air was cold and gray as a knife. She paused for a moment, looked uphill to where I presumed Mangin was, then concluded. "Weapons for all of these are standard air guns and pellets of nontoxic, washable dye. My partner and I are to be observer-judges. The people you designate can dispute any decision they think is unfair. We have judged many such contests. You will find us unbiased. Usually the dye speaks for itself. We have release forms."

She handed me a sheet of standard disclaimers and a pen. I signed without removing my glove. The pen made odd lines and curlicues. Without the glove my hand couldn't have held it.

Brad was circulating among the dentists. B&T had them divided into two groups of five and another of four. I looked up the hill. For an instant the dead earth and tree skeletons were covered with grass and leaves rustling before a summer storm.

The video people checked the cameras on their hats and the recorders on their wrists, adjusted their backpacks. The kid who had ridden up with us stuck close to me.

"Ready?" asked Risa.

I nodded my head. The two observers exchanged glances.

Brad said, "It is now 1:36," and everyone checked their watches. Then the two of them pushed the gates open and a team of dentists started up the hill.

I followed with the twins, B&T and four more dentists. The last team brought up the rear. We reminded me of a herd being led to slaughter. I thought of Morgan telling me to stay in the city and of Jackie Fast and Drew, and put my gloved hand on the gun. My foot hitting the ground felt light, insubstantial.

These acres were all that was left of the hundreds that Mangin's family had once owned. The trail we followed had once been a paved road, a winding driveway, now overgrown. Bushes moved ahead of us. Two of the forward team fired. Neither hit the tiger cat that scooted with its tale down. Everyone laughed.

It was 1:42 P.M. Mangin was somewhere on this hill.

"Spread out," one of the dentists was telling the others.

I alternated between assuring myself that they weren't in any danger and wondering why I cared. The twins moved easily, looking around learning as much as they could, absurd and oddly graceful in their robes. I told myself they weren't in any danger either. But I knew I was. At that thought I felt my guts twist and saw green grass and smelled summer again.

Looking down the hill, I saw Risa and Brad following us, saw our cars in the lot, the houses beyond. A door slammed, two children in bright parkas in a backyard pointed at us, traffic moved on curving suburban streets, rolled on an access road. For that moment, it seemed no more than a game. Nothing was going to happen except a few people getting hit with nontoxic dye.

Then I slipped off my glove and put my hand on the gun in my pocket, and the suburbs became open ground with small clusters of stone houses and stands of trees amid cultivated fields. The sky was still gray, and I still climbed a hill. I looked to the top of it and saw a castle through the trees of its garden.

Capriole, Mangin called it. Mangin's Roost, the neighbors had said. I stared at stained-glass windows, staircases winding around towers, topiary gardens. We were inside the outer walls, which were at the bottom of the hill and looked mean and shoddy compared to the buildings at the top.

Swallows sailed before a summer storm. Women on the stairs shivered in lace gowns; men in boots and bright colors laid hands on nets and stakes. Silver light bounced off them. Their long El Greco faces shone with tension and excitement.

I saw them in a prism and only for a moment. Then a horn sounded behind me, and winter cold wiped out the scene. Saturday Christmas-shopping traffic flowed like a river on the highway. Nearer at hand on the suburban streets, a car blew its horn outside a house. We were far enough up that the car and the house had begun to look like miniatures.

Our rear guard was spread out and walking backward toward us. None of Mangin's crew had appeared so far. The only sounds were of our party heading for the summit, the wind in the trees. The roadway had eroded, stones thrust out. Ahead, the road curved, a potential ambush spot. The advance party had stopped. At the curve, one on either side of the road, were a pair of stone posts. Carved on each was a goat, standing on hind legs, neck hair bristling.

The road went left; the ruins stood in front and to our right. B&T looked at me, and I nodded to the right. We started for the underbrush. One of the rear guard called, "Hey!" We saw Mangin's people for the first time below us. Seven or eight figures climbed the hill behind us, not making much effort to hide, not trying to get too close, just trailing us.

In summer the ground would have been hard going; even in late fall it was overgrown. This was their chance to hit us on our way uphill. It seemed they weren't interested. We reached the foundations of outbuildings. Some tall pines blocked the light. Part of a wall still stood with gray branches reaching through its empty windows.

Then a dentist up front whistled, pointed in front of him. We moved forward, and I saw a large smooth surface, perhaps twenty-five hundred square feet of white marble with a black diamond pattern on it. I guessed that it had been Mangin's dance floor. At its far end was the tower, which was actually the rough pile of stones left after the fire. It could be scaled but not easily. The marble floor was unmarred by debris and scrubbed absolutely clean. It gleamed except for a blotch at the far end. If I squinted, walls appeared all around the floor.

"How does Mangin do this?" a twin asked in a Swedish accent. She was looking through B&T's glasses. Following her sight line, I noticed a pole about forty feet up jutting out of the tower directly over the blotch.

"I think we got something," one videoteer said to another. I realized that the pole was an iron bar with a head impaled on it.

"Is it real?" Erik asked.

"I know you'd be disappointed if it weren't," I answered in Rosko's voice while fumbling with the glasses. The eyes bulged, the mouth was rigid in a scream, but I recognized my old friend Billy Gee.

"It makes a nice shot," said a camera woman.

"I bet in close-up it's going to look fake," my videoteer answered.

My watch said 1:58. The game had been on for over a quarter of an hour without a shot being fired in anger. Standing on a slab of granite jutting out of the ground, I could see downhill. Figures moved toward us slowly, spread out. Our position was the perimeter of the ballroom floor. It stood on high ground; bushes and trees gave cover. Several dentists climbed into nooks low on the tower. It would take a lot to dislodge us from there. I kept my eyes away from Billy Gee.

The twins sat on a pile of bags and coats. They stared openly at the head while my people stole occasional looks. Some of the videoteers were downhill with Mangin's crew, which had halted. B&T trotted over to me.

"Half their force is on the other side of the hill. He's divided. We can move against either . . ." He trailed off when I didn't respond.

Mangin's people had stopped about a hundred yards away. My dentists started taunting, daring them to attack. The other side waited silently for a signal. Several of them were familiar, and they were not the kind to waste their Saturday on a useless game of Take the Flag. They were hard-eyed people who had survived the rise and fall of a hundred scenes. They had come out here on behalf of their own best interests.

Risa and Brad had taken up a position off to the side of the dance floor. Between the two forces were the videoteers, one of whom shrugged and tried to bum a cigarette from another. None of them were filming. As far as they were concerned the day was mostly a bust. If this was as far as it went, I was inclined to agree. But by the way Mangin's people kept staring up at the tower I knew there would be more.

My watch read 2:10 and felt heavy on my wrist. That's when I could stand it no longer and followed the enemies gaze. Another head was outlined next to Billy Gee's. Mangin, his face long and flickering as a candle flame, looked down on me, his mouth smiling and his eyes alive with greed.

"Here they come," B&T told me. Shouts from a couple of dentists indicated that the attack was coming up the other side of the hill also.

Mangin's crew started forward using cover to coneal their exact position and numbers but not disguising their advance. They reminded me of beaters on a royal hunt. The twins, I realized, were the prize. But I was the prey.

That made me reach into my jacket pocket. Friday it would have been for my pills, but that Saturday it was for the gun. The polished bone leaped into my palm. Turning so that no one could see, I drew it. Air pistols popped in the cold air.

"Got one! I think I got one," someone yelled as bored videoteers's filmed and the Mangin's beaters moved up the hill toward us. Then they were all gone.

Wind raced, thunder rolled, the summer sky was dark with an approaching storm. Figures in lace shivered at the sudden chill. Women stood on balconies looking down on the marble floor of a courtyard. Men with tapering fingers and clothes in colors that leaped at my eyes, unfurled nets, grasped silver stakes. I was among them, standing so still that they couldn't see me. I reminded myself of Billy Gee Thursday night.

At that thought I raised my eyes and saw his headless body hanging on an iron spike on a gray stone wall. He was skinny, naked; legs, arms, and crotch seeming to melt away into phosphorus. For the first time I felt sorry for the kid.

Mangin stood on the stairs with others dressed in black, and I remembered a phrase Jackie had used: "the Undying Cabal." His hand pointed, his fingers wavered like smoke, his mouth opened to shout an order, and noise grated in my ears. Mangin looked right at me and spoke softly, a whisper that I could hear. "The storm has brought you to the killing floor."

Then a dozen brightly dressed men were in motion on the black-and-white marble floor. An explosion of light made my eyes blur; another, and I was twirling to get away. Their shouts tore at my ears; the torches they carried blinded me. I knew this was the Chase. The courtyard covered the same area as the abandoned dance floor. One of the Chase raised a silver net and squinted trying to find me. Spinning on the marble to face him, I aimed my bow gun.

I stood beneath the stairs where Mangin and his friends watched. He picked me out, pointed a finger and said, "Leal!" so loudly the word numbed my hearing. A wind whistled into the court through iron gates, rain drops fell, and torches flickered. I tried to aim the gun at him, and a hand grabbed mine. At that moment, I was aware of snow falling on my shoulders and people screaming all around me.

"Those lights. There go those lights again."

"He's hit. I hit him. There's the paint."

"Rosko? Are you OK?" B&T held my gun arm up in the air still in character. "You were twirling like one of them dervishes."

"You looked like you were trying to duck those flashing lights," one of the dentists said. "Aren't they something you arranged?" She looked scared.

"Mangin's people took one look at you and ran," someone was whooping. "You sure spooked them."

"I got one of them," said a dentist with yellow paint all over his face. "Get the judges to look right at the bottom of his vest."

"How many did we get? How many did we lose?" I tried to pull myself back to the world, to the game of Take the Flag, to Cancer.

"Two and two." B&T told me. "Everyone started watching you. Mangin's people came right over the top. Then they saw you aiming that thing at the lights and they ran." He gave a little laugh as if he were in on the gag. His eyes looked less certain. "You should stop waving that gun," he whispered. Realizing it was still in my hand, I stuck the bow gun back in my jacket pocket but kept my hand on it.

"Three, we got three. Where are the judges?" The paint-splattered dentist kept yelling.

"Did you get that light action?" A videoteer who had come up the hill with Mangin's people called. Everyone else was very quiet and looking at me. The attackers had stopped quite a way downhill. A couple of snowflakes fell. The hills and houses of Westchester rolled below us. The gun pulsed against my ribs. I felt alive, my heart fluttering, breathing the cold air in short, excited gasps. Then light exploded in front of me, and someone tried to tear away the gun.

Long, wavering hands pulled me back into Capricorn. I twisted away and noticed a white design on the black marble. Pairs of crabs touched their crossed front claws. Rain fell in large warm drops. A figure in a red shirt with a gold-sun pattern held a lantern before me, tried to shine it in my eyes. Before he could blind me, I raised the gun, pulled the trigger, felt tendons lighten, springs snap. The sun dissolved, the man's mouth opened, and his howl grated in my ears.

Other lights darted at me, but with a rush of wind, rain came down like a sheet and doused a lot of them. For a moment I felt invisible. Then I heard a low whispered "Leal" and knew I wasn't. Turning, I found Mangin moving down the stairs, his eyes on me with unblinking intensity. All the awkwardness I remembered him having was gone. Thunder tore at me, and voices chanted at a pitch that almost split my head.

Mangin moved fast, pointing right at me. The others in black were a step or two behind him. I recognized people I had seen Thursday night at Toys when a flare went off in my face, and I was blinded. Twisting my head, twirling to the side I aimed and shot in what I thought was Mangin's direction. "Not regulation!" a preppie voice screeched in real panic.

On the hill in Cancer, my watch had fallen off, I had walked out of my shoes, my clothes hung from me. One of Mangin's team stared in horror at the front of his vest spewing feathers. An acid pellet had burned away the fabric. One of his teammates, a fairly prominent light sculptor, stood looking down the front of the gun. My instinct was to draw back the bow and shoot him in the face, but I couldn't move my arm.

"Rob, don't!" B&T had hold of my sleeve. That was what had dragged me back from Mangin.

"Not regulation!" The preppie screamed again. Cameras recorded the scene. Snowflakes fell, and feathers blew around the wind.

"You want regulation." B&T aimed an air gun at him. Paint splattered. "You got regulation." The other one started to run, but the fight had ended elsewhere, and my dentists made short work of him.

"We got two more!" someone shouted as the casualties ran away, but most of the dentists were staring at me. So were the twins and B&T. Risa and Brad watching intently made no effort to stop my using the gun. Instead they lumbered a little farther off, as if fully aware of how dangerous I was.

Erika got up from the flat stone where she sat, walked toward me very deliberately, and touched my cheek with her palm. We both felt a slight shock at my actually being there.

"Did you get that light? It's hard to adjust, it's around him so fast," one camera woman was asking my videoteer.

"Joel and I are going to wait in the car," a dentist with a paint-splattered vest said, looking away, not meeting my eyes. They left, and two others went with them.

"Hey, you haven't been hit!" B&T yelled at one. As they walked off the marble, another dentist joined them. "You're walking, don't come back!" B&T shouted. Then we were down to eight dentists and a couple of those looked miserable, as if they wished they had the courage to go home.

"It's hard to get a light adjustment. It's like a cloud. I'm not sure I'm getting Leal," my cameraman said.

"Mangin," Erika told Erik. She said other things, but they were in Swedish. She rubbed together the thumb and fingers of the hand that touched my face. He watched me with interest.

Downhill my dentists passed by Mangin's crew. The non-casualties held up their hands in surrender. Vain Video, fascinated now, took up positions from which they could cover all angles. Mangin's people waited as snowflakes fell.

"Rosko, we can make a rush down one side of the hill, get back to the cars," B&T muttered in my ear.

"Three cameras on him," a videoteer said. Below Mangin's people, through bare branches, the landscape was winter brown; bright cars moved. One of the attackers watched the top of the tower through binoculars. Then I saw green grass again.

"We have to stop this thing. Mangin isn't even here," B&T whispered. "Jesus, Rob, will you say something!"

Even a whisper would kill me in Capricorn. The rain there had let up. I heard something behind me breathe, "Come over the Transept," and turning I saw Mangin. Two of the Undying Cabal followed, one with a silver net, the other with a long silver spike. At that moment the Westchester landscape turned into four stone walls.

From far away a dentist yelled, "Here they come!"

My gun was out and aimed in Capricorn. I fired at Mangin's chest. He undulated out of the way. But one of the Cabal behind Mangin wasn't fast enough. His hand was hit, and he dropped the spike with an echoing cry. Mangin jumped on me as I tried to draw the bow back again. Rain still fell but I couldn't feel it. Bright cloth and El Greco faces moved in the background, looking for me by lantern light. Someone flung a net, which passed right through my head.

Then I fell out of my clothes and came down on the floor with Mangin on top of me. He was big, but I couldn't feel his weight. The gun slipped out of my grasp as he put a knee on my wrist and drew a knife made out of gleaming bone. "Blood of the Crab," I thought I heard him say and remembered Billy Gee's body above us and his head back in Cancer. The cries of the one I had shot grated in my ears as I was blinded by the bobbing lanterns of the Chase.

Mangin put the knife to my throat with one hand and grabbed for the bow gun with the other. Squirming away I managed to send it sliding over the floor. As it left me, the noise and light died, and I heard horn calls long and mournful as the sounds of dying elephants in the distance.

Mangin heard that, too, and hesitated for an instant. At that same moment a snowflake hit my face, and B&T called my name. I felt cold marble under me and knew I was back in Cancer. For a moment I felt Mangin's weight on top of me. He looked around at the crowd of dentists and cameras, then quickly put something in his mouth and bit down.

"Who's that he has with him?" someone asked. But before the words were spoken, Mangin had turned to water, fading in the winter light.

"They didn't even wait for us to shoot. Just turned and ran!" A very dumb dentist yelled.

"Rob, what are you doing?" B&T asked. I swam in my own clothes, rolling on the ground alone. Snow got in my eyes as I looked up at the faces and cameras. Mangin was gone as was the gun. B&T gave me a hand up, helped get my clothes straightened out. He was like my nurse, I realized on that gray afternoon. "Was that Mangin I saw?" he wanted to know.

"Right next to the sucker, and I still lost him," a videoteer told another.

"We've kept the flag! We've won!" screeched a paint-splattered dentist.

"I've had enough. Our 'game master' here, whoever he's supposed to be, is out of his fucking mind," another said while walking away.

I shook myself and felt like I was waking up. In the brown grass beside the floor, I saw the bone and sinews of the bow gun. "Get those goddamn cameras off me!" I said, as I walked over and bent to pick up the gun. I felt it come to my hand like a pet. All of its capsules were used or broken. For a second I saw the castle walls and heard the mournful horns. Then I stuck it in my jacket pocket and kept my hands off it.

"I want my fee returned," one dentist was telling me, looking so scared he wanted to cry. I turned my back, and

B&T dealt with him. A videoteer was talking to me, but I couldn't focus on her. My dentists were melting away. No more than four of five remained. But Mangin's team had disappeared also. I wondered if there were underground passages.

Snow continued to fall. The dark came up, as it does in that season, faster than I'd expected. Lights went on in houses below us and on outdoor Christmas displays. Some of the cars were gone from the lot. Nothing that anyone said registered until I saw Erik and Erika standing in front of me.

"We will go with Mr. Armbruster now," Erik said. Erika reached out again and touched my face. This time neither of us were surprised that I was there. I had begun to sweat and feel sick from lack of drugs.

Armbruster's people were coming up the hill. Immersed in their own particular fantasy, they were dressed in pseudo medieval style. They sensed something was wrong and were very quiet. "We claim these as our own rightful rulers," said Amrbruster in his deepest, most portentous voice. Under his breath he said, "I'll have them back to you this Thursday."

Everyone looked at me, waiting for a line I didn't have. My mouth was dry, my throat wouldn't work. I waved my hand in front of my face and stuttered, "The . . . the . . . that's all folks."

On the way back, B&T and I were alone in the car. The radio dial yielded no Chris Kane. B&T watched me a lot but said nothing. I didn't touch the gun or even think about it until we reached the bridge. Then, unable to resist, I reached into my pocket.

In the distance the electric lights of suburbia twinkled. At the same moment I flew in the air over a countryside, the sun of a late June evening bursting out from behind rain clouds. Below, people stood in fields, looked out from the porches of their houses. They pointed as I sailed out of the north. They waited with horns on the hills and blew their long, sad calls as I passed. My heart turned over, my breath grew short, and I took my hand off the ivory butt.

The phone was flashing. It had to be Joan. I hesitated before picking it up. "Who's after me now?" I asked.

"Police from the Manhattan D.A.'s office, Sandy Burrell, a whole bunch of media." She ran off some names. "All wanting to know about you and Jackie Fast who's still missing. They have a warrant out for her and are talking about one for you. Also someone is watching the house from out front."

None of those things interested me. "Anything else?"

"A few music writers, a couple of producer types, and Chris Kane's old agent have called. All wanting to know if you'd heard from him lately." She paused. I was afraid she was going to tell me I had disappointed Dr. Thorax again. Instead she said. "Jason Beautemps called and mentioned Jackie *and* Chris Kane."

That interested me a lot. Since Joan didn't mention the good doctor, I didn't bring him up. "Thanks. I'm sending B&T back to you. I'm going to look up Jason and relive some old times. Have . . ."

"Robbie you need to rest. Why don't you come home. We can have dinner, maybe talk."

"Have a nice night as I was saying. Lock up if you go out." I hung up and turned to B&T. "Why don't you try to get Joan to go out somewhere. Turn on the security system and take a night off. She says there's someone watching from across the street. Probably something to do with the trial."

"What about the car that's following us? They've been somewhere behind ever since we left Mangin's." He looked at me, waiting for an answer.

It occurred to me that I didn't know. I felt the way a client was supposed to feel, uncertain, enjoyably on edge, part way into a movie. Remembering the car outside the gatehouse, I asked, "Blue Buick?"

"No. Black, not big but fast. It's hard to see. There's a guy with gray hair and a younger woman, dark." He stole a look at me and asked. "Had you set any of that up with Mangin? I mean you looked like you didn't know what was going to happen. Were those hologram images? Where did you go? I had hold of your goddamn arm, and you just melted. I could feel your heart pounding." He sounded curious and frightened at the same time.

"Yeah, we had it set up." I gave him the Rosko voice and a tired, dirty chuckle. "All set up." B&T looked at the rearview mirror and didn't believe me. "Look, somehow it's going to be OK. The important thing for you and Joan is to ease off. Let what happens to me happen."

I went back to playing with the radio and ignored his attempts to start conversations. A couple of times I tried for Jason and got his answering machine. When we reached Manhattan, I asked B&T, "Are they still with us?" He nodded. "Get rid of them. When you do, I'm going to get out."

"I think it's some kind of heat," he said. When I didn't reply, he exited at midtown, slowed down for city streets, made no moves that showed he saw them. We were on Broadway not far from the house, when he said, "I have them right behind us. I'm going to take this next right real sudden. They're going to go past. Is that good enough?" B&T was very quiet and serious, and I knew he was trying to think things over.

He made a fast turn, accelerated down an empty block and stopped at the other end. I leaped out saying "Thanks, B&T, for everything today." This was the kind of game he usually liked but he wasn't smiling. Then I walked one way and he drove the other.

After hopping a cab and slumping in the back seat all the way over in the West Village, I went to a bar where I wasn't known, tried calling Jason, and got his answering machine. I downed a brandy and did some coke in the men's room. I left and walked down Hudson Street, putting my jacket collar up against the cold. I was reminded of being a kid in New York on a Saturday night with a number to call and an idea that anything could happen.

Kids walked past in full Carnaby drag. Some of them wore headphones. I wondered if any of them were hearing Chris. One difference between when I was a kid and now was that if I had been wandering the streets back then, Chris would have been with me. Then for a moment I thought I heard his voice:

Hearts inside each other's hearts,
Shivers down each other's spines.

Another bar, another brandy, another trip to the men's room. On the way back I called Jason, got the answering machine, started to leave a message, heard a click and, "No time to talk right now, muffins. There's an event at Bus Stop this very evening. For the Feral Cell. People say Chris will show. Maybe we can both get some questions answered."

He hung up and I went back to the bar. The bartender was a familiar face. He was on the phone and turned away as I approached. That, I realized, was because he was calling someone about me. I left my drink and change and was out the door.

That lyric I had heard or imagined was a fragment Chris Kane had written young and never set to music as far as I knew. If Chris hadn't done it, I had to know who had. Out on Hudson Street no cab was in sight. I plunged on, walking as fast as I could. No one followed me through the Village. Touching the bow gun brought a distant tingle and suggestion of a soft summer night.

Bus Stop was way over on the West Side, unearthed during a factory-area gentrification. An old Greyhound terminal used as a warehouse, all stainless steel and art-deco streamlining under the accumulated paint and dirt. Its interior looked like the outside of a 1940's intercity bus. It had been on the edge of being trendy for a while but had never made it. Maybe because until that night no one had ever discovered the perfect event for it.

When it first opened, the door people had dressed as bus drivers, and there was a lot of that kind of tiresome detail. It seemed to me I remembered the owners going bankrupt. That night the door people were amateurish kids who didn't seem to see me. I had been going to tell them I was with

Jason Beautemps, when one of them, a vaguely Sun Bumish girl, did a double take and waved me in with an expression of awe.

Once, that would have made my night. Right then I wondered how she knew me and what it was she had heard about me. As I came in the door and looked down four steps to the Main Waiting Room, the loudspeaker, authentically muffled and scratchy, blared, "Now arriving, Robert Leal, game master." People looked up, but they didn't interest me. Jason was talking to the brother of the girl I had let into Toys Thursday night.

I went down the stairs. The loudspeaker blared the next name, and I'd had another couple of seconds of the fifteen minutes of fame Prince Warhol promised to each one of us. I threaded through the crowd, which had a tense, expectant feel. Warhol himself was not in evidence.

As I reached Jason, the kid gave me a tight smile that showed chipped teeth. He took both their glasses and headed for the ticket windows, which were the bar. "Raul, please bring the game master a brandy," Jason told him. "Cute and dangerous," he murmured. "This one thinks he's a revolutionary. Can I find them or can I find them?"

"I give him six weeks," I said and thought of Billy Gee.

"Which is more than you've given yourself, dimples." Jason kept an eye on the old-fashioned arrivals-and-departures board. This carried joke notices, like 11:12 FROM KUALA LUMPUR SLIGHTLY DELAYED and ECSTASY EXPRESS DEPARTING 12:30 A.M. "I hear you managed to keep Mangin's hands off your twins."

"The twins were the dessert. I was the main course."

"I'll bet that now you even have some idea why."

I looked around. The wall clock read a few minutes to twelve. The raw sound system played the Boxtops doing "The Letter." "Looks like a nonevent," I said. "Has Andy been and gone?"

"Andy's been getting slower and slower. Capricorn is one he's missed entirely." Jason threw that out to get a reaction.

"I caught part of that show this afternoon," I said as if I hadn't heard. "Do you have that tape for me?"

"That tape has suddenly become a very hot item. Lawyers saying they represent Chris's family got an injunction against the distributors. Fortunately copies can be made of the ones already in circulation. When Raul brings you a brandy, he'll also slip you the cassette." Jason's eyes traveled to the announcement board again. So did others' around the room. "What's Capricorn like?"

As I oriented myself to the scene, I noticed that the crowd was a bit younger and maybe a shade scruffier than usual. Among the usual bored and media-numbed were quite a few who looked alert and expectant. "Scary," I said answering his question.

"Scarier than Cancer?" asked Jason looking at me hard. Raul was back, handing me a drink, smiling as he palmed the cassette into my sleeve. The crowd stirred, and everyone looked toward the board. 12:01 A.M. FROM CAPRICORN ARRIVING ON TIME, it read. Then the lights went down, the sound system played "Death Drops in for Tea," an arrival gate swung open, and the loud speaker blared "THE FERAL CELL."

A lot of people looking at the gate saw nothing. "Something is there," said Jason squinting. I could see forms moving through a night woods. I touched the gun and made out half a dozen figures stepping quickly, eyes darting, hair flowing, hands like smoke. Something about them reminded me of a pack of wolves or maybe dogs gone wild. The Feral Cell watched us as we looked at them. "Do you see Chris?" Jason wanted to know.

I didn't, but I spotted Morgan and thought she reminded me of something I had recently seen. She saw me and stepped forward, putting something to her mouth, passing out of the living diorama and through the gates. I was aware of Jason and a lot of others staring, of "Moon Dance" playing on the sound system. Keeping my left hand on the gun, I reached out with my right to Morgan and found her hand. The crowd stirred around us.

Jason said, "Rob!" full of wonder and envy.

For an instant Morgan looked trapped, wary. I gestured toward the main entrance, and she nodded. Most of the crowd still squinted at the arrival gate. But when I turned at the door I saw some eyes following us: Jason and Raul and a few other kids and a man and young woman who looked familiar to me.

Out on the street I said, "My place?" She nodded, and I raised my hand for a cab. She breathed what sounded like "too fast" and led me away. At the end of the street the silent Hudson flowed, and the traffic of the West Side Highway rushed like a river. On the block, patrons of Bus Stop got out of cabs, people from other clubs came and went, a Sex-anon meeting was breaking up, the attendees trying not to cruise as they left.

Few saw Morgan, and not many saw me as we walked. She traveled fast, alert. The streets, the taxis and lights, the voices and short blasts of music from radios heard when bar or club doors opened imposed themselves on another landscape. There, trees melted in the dark, house lights blurred, figures followed us, long and loping.

"For your safety," Morgan murmured as we crossed an avenue against the lights.

The long day, the excitement and fear, had left me strung-out, the drugs and booze had numbed me. My legs moved by themselves. Against the lights of a Korean fruit stand, a figure in gray-leather tunic and pants stopped to watch us pass.

Morgan tugged at my sleeve. "Don't touch the bow gun," she told me in a soft, echoing whisper. I let go of the gun butt and the figure faded. Heading home on that Saturday night, Morgan moving like a gray wolf beside me, I knew I was dying and had never felt as alive.

Remembering Mangin and Toys and what Joan had said about my place being watched, I took a detour and came down the street above mine. From there we could go down the alley to my back door. Two guys walked ahead of us sharing a joint. A car full of black kids rolled by. No one sat in parked cars, no figures lurked in doorways.

The alley received all its light from the two streets. I watched someone walk past the far end as we approached my back door. Morgan looked long into Capricorn. "You sleep in the shadow of the Beast." She showed her teeth in what could have been a smile. The back door was just off the alley. We went down the few steps. Shapes moved in Capricorn. A red safety light burned in Cancer. Something scuttled away behind garbage cans.

I jumped, then fumbled for my keys. From Capricorn came the sound of horns. Morgan tensed. Getting in the back involved deactivating the security alarm and opening two locks: three keys. From the street came a rush like a flood. I turned the alarm off.

Horns grew louder. The second key opened one lock, but I couldn't locate the third key in the dark. The rushing sound was metal wheels on concrete. Tall figures rolled into the alley. I jammed a key in the lock as a girl laughed.

"Read this, Leal," she said and tossed something that glanced lightly off my elbow, as I twisted the knob and pushed open the door.

The skaters rushed away, and I bent down for what they had thrown. It seemed that no one was home. My hands shook as I got the door locked. What had been tossed was a wallet and a plastic covered I.D. both covered with something sticky. As I focused on the face and name of Desmond Dupree, the sound of the skates reminded me of who he was. "This guy was my cab driver yesterday."

Morgan nodded as though she understood. "Blood of the Crab," she whispered.

City light was at the windows and the skylight. Red and green appeared when I flicked on my console. I remembered the tape in my pocket, fumbled getting it into the deck, had trouble pushing the buttons. As I walked to the bed, I staggered, reached for my drugs, coughed.

In that glow Morgan was a silhouette. They say those actors evoke the most who are least defined. She was all the faces seen in the windows of passing cars and longed for, the shapes caught under a street lamp half a block ahead and never caught up with. She reached out for me, and her breath came in little pants that I could feel on my cheek. "Do this," she whispered. "In Capricorn we crabs must swim."

Morgan drew me down to the bed, opened my jacket and shirt, took the gun out of my pocket, and placed it on my chest. I noticed that it felt warm and that she touched a bone knife on her belt. Chris sang softly in the dark. She put her arms around me. The fast breathing made me light-headed. The bed seemed to swirl below us. Morgan held her face close to mine. She breathed into my mouth as Chris Kane sang about loss and hope:

Running from the suburbs where,
Straights all cried, 'Beware, beware,
His flowing eye and flashing hair'.

Tripping down the road to hell,
Wrecked and laid and saved as well
As betrayed by the Feral Cell

Every part of me came alive, and something that I remembered as being life spread through my body. At some point my clothes fell away, and I felt ground under me. Moonlight almost blinded me; rustling leaves echoed in my head. It was like I was sixteen on a summer night, out of the car and on the grass.

When Morgan drew off her clothes, I could feel them almost alive brushing over me. I focused on her face and saw it float, shifting as though reflected in water. Then I took a deep breath and gasped as my lungs filled up.

I thrashed coughing on top of my bed. Morgan's hands reached out and drew me back into the summer night as Chris as familiar as déjà vu sang:

When I on honey dew had fed,
Too numb to hope, too dumb to dread,
Screaming for dope, I got life instead.

"Breathe with me," she said and blew air into my lungs, and I was back in the moonlight, holding onto her. I could feel her ripple over me, see her eyes constantly alert, smell summer like perfume. There was a moment when I wanted to swim and come like a salmon. But trying it broke the rhythm of my breathing. I heard Chris singing a new song of his own and knew I was falling into Cancer.

Betrayed and saved
By the Feral Cell.

Then Morgan drew me back to Capricorn. And as when I was sixteen I wanted to practice until I got it right. After that I sat panting like a fox and looked around to see blue lights and long, white-clad figures holding them. I started, but Morgan stroked my back to calm me, "Caprii," she murmured.

One of them had a shallow bowl, which he handled carefully, his long face wavering in the moonlight. Morgan dipped her fingers into the bowl. "Only this will keep you here," she said and placed her fingers in my mouth. Something burned and froze me, and I almost fell back to where Chris Kane sang "Death Drops in for Tea."

It took her many more tries before I could swallow and feel it pass into my throat and stomach. The night was alive in Capricorn. "Honey dew," I said, "milk of paradise."

Morgan looked at me. "That's what he called it also the first time."

I knew who she meant. "Chris." I choked on the air. "Where is he?"

"He said if you asked for him, he would find you." Her voice sounded very far away as she said that. At some point the Caprii and their blue lights disappeared, and Morgan left me. Once I woke up to get under the covers and saw gray morning through my skylight.

Then it was much later in the day, and someone was unlocking the door of my room. I reached by reflex for the bow gun and remembered Morgan taking it to be reloaded. Joan and B&T entered with someone else, a man trying not to look as pissed off as he felt. I couldn't focus on his identity.

"Rob," said Joan, "Dr. Thoreau is here. We're going to take you to the hospital."

I couldn't get my throat to scream as Thorax said, "We suspect that you have a massive abdominal cancer."

CHAPTER Five

They had trouble getting my arms into the sleeves of a shirt. My hands had no strength. I couldn't produce words.

"We will have to assess the extent of the problem," said Dr. Thorax. "Nothing we've seen so far looks untreatable."

Cancer, both world and disease, was a dream. I was aware of a pair of eyes looking into the room from Capricorn. They were real. Mangin's long, pale face took shape beyond the walls of my loft. He sat in the summer sunshine on a big black horse and seemed to be peering in my direction.

"Rob, just find out how bad this is and what they can do for you," Joan told me behind tears. Out of love, she and B&T—trying to save me from one danger—were getting me away from another.

B&T was quiet and down as he packed an overnight bag. Seeing him include my drug box, I realized that for the first time in a long while I didn't feel that need. Taking the Chris Kane tape out of my deck he held it up and tried to manage a smile.

I wondered how Chris was going to find me at Cedars of Lebanon Hospital. In Capricorn the sun shone on the long faces and bright clothes of the Chase as they spread out around me. Mangin and several of his black-clad friends watched me like cats with an injured bird. Then I remembered that Cedars was where Chris had gone also.

On my desk Desmond Dupree stared up at me through the blood stains on his I.D.: Someone who had the misfortune to let his path cross mine. A drawer was open, and I managed to claw the picture in and push it shut. I could feel the hair on my neck bristle.

Dying brought out nothing noble in me. All it did was make me afraid. Death itself didn't bother me as much as the humiliation of sickness and the waste that I knew my life had been. Outside my house, I felt someone watching from down the street at Toys. I'd gotten trapped between sickness and the Chase and doubted that Chris would recognize or want to know me.

"You're in good hands, Robert. I'll see you uptown this evening." Dr. Thorax was uncomfortable out of his office, standing on the street with a patient who was trying to ignore him.

That Sunday afternoon the city seemed half-deserted, as if a good part of the population had fled or died. "New York's going bad," I mumbled. Joan, sitting next to me, patted my arm.

"Don't worry about the dentists," B&T said. "We can take care of them for tonight. Then you can think about what you want to do next." The dentists were of no concern to me. In silence I looked out the window for flashes of Capricorn. The speed of the car bothered me. I felt like I wasn't traveling as fast as it was.

Uptown past Eighty-sixth Street the ground began to rise. On top of a hill in the upper Nineties, stretching over half a dozen city blocks, sat Cedars of Lebanon. It is an old institution, a hospital for surgeons on the outskirts of a city. It's symbol, a roll of bandages and a scalpel, flew on the flags over its new pavilions and old wings.

As we got out of the car, a gust of warm air blew from Central Park across the street. At the same moment I saw Joan and B&T catch glances of a silver van that sailed up

Fifth Avenue. "Shit. I thought we lost them way back downtown," he said. She gestured for him not to worry me. He said, "I'll stay with the car. Talk to you tonight, Pops," he added. "The dentists are gonna find out about how being Dr. Cobalt's son messed Danello up real bad."

Joan came inside and got me admitted. Forms blurred before my eyes. Pens slipped out of my hands. We walked from office to office down endless halls, sat in waiting rooms. Joan filled out the forms, signed my name once or twice when I couldn't.

Then I was in a hospital room. A couple sitting with a patient in the bed by the window looked up. Joan drew the curtain and helped me get into ridiculous pajamas. Then I lay on the bed feeling numb.

"Rob, who's after you?" She looked me right in the eye, and I looked away, felt as if I had been caught. When I'd first met her, the style for girls and boys had been forties B-movie dumb. Looking in those dark eyes for a few seconds would tell you Joan was far from dumb. But somewhere along the line I had begun to take her for granted, to forget that she could see and think as well as I could. At least.

"Mangin," I told her. The word got stuck in my throat, came out as a whisper.

"Benjy Mangin?" She was startled. Then she smiled, and I remembered he had made one of his forays into the city when she was first around the clubs. "He was a creep twelve years ago. Everyone wanted him because he was supposed to be loaded. The reaction was almost always the same, once people got close to him, they found out they didn't want to know him. I remember that all of a sudden he had to go away. There was a girl. And a guy?" It was as if Joan was humoring me with a bedtime story.

"She was an artist?" I remembered photos of a black woman in the papers, a leather mask, a sensational disappearance.

"She was a sculptress, what was her name? And there was an art dealer involved with a French guy? Charles? One of them disappeared; the other was found dead. People talked about voodoo. Celeste something was the woman's name. She was Haitian."

"What about Mangin?" I wondered how many deaths lay around him.

"Everyone said he was involved with both of them, and he was the last one seen with them. A bloody statue was in it somehow. And mutilations. It was a *New York Post* favorite. Everyone knew Benjy had done something bad. No one could figure out just what."

"He got off?"

Joan nodded. "His lawyers just swooped in, and I don't think he even had to appear in court. I remember it was the first time I understood what real money could do." She pulled back the curtains around my bed. "We can beat him, no matter what game it is," she said, smiling at me.

The couple with the other patient looked up and nodded, gave tentative smiles. Their patient remained unconscious. We nodded back, and Joan said, "It has to do with Jackie Fast and her friend Drew, doesn't it?"

I remembered Jackie sitting in the garden telling me about one passing Capricorn along to the next like a disease. I whispered, "You and B&T have to stay away from this."

Joan ignored me. "Sandy Burrell's going crazy looking for Jackie. No one has seen her since she left court Friday. Sandy thought it was a good idea to admit you here, get the heat off you."

"All settled in?" Jolly Dr. Thorax appeared with a clipboard in his hand, much more at ease here than downtown.

Joan stood up saying, "We have to get ready for the dentists. Is there anything you want me to bring tomorrow?"

"All the information you can find about little Benjy. And his grandfather's scandals. Newspaper stuff, pictures." My guts went cold when I remembered Mangin's face. Joan kissed me and was gone.

"Let me try to explain what we'll be doing tomorrow," said Thorax. "You haven't eaten today?" He stood beside my bed. Across the room, the couple pretended not to listen. Through the windows I could see night over Central Park.

"You will be on a liquid diet tonight," Dr. Thorax told me as I looked past him. "We'll give you something to clean you out." I felt no need for food or drugs right then. But whatever I'd drunk in Capricorn the night before was fading. I wanted to be left alone. "Remember that nothing we've found so far is untreatable. Your prognosis is not all bad."

"Minus a few organs and my hair, I have maybe a fifty-fifty chance of making it a few more years." I spat that out.

"There are people in this hospital who'd give a lot for those odds." The doctor's eyes went to the other patient. "I'll be around tomorrow to introduce the people who'll be involved in treating you. Any questions?"

I remembered to shake my head and went on looking out the window. "Remember, Rob, abdominal cancer if caught in time is not a sentence of death." When I didn't answer he asked the couple by the other bed, "How's the patient doing?" They made appreciative noises, the kind Doc Thorax liked to hear. He said good night and left.

After a while I got up and went to the windows. Streetlights shone on sidewalks in Central Park six stories below me. I nodded vaguely to the couple at the other bed. Their patient was gaunt and ravaged-looking, face pale, clumps of hair gone. But he was just a kid, I realized, no more than twenty one.

"This is Gary's fourth major surgery in the last two years," said his mother. On a walk in front of an empty bench two skaters circled slowly under skeleton trees in the park. "There are cancers now that just seem to strike teenagers," she said. It seemed I had seen something about that on television, but my attention was concentrated on the skaters. I couldn't make out their faces, and it was too cold for them to be wearing their Sun Bum outfits. But seeing them brought back Desmond Dupree, the Friday afternoon traffic jam, the rush of skates in the alley.

"Poor kid," added the father. I nodded, tried to put compassion into my smile. Capricorn was near, I could feel it.

The city glow faded, the lights of Central Park got blotted out. The land rose, and I saw summer evening light reflecting off the windows of scattered houses. "A complete ileostomy this time," the father said.

"His surgeon is a partner of your doctor," said the mother. Faintly from somewhere uptown I heard the horns of Capricorn. Below, long-faced people in white pants and shirts looked up and pointed at us.

"That's everything removed below the stomach on down," said the father. "He was operated on yesterday." The kid was conscious but not paying attention to us. In a state of semi-shock and drug stupor, he lay halfway into Capricorn.

They brought a tray and left it beside my bed. I pretended interest and wandered back there. Dinner was tea and pineapple juice and jello. I felt the edges of what I had drunk in Capricorn fading. As it did, the pain and need that would make me want drugs started eating at me.

Concentrating on my growing panic seemed to make the sunset in Capricorn clearer. I lay on my bed and watched it through the ceiling and walls. I wondered if I wanted to have Chris see me as I was. He belonged to the time when anything was possible and death was unimaginable until it came for him.

What had I done with the nearly fifty years I'd been given? Found a racket somewhere between acting and pimping. Gotten so afraid to look at myself that I'd die in agony rather than do it. In the twilight on another world, people pointed fingers that wavered like candle flames as they saw me against the sky.

A soft voice said, "Could we talk, Mr. Leal?" I jumped. A man, a small oriental, dressed in pajamas not much different from my own smiled at me. "I'm Mr. Montoya, your night nurse." The kid in the other bed was sitting up, groggy and unfocused; his parents spoke to him quietly. "Dr. Thoreau wanted me to talk to you about what's going to happen tomorrow."

"Tests," I said and shrugged. "He's mad because I don't

get as excited playing his game as he used to get playing mine." I stared out at Capricorn.

"You are excited about something, though, Mr. Leal." Montoya was reading my blood pressure. "You should try to stay calm. Do you want something to help? No? Compared to some here your chances are not bad." We both found ourselves looking at the kid in the other bed. Instinctively I knew what they were doing for young Gary was entirely a holding operation. "But it is necessary to concentrate, to understand. The body responds to the mind."

Montoya's Spanish name and oriental face reminded me of a video image: grafitti on the walls of a tropical city. "Are you from the Philippines?"

"Manila."

"It went bad." Manila had been as one with Beirut and Belfast, with Caracas and Berlin, a place of riots, bombs, wrecked streets, the subjects of television-news specials. I was vague on exactly what had happened. Had Mangin visited? Did people see Capricorn?

"My family left before that." Montoya stopped smiling, and an understanding came into his eyes. "I will talk to you again." He turned to the other bed. "I will be taking good care of Gary," he assured the couple.

Lying back, I tried to concentrate on the other world. Night had fallen there. It was darker than the city glow outside the windows. "Good night, Mr. Leal," Gary's parents said. "I think he'll be pretty quiet tonight."

Montoya and others appeared. Things were done to me, all of them indignities, some of them painful. They gave me purges. I had taken no drugs in almost twenty-four hours. I had eaten nothing in days. Halfway into Capricorn, I could feel the hospital pulling me back to Cancer.

After they left, I went to the window and looked out at the park. At first it seemed empty; nothing moved in the pools of light along the walks. Then a figure twirled half a dozen times, and ended staring directly up at my window. The kid in the bed stirred, and we looked past the skater into another world.

It was night in Capricorn, but I could see in its dark. A distant swath of flickering lights moved like a blade over an open field. Nearer at hand were stationary pinpoints of blue light. Concentrating on them I saw that they hung over the gates and porches of stone houses. A man standing in a doorway blew three short blasts. On the last he looked up in my direction and did an awestruck double take.

The swath flowed toward him. My sight was like a cat's when looking into the Capricorn night. The flowing light was dozens of lanterns held by horsemen trotting across an open field. I spotted bright silks and pale faces as at Mangin's Roost or outside my bedroom earlier that day. The Chase was out. "Did they give you lots of morphine?" asked a slurred voice at my elbow. Gary watched the same thing I did.

"No."

"Some kids downstairs are so far gone they see this stuff all the time. It happened for me the last time I was here. After major operations they give morphine. Real good. I was on it for a week when I lost my leg. It's fire and ice, peace and pain."

Trying not to look at the aluminum crutches against the wall, I asked, "Did you ever try going to Capricorn?" Gary's eyes went further out of focus, and he shook his head.

The Chase was headed toward the houses below my room. People in that crossroads village didn't yet see the horsemen. They watched from their windows as two women in white smocks and pants walked toward a huge tree that grew where Cedars of Lebanon stood. They carried bowls, which they set down on a flat stone. The man who had seen me blew a last long call. I knew the bowls they carried held the milk of paradise.

The kid on the bed writhed in pain. His buzzer was in his hand. "Gary, what's wrong?" Montoya crossed the room without looking at me. Central Park shone through Capricorn. The skaters still cruised under the street lamp.

"I need a shot."

"In a little while. Let's sit you up. Wash your face."

Amidst the Chase I saw a figure in black, a member of Mangin's Undying Cabal. Montoya didn't notice me as I moved away from the window, but the Chase did. They looked up and pointed as I let the ache in my guts and the terror along my spine draw me out into the hall.

No one saw me move along the corridor and push with all my weight to get through a door under a red exit sign. A summer night existed just beyond the cement service stairs I descended. The door on each floor had a sign. Two flights below mine one read CHILDREN'S ONCOLOGY. This was ground level in Capricorn.

On the door was a window. I looked through it into the children's cancer ward. In the hall two attendants pushed a rolling stretcher; a nurse moving beside them held an apparatus attached to the patient. On the stretcher was a kid no more than nine or ten, skeleton thin. Her huge round eyes looked past their pain and found me. The wake of that dying child's passing drew me into Capricorn.

I remembered to take short breaths as my pajamas fell away. The women in white smocks and pants left the bowls and backed away reverently. The tree above us and all the trees around it appeared to have human faces. These seemed to smile down on me as I bent over the bowls.

Suddenly the horn blew. The man I had seen before stood on the porch of his house. Men with staves and scythes ran out of the houses. Windows opened and people crawled out onto their roofs. The Chase was headed for me. I heard a sound like muffled sirens that was their yelling. Their torches flaring in the night blinded me.

Then something tenuous as smoke dashed from bushes in front of them and tried to dart away. As I crouched I saw gray clothes fall off, saw a naked woman running toward the houses, and recognized Jackie Fast. The Chase turned their attention from me and went after her.

Watching, I understood that the people in the houses were prepared to guard Jackie from the Chase. Without real weapons some of them ran forward. Two of the hunters were no more than a horse's length behind her. One rose in the saddle, and silver flowed through his hands, caught the light of the moon.

I tried to yell her name. I choked on the air, and a scream tore out of me. The silver net fell over Jackie's head, carried her to the ground. All action stopped for a moment, villagers and Chase stared at each other.

Then a black-clad Undying Cabalist riding with the horsemen gave orders. Half a dozen hunters leaped off their horses. Some secured Jackie, binding her in the net. Others crouched low and aimed metal tubes at the house. I recognized these as being some kind of weapon.

The rest of the Chase spurred forward with swords drawn against the villagers. The night shimmered; their torches and long pale faces wavered in the dark. The villagers stood firm. Jackie was thrown over the back of a horse. The villagers made what sounded like a low moan. The man with the horn blew another long note.

A figure on a roof raised an arm, threw. A horse reared and plunged; a hunter grasped his arm and gave a loud screech. A man armed with a stick was knocked down by the one from the Undying Cabal. The weapons fired, flames exploded against a house, a window broke in another, and light flashed inside. Having given the villagers something to keep them occupied, the Chase turned away and started after me.

As they did, a figure in gray leaped down from the tree and stood beside me, a long bone knife in hand. His hair flowed as if it were underwater; his face flickered in the night. And I knew. "Chris!" The name echoed.

He looked at me, and his mouth moved. Sound seemed to drift out. "Asshole," he said, "you drew them this way." He moved away from me, right at the Chase.

Then horns sounded on all sides and pinpoints of blue light danced in the dark. The hunters who had dismounted leaped back into their saddles. The ones who held Jackie spurred away, heading south, and Chris went after them. People dressed in white like the villagers, armed with farm tools, ran out of the dark. The blue lights were from the small lanterns they carried.

Gray forms moved with them, their faces pale, their hair and clothes flowing as they swam in Capricorn: the Feral Cell. The fires from the burning building blinded me when I looked in that direction. Before the flames were doused, the stairwell outside Children's Oncology, my clothes piled in the doorway, loomed up threatening to pull me back. I swam panting toward the Capricorn night.

Around me, the faces of the Feral Cell were like silver masks; their fingers and feet trailed away like candle flames. It was hard to tell them apart. Then a head tossed, a face smiled, and I found another face I knew.

"Morgan!" I tried to whisper the name. But it came out in a grating roar. The rest of the Feral Cell went off after the blue lights and disappeared into the dark. "I saw Chris." I choked on the air. "He didn't stay." The lost sound in my voice surprised me.

She gestured toward one of the bowls. "Drink." They were half-full of the dark liquid that I remembered from the night before. The faces sculpted out of the leaves on the trees seemed to nod their approval. I crouched down furtively and tried to gulp between breaths. It burned my lips and froze my tongue. Behind me in the distance danced the corridors and night lights of the children's cancer ward.

It took a few tries before I forced the milk of paradise into my throat then into my stomach. The people of Capricorn watched, motionless, fascinated as if I were something rare and wonderful. I lapped like a wild animal until a hand touched my shoulder, and I found Morgan kneeling beside me.

"Rest," she whispered. "The Feral Cell has lost and gained tonight." For a while I subsided into a kind of dream, curled up under the benevolent faces of the trees. I could still see snatches of Cancer. Children tossed in their sleep, awoke in pain, or just lay lonely and afraid in their hospital beds.

Then Morgan whispered, "Awake," and held my arm. We

were alone. Small blue lanterns shone outside a couple of the houses. Morgan helped me drink from the other bowl, then bent to drink from it herself. As she did, I saw a lighted corridor, heard someone walking quickly in rubber-soled shoes. An orderly carrying linen stepped right through us as we stepped into Cancer.

In the stairwell I struggled with my pajamas, suddenly aware of the cold. Morgan looked around quickly like an animal in a new place. She glanced through the walls at the skaters out in the park. From her belt she drew the long knife with the bone blade and handle.

"I'm getting out of this place," I said. My slippers seemed to keep falling off my feet.

"The Caprii saw you here," Morgan said. "They will want to dress you tomorrow night and return the bow gun to you."

"So why don't I stay in Capricorn?"

"Days are safer for you here."

"Chris thinks I drew the Cabal to Jackie."

"These things are not your fault nor his. Quiet now."

"Will he get her back?" I asked. This seemed like a game, one that I might have made up myself.

Her expression would have been a smile except that it showed too many teeth. Morgan said, "Crab and Goat are very close in the shortest and the longest days. You and Jackie felt the pull of Capricorn. Cancer has made Chris . . . restless." She stared out in the direction of the park, her fingers touching her knife handle. "Rest now. I will guard you until Chris returns."

I could see beyond the hospital walls to the skaters under the streetlight and at the same time glimpse the Capricorn night, moonlight, and stars shining behind Morgan. She stepped under the approving faces on the trees and down the hospital corridor at the same time.

I went back up to my room and found Montoya sitting with Gary.

"Mr. Leal, where have you been?"

"Taking a little walk."

"You are not supposed to do that. I've been looking for

you for the last hour." I nodded my understanding, went to look out the window. "You're my responsibility here." The skaters stood looking up at my window. Montoya, small and serious, sensing something, put his hand on Gary's shoulder as if to protect him.

Then Montoya led me to my bed, pulled the curtains, and brought out a medical tray. "These are procedures you must follow tonight and tomorrow morning," he said trying to take my blood pressure and frowning. "You think that there is some other way out of this than medical treatment?"

"Sticking apple peels in my shoes and facing the east? Thinking good thoughts and eating brown rice? That kind of thing?"

"Something like that." He was having trouble hitting my arm veins with a needle. I could have told him not to bother, but the things of Cancer had stopped concerning me. "What do you do, Mr. Leal?" he asked.

"I play games. All the time."

"Is that what you think you are doing now?" I understood he was trying to help. I had once seen a paramedic keeping up a conversation with a man who'd had a heart attack, holding him awake and alive.

It was hard for me to focus on Montoya's words. "My treatment is not of this world," I finally managed to say. He said some other things that I didn't hear, floating as I was half in Capricorn.

After he left, a purge he had given me began to take effect. On one of my trips back from the bathroom, I went to the window. Something moved in the silent park.

"What was that you were drinking?" Gary sounded like he was talking in his sleep.

I knew what he meant but pretended not to. "From Montoya?"

"No. Before when you were licking stuff off a plate." If I looked carefully the park disappeared, and all I could see were the blue lights on the houses of the crossroads village. Summer dawn was almost in the sky. "Do you know those people you were talking to?" asked the drug-remote voice from the bed.

"I grew up with one of them," I said and wondered if I was passing a kind of curse onto the kid. But how much time did he have anyway? What I had was maybe a kind of cure. "He di . . . he had leukemia when he was about your age."

"When was that?"

"Nineteen seventy two. He had a couple of hits as a rock musician. His name was . . . is Chris Kane." I wanted to see if the name meant anything.

Gary said, "He was supposed to have died. That's what everyone thought, right? They talked about it the other day on the radio." Out in the park, something moved beyond the lights where the skaters stood guard. "Can you find out how he did it? Will he tell you?" Gary asked.

It felt like someone drowning trying to grab hold of me. I realized that we were both in great danger and that hope was not something to be tossed around casually. "I don't know," I told him. "Let me give you this tape he just made."

"Fire and ice, heaven and hell," Gary said as I brought the tape, loaded it into the headset on his pillow. He gave a moan and rang for Montoya as his pain cut through the drugs. He said no more to me. It was as if he had awakened from a fever dream of which I was a part.

Before the nurse could show up I lay on my bed and looked at my dying for the first time. On some level, my body and brain had known what was happening to me. Because I could see no acceptable way out, I'd refused to acknowledge it. Medical treatment seemed like death by inches. Gary pleading quietly for more morphine proved that.

Now that I had found hope it was something that I previously would have considered a hallucination. The thing that made me believe in Capricorn was Chris and his music. With some part of my mind I believed he had drawn death toward me.

We met in junior high school just about when the politicians like Kennedy and King started dying. Then it was the musicians like Redding and Hendrix and Chris Kane. Then death took my family. Chris somehow was the link between music and my family. My parents had liked him. He went two years before my mother. My father died a couple of years later. Realizing that was an answer of sorts for me, I dropped into a kind of doze.

Next morning, I woke up with the Cedars of Lebanon. Breakfast carts rattled in the hall, supplies of fresh sheets arrived, stretchers hauled people to surgery, doctors and nurses spoke brightly and alertly.

A tall Islands black woman shot Gary up with morphine and told him, "Today we have to get you up and walking so you can heal."

Outside looked cold and gray. Inside, I knew, must be warm, but I couldn't feel it. On a meadow over in Central Park, half a dozen cops led their saddled horses. The police smoked cigarettes and drank from paper cups. Morning fog lingered. Out of it, as if by magic, a dozen kids appeared, mostly girls in their early teens. They took the reins from the cops and led the animals across the field.

I looked at Gary, who stared back blank-eyed. Caught in the morning light, his patchy baldness, huge helpless eyes, gaunt features made him the representation of the ageless, timeless victim. "How's it going this morning?" I asked. His lips moved, but no words came out, and I knew he wasn't seeing Capricorn at that moment.

"Robert?" I turned and found Dr. Thorax standing with two other men and a woman. All of them wore white lab coats, the mark of medical people and meat handlers. "This is Dr. Wang and Dr. Feingold," the woman and one of the men nodded, "who will be doing the testing. And this is Dr. Millstein for surgery, which I think will be indicated." Millstein was short and dark. He held his hands away from his body, ready: a dangerous blade man.

I watched him watching me as Thorax spoke. Millstein sized me up, the hired killer observing as his client showed him the intended victim. Somewhere I had read that the ones in charge of medical schools looked for aggressive kids to be surgeons: ones bright enough to learn some biology and not afraid to stick a knife into another person.

"Now, are there any questions?" Thorax asked, and I remembered to shake my head. "They'll bring you down to Dr. Wang's section shortly," he said frowning gravely. "I'll be talking to you later today when we know more." They left, and I imagined them out in the corridor raising their eyebrows. It reminded me of Sandy Burrell with poor Jackie Fast.

With that, a shadow passed over the brightly lit room. A cloud had crossed the sun in Capricorn. The phone started to ring. It took me a couple of tries to get the receiver off the hook.

"Hey, Dad, how's it going?" B&T was calling from a telephone booth.

"I take it the phones are tapped. Maybe this one is too." The world was closing in on me. "How did you do with the dentists?" I didn't care about that. But the sound of B&T being B&T was going to be something from Cancer that I would miss.

"About half a dozen of them showed up, the real hard core. They had a lot of questions about what Rosko and me were doing Saturday afternoon at Mangin's. They wanted to know where Cobalt was. I gave them a lot of crap about being brought up as an adopted son. We kept dropping hints that Cobalt was somewhere nearby. It came down to them wanting to go into your room and look, and me pretending to stop them.

"The dentists got so interested in getting me out of the way, they didn't notice Joan slipping off. When finally they did pile into the room, they saw Cobalt in cape and hat closing the skylight and making it over the roofs. It really worked because Joan had figured out something about Cobalt: he's all cape and hat!"

And life could go on without me. Something ripped in my chest, but I managed to say, "I think you have the idea."

"There's something else. Jackie Fast didn't show up in

court this morning. There's an all-points out for her. Sandy Burrell says they wanted to talk to you real bad, but she managed to put them off because of your being in the hospital. So it kind of works out . . ."

"Mr. Leal? I'm Felicity Palmer, your day nurse," the West Indian who had tended Gary stood at the foot of my bed. "You are due for preparation and tests." A short beaming black woman stood with her. "This is Barbara, who will go with you."

"Sounds like you're busy," said B&T. "We'll be up later. Joan has the stuff you asked for." He hung up.

"Will you be able to walk or would you like a wheelchair?" asked Felicity.

While I pondered that, the two women looked out the windows to the park. Police cars had appeared. Cops searched the bushes near the street lamp where I'd seen the skaters the night before. A couple of the mounted police stood with a pair of kids who clung to each other and stared at two body bags. They had obviously found some corpses. The rest of the cops held the horses and watched. "Why would anyone think it was safe to skate in the park at night?" Felicity wondered.

"I'll walk," I managed to say and remembered Morgan and her knife.

Capricorn was all around as I was first flushed out and then brought through corridors and tunnels to another hospital building. Lack of food and sleep, the purges, and my sickness should have made me feel very bad. Instead I seemed light enough to float. A couple of times Barbara lost sight of me. Once or twice in the clinics where I was tested, people looked right through me and asked, "Is Mr. Leal still here?"

Once when I was alone, I turned suddenly and saw Morgan watching me from some kind of shaded place. "You got them both," I said.

Her eyes flashed, her mouth moved, and I seemed to hear her say, "They were the ones who killed Desmond Dupree. They have given their blood."

"Yes?" For me there was no turning back, but I had to know.

"Blood of the Goat binds us to Capricorn. Blood of the Crab binds us to Cancer." It sounded like a maxim. I looked again and couldn't find her.

Only after standing guard on the Transept myself did I understand what it cost Morgan to watch over me like that. That day I watched for her outline as she crouched in shadows to avoid the blinding sun of Capricorn. As they drilled my bones for marrow samples, I squinted and saw figures move over light-flooded fields.

Once I lay with a hose up my ass watching on a screen as a barium enema spread through my colon. "The dark egg shape is the tumor," Dr. Wang told me while I worked up the courage to think about the Blood of the Goat which I had drunk.

That clinic in Cedars of Lebanon Hospital was up in the branches of the grove of trees in Capricorn. In their shade it was dark enough for me to see that their leaves had been sculpted to look like human heads with faces. It seemed I was visible there. On the ground I saw a man in red-and-yellow doublet and cloak back up toward his waiting horse, while watching me in fascination and terror.

Morgan leaped from a high branch drawing her knife. The man from the Chase turned to run, and the bone blade buried itself in his side. He threw up his hands, took several stumbling steps, and fell into the sunlight. Shielding her eyes, Morgan went after him as I was disconnected from the machine.

"It's size would be classified as massive," said Dr. Wang. "The question is the extent to which it has penetrated the intestine wall." I saw the tumor jutting out of my colon, felt cancer in my liver. "The Duke's scale is A to D in range of prognosis from good to bad."

Neither Morgan nor Chris had reappeared when my tests were over and I was being led out of the elevator on my floor.

"Mr. Robert Leal?" Two men, one black one white, both

obviously cops stepped forward. "Manhattan D.A.'s office." The black detective told me their names and showed me his badge. He was a sergeant. "Sorry to bother you here. But we wonder if we could talk."

"My lawyer...," I said as an automatic response. Then I remembered that the assistant D.A. on the case hung around Mangin. This wasn't a question of law.

"This has nothing to do with you personally, Mr. Leal." He gave a significant pause. "Yet. Just some questions about Jackie Fast." A door to an empty office stood open. The sergeant gestured me inside.

"Such as?" A question for a question. I stood where I was.

"We wondered if you had seen her after you left the courtroom?"

"Not as far as I can remember." A lie was simpler than the truth. And I had a feeling that the one who sent them had a better idea than we did as to what had become of Jackie.

"We know you and she were old friends. She made no effort to contact you in any way?" I remembered the phone call, the lines that were tapped. But it also occurred to me that one way or another the problems of this world weren't going to matter much in a short time.

"I don't recall anything like that." I realized that these two were hacks of their profession, competent enough but not about to break routine and go looking for trouble.

"We're trying to find the last one to have seen her," said the white cop. "We traced her movement Friday night as far as East Ninth Street." They both looked at me hard. "Some of her belongings were found in the garden of a restaurant there."

"I'm sorry, gentlemen. I have to lie down." As I turned I couldn't resist a throw away line. "People say she's been seeing too much of Benjy Mangin."

Several skateboards leaned against the wall outside my room. Inside were Gary's friends, Sun Bums, who had left them there. A box played my Chris Kane tape:

In dreams it was so easy
I'd stride across arena sand,
Facing down that skull-head man
As the hip all cheered to see.

Then with no word of warning,
He came and fingered me.
Before I got my pants on,
Death dropped in for tea.

The sight of Sum Bums with their dyed-blond hair and shorts reminded me of the skaters. But I realized that these were more like the genuine article: the harmless kids we had all come to ignore.

Seeing them and hearing Chris's voice, I remembered him as a kid their age. Tea was what he called whatever he had when he first woke up because that happened at four or five in the afternoon. What he usually had was whatever had not been smoked or dropped or drunk the night before. "Tea time," he would say in a fatuous English accent, wandering around my place in his underwear.

That was in the late sixties when he was 4-F and I was in school and had an apartment on Seventh Street and Avenue A. He was in the group Sleep Rope Dancers, and they let me sing back up.

I lay down on my bed and noticed that one of the girls sitting with Gary looked familiar. She smiled at me and said, "I've seen you in videos." I wondered where I knew her from.

"You own the Feral Cell tape," said a boy. "It's life and death." Had we been so polite when we were young? No, we were arrogant. Sun Bums asked only to be liked. Chris and I had behaved as much like desperados as possible. Listening to that soft, insistent voice, I pictured him on a late afternoon getting a call from a doctor that told him his life was going to come up short.

"You're a friend of Chris Kane's?" said the girl, and I nodded. "I let you into Bus Stop the other night," she added.

"Rob, how are you?" Joan came in wearing a light jacket and carrying a folder. "This is more stuff on Mangin and family."

"Two stiffs in the park," said B&T throwing a *Post* down on the bed. "When are you going to behave, Dad?" The murders were the headline. Smaller type announced Jackie Fast's disappearance as an inside story. "You don't even rate a mention," he said.

Across the room Gary sang along with Chris on the tape, his voice quavery and stoned:

Betrayed and saved
By the Feral Cell.

Joan and B&T sat beside me on the bed. I fumbled but finally got hold of their hands. I wanted to say that they were the only ones I loved. An image came to me of Jackie Fast writhing under a silver net. I remembered what she had said about passing Capricorn on as if it were a disease, and I let go of their hands and started to shiver. The purges and testing seemed to have diluted the Goat's blood in my system. "I want to leave as much as I can for you," I told them. "Sandy already has the papers."

"Jesus," said B&T.

"Rob . . . ," said Joan. It felt like I was cutting the last ropes that held me down. I was set to float away.

"I'm not going to die," I told them. "I'm going to disappear. There may be one last favor I'll want from you." I stopped talking when I saw the look they exchanged. They made conversation for a while. The sun went down outside the window, while through the walls I could see a summer evening.

Gary's friends said good-bye after his parents arrived. The girl from Bus Stop nodded and smiled at me as they left. Then this tired-looking couple and their dying son sat and watched television. Joan and B&T left when Dr. Thorax appeared. Gary's parents seemed to be able to understand what he told me, but I couldn't concentrate.

My television was on without sound. The news had publicity images of Jackie Fast looking glamourous and footage of her as a haunted figure hustling in and out of court. Then I saw shots of body bags being taken out of Central Park and pictures of the building I was in. It felt like the noose was being drawn on me in Cancer.

Dr. Thorax left after saying he had scheduled me for surgery on Wednesday morning. Outside their houses on the crossroads, children squinted to see me hang in the dusk like the evening star. Fighting down rising panic and pain, I waited for the Feral Cell.

I thumbed through the material Joan had brought. Some of it was from a book about the robber barons that had lots of pictures. It devoted a chapter to Beast Mangin. He was being contrasted with Andrew Carnegie, who had been born poor in Scotland, made his fortune, and spent it on good works.

Mangin rose up by various accounts from Wales, Malta, or Croatia. Nice ways of making a fortune don't exist. His were particularly vile. And he spent every cent of it on himself. Enemies said that he could cut your throat while looking the other way.

I had trouble focusing. For a while I stared at the pictures of the house and grounds of Capriole, the estate that came to be called Mangin's Roost. The mansion was an ornate folly built of imported wood and marble, the horned goat's-head image was everywhere.

Again I was hypnotized by the photo of Mangin and his last wife. His face was obscured by a full beard and the brim of a silk hat. But his eyes were the ones that had stared at me Sunday in my own room, the eyes of someone who wanted to drink my blood. Antonia Ferrar's face was also one I had seen very recently.

Then the phone rang, and I managed to pick it up on the fourth or fifth try. "You saw Chris. I just heard all about it from my scouts," said Jason Beautemps. "But I knew that you'd seen him when you stopped calling for more information."

"What can I do for you, Jason?"

"I want the interview with him."

"Letting you get closer to this isn't doing you any kind of favor."

"Maybe you can answer some questions," Jason said and began firing away. "What was he to you, what is he? Great and good friend? Blood brother? Didn't he die back in '72? If not, why didn't he get in touch with you sooner? Do you have to die to get to Capricorn? Doesn't it feel like New York is going bad? Did you know that more kids are dying the same way Chris is supposed to have? Don't you agree that this is a little more important than last night's opening? Rob, I gave you what I knew, now give me something."

"Thanks for the tape." I was going to disconnect Jason when he beat me to it.

Before he hung up, though, he said; "Mangin is giving a big reception at Toys tomorrow night. It's for the Undying Cabal. You are quite definitely not on the guest list."

I lay back feeling cold pain in my guts. A pair of eyes watched me. I jumped. "Wake up, shithead," whispered Chris Kane. "Let's take a walk."

CHAPTER
Six

The dying body and bald head were gone. Now he was thin and lithe with long silver hair. Years had done their work on me, but Chris looked like a half-dollar struck to commemorate all our lost youths. He had gotten bigger in my memory; seeing him now I remembered that like me, he wasn't as tall as he would have liked. Only his eyes moved, and they moved a lot, wary. Feral.

"Who thought up the name *Feral Cell?*" I asked as though no time had passed between us.

Chris pointed his thumb at his chest and almost smiled. "In Capricorn I felt like a house pet gone wild." He breathed the words out slowly.

"You're like a secret society, a conspiracy of things that go bump in the night."

He looked impatient. "Cancer is tame cells going bad," he whispered. "Those cells changing are what let us over the Transept into Capricorn. So the name works that way too."

"At first I couldn't believe it was you." I bent down for my slippers, feeling weak and dizzy. "But that album . . ." Something almost like contempt in his eyes shut me up.

"Morgan wanted me to contact you. But it was better that she did. She guided me over the Transept my first time." He was nearly translucent. I could almost see right through him to the door and the hallway outside.

Gary stirred in his bed. "Chris Kane?" he asked.

Chris stood absolutely still watching the kid.

"He's listening to your tape," I whispered. "They don't think he's going to make it. Can you do anything for him? He can look into Capricorn." My concern surprised me.

"I've seen him." His whisper was fierce, angry. "He couldn't last. Not the way things are. Anyhow, we decided we needed you."

"The music is fire and ice," Gary told him in his stoned, dreaming voice.

Chris's face softened. "Sleep now, however you can. Maybe the Feral Cell can help your dreams." The kid closed his eyes, and Chris led me into the hall. An orderly pushing a cart full of fruit juice went past without seeing us.

In a burst of something between memory and déjà vu, I felt years dissolve. The first time I saw Chris was in a junior-high study room. My family had just moved into town; he had just been tossed out of private school. He had looked at me and jerked his thumb toward the door. Fourteen and desperate to fit in, I followed. Over thirty-five years later it felt like we were sneaking down school corridors when we were supposed to be in class.

"All those years," I said and remembered the last time I had seen him in New York, his eyes huge and full of pain. He hadn't wanted to talk to anyone, even me. "All the goddamn years I thought you died of leukemia?"

"I went where that couldn't hurt me."

"Did your mother know?"

"No. There was a real corpse and a real death certificate, and I had a sealed coffin shipped to Canada. She'd gotten into Christian Science, so I knew she wouldn't open it. I made a clean break."

"Why didn't you say something. Tell me you weren't going to die before you disappeared?"

"Who are you telling?" We reached a door with a red exit sign. He leaned hard against it. "Come on, push." It took all our strength to get the door open. I thought I heard Montoya's voice but didn't look back to see. The stairs were a steel cage. Through them shone the lights and stars of another world. I smelled damp wood and grass; a summer shower had passed in Capricorn.

"When I saw you a few weeks ago floating in the night I didn't recognize you. Not with that lousy disguise." Chris looked at me, questioning.

I thought of the reasons I had become Dr. Cobalt, and how hard they would have been for me to understand when I was twenty-two. All I could do was shrug and say, "It was a living."

Chris and I had met in '64 in a Long Island town too small to hold us. We were the first to dress like the Rolling Stones and buy Yardbird albums. We were sort of tough, sometimes crazy, often scared. Chris was six months older and dared me into Hombré wine and grass. He needed an audience and I needed an older brother.

I had wanted to explain to Jason Beautemps that Chris and I had grown up like parts of the same person. When I thought he was dead, part of me was gone. Now he was back and couldn't understand what the years had done to me.

Then the door we'd come through opened, and a voice that sounded familiar called, "Robert Leal?" Once again we were cutting class, Chris leading the way, shimmering like a fish seen through water. I shivered in the steel and cement stairwell. Someone was hurrying after us as we reached the third-floor landing and the door that read CHILDREN'S ONCOLOGY. I remembered that I was dying of cancer and being led by a ghost.

"What happened to Jackie Fast?" I asked.

"The Cabal killed her." He breathed the words. "You saw her fall last night. Blood of the Crab is precious to them. It's how they cross the Transept to Cancer." He saw me hesitate. I was remembering Mangin, who up in Westchester promised to drink my blood. "All the Feral Cell promises is that you can run in Capricorn as long as your luck and skill let you." Feet pounded on the stairs. He put his hand on the knife in his belt. "If that's not enough, wait here and let them take you back to your room."

I shook my head. He nodded and told me, "Empty your lungs of Cancer." As I did, my pajamas and robe began to slip away, and I felt shame. My nakedness didn't bother me but my age did. Next to Chris who was somehow both twenty-two and timeless, I seemed old and dying.

"Why do you keep your clothes?" I asked, sputtering as I tried to talk.

For a second he looked amused. "Good tailoring," he said.

I saw activity in the houses, saw their pinpoints of blue light come on under the last traces of sunset. "What does the knife do?"

He stuck it back into his belt. "It's carved by Caprii from a bone of the goat. Grasp it in Cancer and it draws you here. Like the bow gun does."

We had been spotted in the village. Two women again approached. One bore a stone pitcher; another, a bowl. They knelt and poured dark liquid from pitcher to bowl, then placed the bowl on the rock. As they did, I looked at the trees, saw faces watch and whisper as the leaves moved in a night breeze.

"Drink fast," said Chris Kane. "The time you have is Morgan's gift to you."

Crouching, I asked, "Where is she?"

"Baiting the Chase. Drink like you drank before." Knowing what was in the bowl, I hesitated but only for a second. Then I lapped and felt my veins bubble, my heart bound. Looking up, I could see deep into the night. Small distant sounds echoed.

"Blood of the Goat," I gasped, remembering Morgan leaping from the tree to the ground after the fallen hunter of the Chase.

"Honeydew," Chris said. "The fucking milk of paradise." He stroked my arm. "Drink a little more, just a little more." He half chanted, "Anyone can glance over the Transept. If they're sick or worried or lose a night or two's sleep, they see things moving out of the corners of their eyes. Only those dying of cancer cross the Transept. Only Goat's Blood anchors us here."

Realizing whose blood it was should have made me nauseated. But it didn't. I drank until my heart seemed to explode, and I felt ready to leap up and swim into the night. "What's next?" I panted.

"The Caprii will dress you," Chris said as I looked up. Two more women approached, each carrying a small bundle. "One size fits all," he breathed and bent to drink.

From their windows and doorways, the people of the village watched as the two women stopped before me. Their mouths moved, and their voices, diffracted, reached my ears sounding like a distant waterfall. The women showed me a shirt cut like a tunic, pants, a belt, and shoes of gray suede like the rest of the Feral Cell wore. The Caprii wore the same outfits made of white cloth and dark leather.

"It's a big honor for this village to dress you," Chris whispered. "You're a hero."

I stood, and they put the tunic over my head. It fell through my body and onto the ground. The faces on the trees twisted in pain. Above us in the dark a child wearing Cedars of Lebanon pajamas floated in a bed of light.

Again the shirt went over my head.

"Steady," I heard Chris say. It clung to my shoulders for a moment. The women let go, and it drifted to the ground. Patiently they picked it up in their long trailing hands and tried again. "We call this the Second Skin," Chris whispered. "It will help tie you to this end of the Transept."

The shirt attached itself to my back for a moment. It felt alive. I shivered and shook it loose.

"They saw you bare-ass and want to dress you. Just like they fed you."

"What's it made of?"

"Get it on and I'll tell you." A horn sounded from the south. Looking that way, I saw a glow in the sky. "Concentrate. Imagine yourself dressed." I caught the urgency in his voice. "They're baiting the Chase to give you time."

The leaves tossed in a breeze that I hardly felt. The tree faces seemed to pause and listen to the horn. The arms of the Second Skin caught mine. The shirt embraced me, held me in Capricorn. "I don't need this," I said panicking. My voice echoed and the shirt fell away.

A goat's horn sounded toward the west and closer to the village. Doors and windows flew open on the houses. "Without the Caprii we'd run naked looking for our Blood. We'd fall back into Cancer or get hunted down by the Chase. Now stand still, shithead!" Chris hissed.

The tunic grasped my neck and wrists; it clung to my chest and back. Once that happened it was easier getting the pants on me. They put the shoes on as I stood flinching and uneasy as a horse being shod. They tied a belt around my waist. I looked down and saw my hands trailing away like thin flames. "What am I wearing?"

"One man's Second Skin is another man's first skin." He said it like an axiom. "We exist in what these people call the Crab Transept—not quite in Cancer or in Capricorn. Blood of the Goat keeps us here. Without it we'd fall back into Cancer. Drinking Blood of the Crab sends us back there immediately. Our Skins get made from ones who died in the Transept. Like our knives, like the gun."

I twitched and my Second Skin trembled. The stairwell of Cedars of Lebanon appeared. The watching Caprii began making a low noise that might have been a moan. The stairs were gray and cold. The thin leather started slipping off my feet. The low moan sounded like a long slow freight rumbling away in the night. Beyond the stairwell door, children were dying. I drew back from that world.

"There's nothing in Cancer for ones like us," Chris whispered. "Our hearts run on a different beat." His voice and the sound of the Caprii pulled me back into my Second Skin.

"This is a blood cult," I said.

"Hey man, we may be a bunch of half-assed vampires, but we're all these people have to believe in." The glow of torch lights moved on the horizon, stirring up the Caprii. "Pay attention. I think you'll dig what happens next."

The man who carried the goat's horn approached us. Two children, a boy and a girl, walked with him. They carried a pillow. On it was the bow gun. Its strings were repaired. The capsules had all been replaced. They knelt before me and presented it.

Wondering what to do, I glanced at Chris and found him looking up into the dark. Following his gaze I saw figures floating in the night, mostly young and doomed, patients on the Cedars of Lebanon critical list.

"Take it," he said. "You won the bow gun back. You're their defender now."

I looked at the bow gun, its bone stock and butt, its strings of sinew and membrane capsules. Carved on one side was the pair of crabs touching claws, and on the other the pair of goats touching horns. "How did they repair it?"

"An old guy in this village made it. They bring it back to him."

"How did he find the . . . material?" More than Blood or Skin I felt that taking the weapon in a ceremony would bind me to that place. And while I wanted life, I didn't want its entanglements.

"I got it for him. When I first came over the Transept, one of the Cabal ruled this place for Mangin. Just down the road from here, I managed to off him. A man living here—he wasn't old then—came from over the mountains. They know how to do this kind of thing."

"How did Billy Gee get hold of it?" The horn calls grew close. Torches flickered in the dark.

Chris turned away so I couldn't see his eyes. "I gave it to him, all right? It was mine. I screwed things up. Take it. You're protecting them now." Being as close to him as I was, I had seen things go very wrong for Chris a couple of times. If his heart got stepped on or a gig didn't go right, his reaction was shock and shame hidden behind anger. It occurred to me that my old friend felt himself to be in disgrace.

"Whatever happened wasn't your fault." I gasped out the words and reached for the bow gun. "No more than finding it was my doing." The weapon seemed to leap into my hand. The Caprii murmured approval at this. Chris still looked away saying nothing. "They feed us, arm us. What are we to them?"

Chris Kane nodded as if I had found something he was able to talk about. "Hope. We're the old gods, the promise of magic help in times of oppression."

"And that's Mangin and company?"

"You've seen him in both worlds. It's Blood of the Crab that lets him go to Cancer. That's us. Blood of the Goat brings him back here. That's the Caprii. The word *Caprii* means *people* and also *the ones attached to the land, the original inhabitants, the ones who remember the old cults*. They're the ones who do the work and yield their blood for the ones who rule."

"What's the Cabal? The Chase?"

"The Cabal are priests, magicians, ones who understand the Transept. Some come from here, some from Cancer. The Chase is the local gentry, the pig oppressors, remember them? Imagine a combination of the Grand Inquisition and a stag hunt." Horns sounded on the outskirts of the village.

"Hunting us is religion and sport?"

"And a chance to reach legendary Cancer, realm of wonders." A line of lights flickered in the dark. The Caprii were lining up around their houses. Chris watched this and said, "You're about to start earning your keep, my man. Try walking in your Skin. We'll do what I was going to do last night." I took a few steps forward and felt the Skin move with me. "Put one foot in front of the other. Whatever you were in another world, here you are hope."

Each step Chris took was a kind of bound. Trying to move the same way, I felt my Skin tug away from my body. We left the grove of trees. I took a step and glided through Capricorn. Looking back, I saw dim lights amid the upper branches, and within them floated dying children. One I recognized: Gary, eyes closed, beating time with his hands, listening to Chris sing.

I could see more clearly in the moonlight than by day in Cancer. The sculpted leaves above us stared with round-eyed wonder, twitching and fluttering in a breeze.

"That's how we look to them," Chris told me. "This is a sacred place. The spawn of the Crab, us, walk here all the time. They sculpt the trees to show that this is a place where friends will feed and dress us."

A horn blew loudly. "That's close!" I gulped the words.

"The Chase rides hard on the short nights." All of this information Chris gave impersonally without looking at me.

As he spoke, the horn blew in the crossroads village. A column of torch lights bobbed and weaved, and the night riders approached. "Doesn't the Chase hear it, too?" We seemed to be moving toward the lights. "What are you doing?" I struggled to keep up.

"The horn's in a range only Crabs can hear. The two worlds and the Transept are on different frequencies. Even the ones blowing the goat's horn don't hear it. The blue lights are only for us, so we'll know where the Caprii are and can lead them in the dark." In the night, flames erupted, and horsemen flickered in the lights of a burning barn. "They'll try to waste this spot. We have to draw them to where we can hunt them."

"I left Cancer for this?"

"You traded death by inches for a chance to run until the net falls." I looked back at the houses, where men armed with axes and staves stood in their doorways, women formed a fire brigade, and kids with rocks climbed up onto the roofs.

"You can slide back over the Crab Transept," Chris hissed the words without looking back. "If you want, drop the bow gun and walk away from your Skin. Find some place to hide, and you'll drift back to Cedars of Lebanon." I heard a long rumbling noise and realized that the Caprii were chanting in unison as I followed Chris across the path of the Chase.

"What are we going to do?"

"Just let them see us. Don't look at the fire." Flames sprouted, almost blinding me as he spoke. "Be ready to run that way." Chris indicated a diagonal direction that would carry us past some stone walls and up a wooded hill. "Trust them to be overeager."

Floundering, I felt the Skin bunch around my legs, the gun pulse in the belt at my waist. That was when a black-clad horseman of the Undying Cabal spotted us and pointed the Chase in our direction.

Chris drew his knife and said, "This is where we earn our Blood." The hunters roared like an approaching freight train. If there had been a dozen the night before, there were thirty now.

Chris drew his knife as he ran. I pulled out the gun and felt the bow set itself. Looking back I saw the mounted figures wavering in their torchlight trot over the field, their lights dazzling my eyes. Silver nets were unfurled, and I turned forward to see Chris standing on the wall, gesturing me on. The Skin pulled behind me as I jumped up beside him.

"Keep moving. We've got them hooked," he said.

At that moment, I wished I could move with enough grace to glide away like a bat in the night. A high squeal merged with the rumbling sound. I glanced back and found Chris catching up with me. The dark horseman was urging the Chase forward. But at least one hadn't cleared the wall. An animal, saddle empty, threw its head in the air and reared. On the ground a hunter writhed.

"One down," Chris whispered.

The land rose beyond the wall. The woods were about a hundred yards in front of us. Then I saw the glittering silver nets. A pack of Chase hunters who had been waiting in ambush urged their horses forward. Several carried nets and spikes. In the lead was a Cabalist with a bandage all up one arm. It was the one I had shot at Mangin's Roost. Seeing him, I gasped and tripped, grazed the ground with one hand, felt my Skin catch at my back.

He looked right at me and raised a silver spike. The air came out of my lungs in a scream, and I began to choke. My Skin bunched around my legs, and I couldn't move. Capricorn was killing me, and Cancer was far away.

Chris shouted, "Bow gun!" and broke the spell. His voice boomed. I saw horsemen wince. Rising, I aimed and fired the gun at the one who had recognized me. On his bad arm the Undying Cabalist wore a small silver shield. With a gesture he deflected the capsule, which bounced away.

It hit the hunter nearest to him and burst. The horse reared; the hunter flailed at his face as he fell screeching. Then the others were around us. A net sailed over Chris, but he ducked, rolled on the ground, came up with his knife, which he drew along the belly of a horse. Animal and hunter went down screaming.

"Move!" Chris's voice thundered. Without looking I knew that the rest of the Chase was closing in.

Caught in my Skin, breathing in short gasps, I was hunted down in Capricorn. The ground shook right behind me as I ran to the woods. Drawing the bow strings, I felt a capsule slide into place. Turning to fire, I saw a silver net float through the air and fall over my head. Heavy as lead it forced me to the ground. The Undying Cabalist stared down at me from horseback, preparing to nail me with a long silver spike.

Then Chris was on the horse behind him, slashing his arm with his bone knife. Screams tore at my ears. The horses of the Chase bucked and reared. A hunter reached out to spear Chris. My hand still held the bow gun. I raised it and fired. Acid spattered on impact. The man dropped his spear, howling. Another hunter turned his horse under a tree ready to run me down. A gray form dropped on him. A bone knife caught the light of the moon. The woods were full of gray shapes as the Feral Cell closed in.

In the direction from which we had come, were blue pinpoints of light. In the dark I saw scythe blades and carving knives. Caprii ran from all directions to confront the Chase.

In the confusion, a couple of the hunters went down.

Others tried to rally around their leader. But when Chris pulled an Undying Cabalist off his horse, the Chase broke and ran. Most of them escaped by galloping south, the Feral Cell and the Caprii parting to let them go.

A long low roar in the night marked the retreat of the Chase. Around me, horses struggled to rise; hunters lay injured. In a few moments all that was left were Caprii staring in awe at about twenty figures in Second Skins and at Chris, who sat on the chest of the Cabalist. He waved an arm, and a Caprii ran up with a gray sack. Chris plunged his knife into the Cabalist's throat. I found I couldn't pull the net off myself.

A young Caprii picked it up easily, as Morgan and a dozen of the Cell stood looking at me, silently panting, their hair floating in breezes I couldn't feel. They were amused I understood, as I got up, stuck the gun into my belt, and asked, "Do I qualify? You letting me into the club?" The words echoed.

Morgan approached. "Welcome to the pack," she said. "If you are far enough into Capricorn to be caught under a net, you are one of us." All gave little barking laughs except Chris, who stood apart and looked away.

Caprii were getting the injured members of the Chase back up on their feet. A crude litter was made for one who was too badly hurt to move. Others had opened the veins of the two Cabalists who had fallen and caught their blood in leather sacks. "One from Cancer, one from Capricorn. Both sides of the Transept are open to us," whispered one of the Cell. An involuntary shudder almost tore me out of my Skin. Again I heard the barking laughter.

Then Morgan brought forward each member of the Cell and whispered a name. As they were introduced they ran their hands over my face and chest. "Speedo," she said as a long form floated before me. "Ruby," she told me as another stepped up to me. At first they had looked too much alike for me to distinguish them. Watching them closely though, I could tell that Speedo was a young black, that Ruby was a red-headed woman.

Morgan was recognizable to me. It wasn't just that I had seen her before in Cancer. Her eyes had stared out at me from some of the photos of Benjamin Mangin the First. "Lurch," she said, and a figure that seemed huge but even more smokelike than the others came forward. "Garbo," she said, and I made out a wispy woman flickering in the night.

"Leal?" she said indicating me and questioning Chris.

"If that's the name he wants," my friend said, avoiding everyone's eyes, staring at the trees. An outline of a head scuttled along the ground like a crab, its eyes staring and frightened as someone hurried dying through the streets of New York.

"Leal then," Morgan murmured. "We need much from you." A couple of their horses had been caught, and the injured men of the Chase were using them to haul the litter as they slunk away.

Bouncing on my toes, feeling like I could fly, I said, "I'll do what I can," just to make conversation. I was concentrating too much just on breathing and keeping my voice down to wonder what they could possibly want.

"We need you to remove Mangin and the Cabal from New York," Morgan told me as the others nodded.

"The guy's got money. He's connected." I could hear my voice rising.

"Chris will help you." She looked at him, and he continued to look away. "He wishes to return to Cancer."

"All I do there is play games."

"All anyone there does is play games," Chris said, and I felt the contempt. "We've seen what you've done. You took the bow gun away from Billy Gee. Spies say you beat Mangin on his own killing floor," Chris said with an expression that said we both knew that was all an accident.

"If we cannot destroy the Cabal in New York, they will destroy our Cancii here," Morgan told me. My mouth opened and closed, but I had nothing to say. "Let us show you what Mangin is doing here," she said.

Some of the Feral Cell had dispersed along with most of

the Caprii and disappeared into the night. The dozen that remained faced south and prepared to travel.

"Show him the House of Usher on the way," Chris suggested and Morgan nodded.

The night was soft, and the moon had set as we moved by the light of the stars through a silent world. Before us, a young woman, slender and dark, shot into the air. Her eyes closed in exhaustion as an elevator carried her up a skyscraper.

"Does she have cancer?" I asked Chris.

"Maybe. Maybe she's strung out. Maybe flipping out. *In extremis* people from Cancer can see and be seen over the Transept."

"And the Caprii see this?"

"Certain places are holy places. Maybe it's lots of people in tough shape at the same time and the same place. Maybe it's the weather. Maybe Cancer and Capricorn coming close together screw up the weather and make people flip out. Not many scientists stumble down the Transept. Those that do have been recruited by the Cabal."

I thought about that as we floated through the landscape, brushing past undergrowth, bouncing over walls. If we didn't go too fast and I concentrated on the short, quick breaths, I felt free of Cancer, both the place and the disease. "Can't we just avoid the Undying Cabal?" I asked.

"Remember what happened to Jackie? You know what the Cabal will do to any of those kids at Cedars they get their hands on?" Morgan and the others had halted at the edge of a grove. Chris stood in front of me. "Remember what I said about pig exploiters?" His voice was fierce.

"There they are," he said and stepped aside. On a rise at the center of cleared ground stood a huge stone house ringed by ten-foot walls. Gaslights flickering over the gates hurt my eyes. "Capricorn has the magic. But Cancer has the technology," Chris whispered.

In the drama of the way he did it was something that started my mind working. I saw a game as I watched and listened to him. The house was a rambling complex, several stories tall in some places. "A town on that site got razed so that thing could be built. All the Caprii lost their homes. Lots died. The men of that house ride with the Chase."

His anger was an embarrassment to me. I was going to say we had gotten used to the powerful doing what they wanted, to ask him where he had been. Then I remembered. Instead I whispered, "It seems like no one's awake."

"They're awake. They're watching for us. Those are the landowners. The ones brought in by the Cabal. See those gaslights? Those are Mangin's gift to his home world. Without them the Cell could go over those walls and destroy everyone inside. Take cover; don't look directly at the house. See what happens when I get close."

The rest of the Cell stayed well back and turned away. I got behind a tree but couldn't help looking when Chris stepped forward. So I was blinded when he triggered an alarm. Light from gas jets flared all along the walls. Noises that I recognized as shouts came from inside.

Chris must have looked away at the last second because he came back and grabbed me as I stumbled around without my bearings. I felt hands like feathers on my arms, heard his voice in my ear. "Mangin showed them a way to harness natural-gas deposits. It's messy and it's dangerous, but it works. He's showing them wonders, man. We need some kind of magic."

I heard a note of pleading and remembered how much Chris hated asking for anything. Squinting at the place from a distance, I saw the lights die down and started to learn the game being played in Capricorn. "The ones in the House of Usher worship Mangin?" I asked as we rejoined the Cell and headed south.

"He brought them here. Down on the coast is Cabal territory. They have a state religion and rulers who don't matter to us. But lots of people down there follow the new gods."

Once we passed the evidence of a fight along a road: a dead horse, broken staves, a dropped sword. "A Caprii party clashed with the Chase." Chris told me. We went down a street of silent buildings. "The ambushers came from here," he said. Over a couple of doorways small blue lanterns burned. I was aware that we were watched from upper windows. "Morgan wants to force the Cabal out with as little bloodshed as possible."

I felt every nerve in my body tingle. Until a few nights before, I had forgotten what it was like to feel thrilled, caught between ecstasy and fear. I remembered how Chris had always gone first, found the new scene, brought me along. Here I was again with my old high-school buddy and the strange new crowd he'd found. It seemed he didn't much want to know me. But they offered me the chance of life everlasting.

The Cell traveled fast. Part of the time I managed their long, loping stride, felt the Skin cling to me as I moved with the pack. Mostly I fell behind and Chris stayed near me. As we headed south, the land rose, and a glow grew on the horizon. Ahead of us on a road, a clump of horsemen picked their way through the dark.

"The Chase is hiding, not hunting tonight," Chris murmured.

Up front, the others had halted and stood shading their eyes. "This is for you to see." Chris motioned me forward. The fires burned on the other side of a valley. I made out tents against the flames.

Morgan whispered, "They rode down from Capriole Castle and set up camp the day before yesterday." She pointed to a spot a little east of the fires. "That is where you live in New York. We were preparing to rescue you when you escaped to the hospital." All of the Cell looked at me; the one called Ruby darted her tongue.

Morgan pointed a finger that trailed off into the night. "Chris calls what they are having down there a revival meeting. The Cabal holds it here where we are supposed to be strong to prove to their followers that they are all powerful. Tomorrow night will be its climax. For it, Mangin will bring the Chase to Cancer. Jackie Fast will provide them with the Blood of the Crab."

Being reminded of Jackie reminded me also of what Jason

had said about a big reception at Toys that night. The thought of returning to Cancer filled me with fear, but so did the idea of my house lying next to the Cabal's hunting tents and of my falling under a silver net in Capricorn. Reluctantly I said, "It looks like I have to go back."

"Even if you don't, I'm going to." Chris said. "And I'm staying. The Cell is helpless here, and I'm fucking useless."

The game was coming together in my mind. It would take all my resources in New York. Whatever happened they were worthless to me anyway. I needed two things: some understanding of my opponent and a product to sell, what with the media blitz I was planning. I intended to show New York a kind of magic.

Morgan looked at Chris, who stared back angrily. "You are not useless," she told him. "You have given us everything from names to a purpose. I found you dying. If you return, how long will you last there before you die? Think how sick you became in Berlin."

"I'll last long enough for people there to see me and know about the Cell."

"How can this be good? The Beast brings the things of Cancer here, and see what that has done."

It was an argument that obviously had gone on for a while. Chris was going back to New York, and Morgan wanted him to stay in Capricorn. I caught faint traces of a French accent, which reminded me of something I had meant to ask. Here was someone who could tell me about Mangin. "When did you change your name from Antonia Ferrar?" I asked her.

She turned to me. "I had lost that name. I wandered this land without a name until I brought him here."

"And the Mangin I met brought you here. I mean it wasn't his grandfather. It's the same man. He doesn't really die, right?" She nodded. The Chase watched us. "What happened? You were his mistress and you had a falling out?" Again she nodded. "Is he immortal?"

"Once he said that a day in Cancer brought him a year of life here."

"Is he dying here like we are there?"

She looked off. "That is the Cabal's greatest secret. But no. The illness is different. It is madness perhaps. Lust for power. I could never find that out."

"What is Cancer to him?"

"A mine of wonders. A place where everything he sees he wants. But where he can barely touch them."

"But he amassed a fortune."

"Several. Under other names in other places and times. But Mangin is his best-known identity."

The way all of them, even Chris, looked to me made me feel like old Dr. Cobalt setting up a game as I asked, "And his influence here rests on his control in that world? So that if this party tonight got ruined, it would cripple him here? Would it help to rally the Caprii here tomorrow night and see him humiliated?"

Morgan nodded. "Yes. But there must be as little killing as possible. If it comes to killing, the Chase are better suited to it than the Caprii." She looked to the east. "We must disperse before dawn." The rest of the Cell, before splitting up into the night, paused to say good-bye to Chris. Ruby murmured pleas that he not go. Lurch ran his hands over Chris's face and said nothing.

"I have known this ever since Llish," Morgan sighed and kissed him. "That we would lose you."

"I want you to be at the camp just after midnight," I told her, aware of being in charge, putting the first part of my game into place. "I'm going to make Mangin very unhappy. I want you to make sure he doesn't do the same for me."

"What are you going to do?" Chris asked. "Destroy him socially?"

"All I'm going to do is set the scene," I told him. "Your return appearance is going to be the big news. The kind of publicity people kill and die for," I added and watched as his eyes, distorted in the spectrum of Capricorn, reflected hope and fear.

CHAPTER

Seven

The rest of the Cell disappeared, and the two of us stood alone with the first gray showing in the sky. "We should get out of Capricorn before the light," Chris said. I tried to look down at the bonfires and said nothing. After a long pause he asked, "What do you want to do?" He spoke impatiently, but his asking meant I was in charge.

"I have to get to my house," I said. "It's watched in both worlds. Any ideas?"

"We go to Cancer a little way off from it. Stay close to the Transept and approach it fast. If it's bright enough there, we'll be hard to spot."

"I'll have to warn Joan and B&T. Let's try Bus Stop." Chris nodded, and we headed west loping quickly. "What does sunlight do to us?" I wanted to know.

"It burns the Skin right off us," he said. "A couple of minutes is bad, an hour or two is death." I followed him silently thinking that over. When the light from behind us became stronger I began imagining it searing my Skin. As the woods turned gray I started to have trouble focusing on things.

Once he halted, listened. I heard a rhythmic drumming. Chris pulled me into some underbrush while a party of hunters galloped past. They had no Cabalists with them and hurried through the dark looking straight ahead as if afraid of what they might see.

"We're not going to make Bus Stop," Chris whispered. "There's another place." He got us into a shallow cave just as the rim of the sun came up and blinded me, and while I was blinking my eyes, he broke the silence by asking, "You want me to perform?"

"A triumphal hometown engagement after a long foreign tour," I whispered. "You've got an album to promote. Think of the ad line: 'Chris Kane: legend or superstition?' "

It was a stupid joke. His eyes drilled right through me. "What happened to you, man? What happened to New York? Everyone talks like an agent now. All anyone wants is the chance to get rich enough to step on the faces of everyone else."

It was the echo of a past I had managed to forget. "It was never any different in New York . . .," I started telling him but trailed off when I saw the amount of pain in Chris's eyes. The conversation sounded eerily familiar, like one I'd had before but not with him. "Morgan acts like she thinks you won't be back to Capricorn." I said to change the subject and because I had to know.

"And about that she's never wrong." Chris said in a flat voice and fumbled with a small sack around his neck. "She brought me down the Transept all those years ago. Even then she knew I'd go back."

"But why now?" It was just dark enough in the cave in Capricorn for me to see. As I looked hard at him, a figure floated through the space. He was a thin Spanish guy with glazed eyes and a shambling step. It seemed that I could see him right through Chris Kane.

"The two worlds finally crushed me between them, man. We can live as long as our wits let us." He poured a few teaspoonfuls of blood from the sack onto a rock. A small natural basin there had been smoothed out and polished. By the Caprii, I realized. "But people in Cancer and Capricorn die. Little kids. Ones who don't even know what living is." He bent to drink, lapping at the blood.

"It's the way things are," I found myself saying. Then I realized why this conversation seemed familiar. I was saying to him what my parents had said to me. Which meant I must have been getting to them the way Chris was bothering me.

"It doesn't have to be," he said, looking at me with those weird, El Greco eyes.

As I bent to drink the Blood of the Crab, another figure floated into view in Cancer, looked at us through bleary eyes, did a stoned double take, and staggered out of sight. "This is the Supermarket," I said. "Over on the river." I bent and drank blood that stuck on my tongue and tasted warm. It killed the tingle of Capricorn first in my stomach, then over the rest of my body. We were returning to New York on a chilly morning under a heavy fog.

A woman with a hollow face swayed at the end of the short cement pier and looked right through us as we came over the Transept. We stepped onto the pier right beside her, and Chris said "Don't jump" so quietly that she didn't really hear him. But she did turn around in what looked like a junked-out daze and take a step or two back from the edge.

A dozen stoned drug runners revolved like planets in the park by the Hudson as the winter sun came up. One of them chanted a jingle:

Heaven and hell's
What I got to sell.
Fire and Ice
Here for a price.

"They keep saying they've broken this up," I whispered, sounding like I thought I was in church. "All they do is chase it from one part of Manhattan to another." We watched as customers came out of the mist and crossed the bridge over the West Side Highway. They had on jogging clothes or still wore suits and dresses crumpled from a night in the clubs;

they were well-heeled or in torn sneakers, desperate or cool, fifteen or fifty, street kids and sleek tourists.

Coke addicts needing something for the day ahead, ones with nerves so jangled they needed downs, junkies and heavy cannabis heads, psychedelic abusers and ones who got off on animal tranquilizers, addicts of old drugs as natural as heroin or as new and synthetic as Salvation—the Supermarket served them all. They made eye contact with their connections and moved off to where the dealers waited.

When I'd first come to the city, ships at the long piers along the river had unloaded cargoes from around the world. Now in the bushes along the Esplanade, in thick fog at the ends of piers, behind the slides in a children's playground, people bought products smuggled in from South America and Asia, from farms in New Jersey, from bagging factories in the Bronx, and chemistry labs in Oakland. Some of them saw us, but to most we were just an eye flash.

"These are ones the Cabal preys on," Chris told me. "Lots of them are dying; lots of them will grab at anything that offers hope. Mangin promises people like this whatever they want to hear. They'll do anything for him in Cancer. Then he helps them over the Transept, shows them like miracles to the Chase, and slaughters them for their blood. No one knows they've disappeared." He spoke in short gasps that sounded like sobs. "It's how I lost the bow gun," he said.

We walked toward the overpass. My feet felt so heavy I had to step with a kind of glide to avoid tripping. Cancer was a thin shell over Capricorn. Looking back I saw the woman on the pier staring after us and seeming to talk to herself. "What happened?" I asked.

"Remember Billy Gee?"

"Yeah. He made quite an impression."

"Billy was a perfect Cabal recruit: young, not stupid, dying so fast he was halfway over the Transept. When the Feral Cell got to New York a couple of weeks ago, Mangin already seemed to have the place sewn up. He's hard to get at, tight security in both worlds."

"You thought a kid like that could infiltrate?"

"I thought I had him for the Cell. The bow gun, when he saw it, astounded him. I already knew I was going to come back here and . . ." He trailed off.

"Wouldn't be needing it."

He nodded. "Billy was angry at what had happened to him, what was happening to his family, his people. I thought someone like that should hold the gun. I didn't tell anyone, just let him take it over the Transept as a sign of trust. I trailed him thinking he was going to Toys. Instead he went to off you. Mangin understood things better than I did. He knew Jackie and Morgan wanted to recruit you. The Cabal had a price on your head. Stupid of me, huh?"

As Chris spoke, we crossed the West Side Highway. Traffic below sounded like a river at flood tide. Uptown and downtown, skyscrapers not yet built when we first came to the city overlooked the valley of low buildings that was Greenwich Village. Behind us, over the Hudson on the Jersey shore, vast condo complexes floated in the fog. Shining right through them I could see sunlight in Capricorn.

"It turned out OK," I told him.

On the narrow streets of the Village, we passed joggers running, trucks unloading early deliveries. I saw Chris turning, listening, sniffing the air. Cars with their headlights still on seemed impossibly fast and bright. Lamps shone in kitchens and shops. The air was full of wet garbage smell and exhaust and morning coffee. Over the truck horns and morning announcers' voices, I could still hear the rushing river sound. As we walked toward Bleecker I asked him, "What happens with our cancer now that we're back here?"

"You can stay for a little while, and it doesn't matter. But when the Blood of the Goat wears off, you start to die again."

"Why do you feel you have to stay?" Near Abingdon Square a door opened, and a party came out of an after-hours club. It was made up of four people in their forties and two kids. Two of the adults were a couple, beautifully dressed, obviously foreign; the other two were stylishly turned-out New York artists. The boy and girl with them were hustlers. The situation was obvious to me; wealthy patrons, or show backers or film producers, a painter or director and his agent, and the live part of last night's entertainment.

Chris watched them move to a limo. The foreigners seemed bored, the artists anxious, the kids stoned. "That's why," he said. "How can a place go that bad?"

What I was going to say was "little by little," when I saw horsemen in bright jackets and heard the rushing river sound grow very loud. Chris saw and heard, too, and pushed me against a wall as a skater whirled around a corner and seemed to bounce right through us. The skater wore a helmet, a leather jacket, and knee and elbow pads. She was a hard-looking kid who turned and squinted right at us. "We must have been spotted at the Supermarket and tracked," I said, as she spoke into a receiver on her helmet.

Chris had his knife out. I put my hand on the gun and was aware of hunters of the Chase pointing to where I floated a few feet off the ground in Capricorn.

The rushing noise came from behind us. Several skaters appeared the way we had come. Chris and I got our backs against a wall and faced up and down the street. Three more skaters rounded the corner and drew up short. The one we had seen first came back with a couple of others. I had the bow gun out, and they seemed to respect that, gliding around at a distance from it.

Two guys starting to unload a truck in front of an Italian meat market stared at the skaters suspiciously but found the skaters weren't interested in them. After looking once or twice to see what the skaters were excited about, they shrugged and went back to work. Brightly colored figures holding glowing silver nets were outlined right through them. Our touching the weapons drew us to Capricorn and the Chase to us.

"Move that way," Chris pointed down Hudson Street due south in Capricorn. We stepped away from the wall. The skaters behind us moved up. I spun and aimed at them. They skated backward, scattering as they did. We started to run. I felt the bow gun and my tension dragging me back over the Transept. A hunter grinned and reached up for my foot. I stuck the gun in my belt, and the skaters closed in.

"Like dogs tracking us," Chris muttered as the skaters fell back in front of us, rolled up behind. We approached the next corner, moving fast; people who couldn't quite see us instinctively crossed the street to avoid trouble.

In Capricorn the land fell away. The Chase had to go downhill. I felt something brush my legs and saw a net. I staggered and fell against a parked car. Chris jumped up on the hood as the skaters closed in.

Then they stopped and looked past us. I got up on the car out of reach of the Chase and saw a black Corvette. A dark-haired woman drove it; a guy beside her showed the skaters a compact machine pistol. He did it very discreetly, but they backed away. We jumped off the car and started to run. The skaters started to follow us. At the next corner, the Corvette drove between us and them.

In Capricorn the Chase waved their nets and trotted after us. Then they, too, stopped. There weren't many of them, and up ahead was a rock outcropping right about where Bus Stop stood. On top of the rocks were Caprii armed only with staves and crooks, but numerous.

On the Bus Stop block, Sun Bums lounged in the morning light, lying on car hoods, on loading docks. They stood as we ran by. Someone inside the club opened the door. "We welcome the Feral Cell," said the girl who had let me in the night before.

"We need blood," Chris whispered.

"We'll get it for you," she said and brought us indoors. I felt the ghost of a pain in my guts and knew there was more to come on this side of the Transept. Inside only a few service lights were on, most of the chairs were upside down on the tables, the place smelled of ammonia. I peered around the dusk. "There's nothing as dismal as an empty nightclub," I whispered.

A familiar voice wafted out of the gloom, "Unless it's a crowded nightclub." A light went on as Jason Beautemps walked toward us across the Waiting Room floor. "Just in time to be interviewed."

Chris looked at me, questioning, and I nodded. "You get an exclusive if you hold it till midnight tonight. We're about to go public."

A woman with a camera appeared following Jason.

"Can you see them?" he asked her. "I just barely can. I want photos, Rob. This is going to be like a Big Foot sighting story."

Raul came in from the kitchen with a glass carafe glowing red. He poured some into a saucer and watched fascinated as Chris lapped at it. I realized that quite a few Sun Bums stood in the shadows awestruck.

"You claim to be Chris Kane?" asked Jason turning on a tape recorder.

"For longer than you've been Jason Beautemps," Chris said quietly.

"Welcome home, Chris. I knew it was you the first time I heard the tape." Jason smiled, then got back to business. "How did you come to record an album after being dead for all those years?"

"I started in Berlin. Which is Llish in Capricorn."

"Was that before the Embargo?" Chris's look was blank. "When did you start recording?"

"It was winter in Llish. The Undying Cabal appeared and raised a crusade against the old religion. You felt it here."

Jason looked at me. All the events of the summer before: riots, famine, snow in June, NATO hesitation, and Russian waffling were called the Embargo. It was a euphemism. No one wanted to say that Berlin had gone so bad that the world refused to be responsible for it. Jason turned up the recorder. "Getting anything?" he asked the photographer.

"A shadow only."

"He'll come into focus tonight," I said, sounding like an agent promising his client could deliver. "I'm planning something to coincide with the Toys opening."

"Have you set it up with Mangin?" Jason asked. "It seems it's to be a very private affair. No press, very few guests."

"I don't think he has the kind of media flair we do. Could you spread the word? I want as much coverage as possible."

"Could you be more specific about what you have planned."

"Let's call it a media assault. I have to set things up. Telephoning is unwise. Some messages need to get delivered. I need people to deliver them." I noticed that my speaking barely made the dials on the recorder register.

"Bus Stop is pretty much run by the kids," Jason said, indicating the Sun Bums. "Raul, are you willing to help these people?"

"We've wanted to help the Feral Cell since the rumors started," said Raul, and the ones around the room nodded. As the interview went on, I started to make a list of the people and equipment that I'd need, fumbling with a pencil as I did.

"Drew Whitley was in Berlin last summer," Jason continued, turning his attention back to Chris.

Chris spoke in a drowning voice as if talking in his sleep. "Drew walked in Capricorn. I brought him over the Transept once, and Morgan did too. I remembered Drew from Max's Kansas City." He bent over the bowl, looked with distaste, lapped more blood. "Things went against us both in Cancer and Capricorn. The Feral Cell got trapped in Berlin. I ended up eating solid food and felt myself starting to die."

"You wrote 'Death Drops in' then?"

"I remembered it. Most of it. Most of it was written before I first went to Capricorn." His sharp panting was as loud as his words. "I remembered all of the songs on the album. You don't sleep in Capricorn. Just kind of doze during the light. Some lyrics ran in my head for years."

"You recorded in Berlin?"

"We started there. The Undying Cabal ran an espionage ring. Mangin was there under a different name. He controlled terrorists, blew up any house that gave us shelter. Drew was brave just staying near us."

I bent over the bowl. The smell and taste, raw and metallic, choked me. I gulped a mouthful and asked Raul, "Can someone take this note to Vain Video? Tell them tonight at my place. Before nine. Absolute secrecy. They can talk terms with Joan when they get there."

"What happened to the Cell in Berlin?" asked Jason.

"We hung on." Chris's eyes came alive at the memory. "Morgan got back into Capricorn and turned things there. The Caprii of Llish rose up and threw out the Undying Cabal. All the people of Capricorn have left is their memories. The old faith. Us."

I beckoned another kid. "This is for Fast Action Street Theater. I'm willing to pay them the usual advance. And tell them, too, that it's going to be for Jackie Fast."

"Where else did you record?" asked Jason.

"Lots of places. Drew shadowed us in Cancer. Turned up where we were going. I'd find him and record some tracks. He was afraid of crossing over. But he had courage. He was sick, and he was trying to help us help the Caprii." Chris stopped and lapped at the blood.

"Here's the address of a sound-system team. They know me. I need them for tonight. Have them bring a set up to my place." I was using every contact I had.

"Why now, after all these years?"

"Because I realized there was nothing else I could do to help the people of Cancer and Capricorn." His voice had gotten stronger.

"Power to the people?" Jason nodded. "Very sixties. An interesting hook this far down the line."

"I need street artists," I told Raul. "Lots of them." He nodded. "Let me show you what I want from them."

Chris fingered his knife and looked past all of us, out through the wall to what had been the loading platforms. I put my hand on the bow gun, felt it pulse, saw the outline of white clothes against a darkening sky. The Caprii were guarding us. "Doesn't anything in this world bother you?" he wanted to know.

Jason nodded, and I was surprised by his answer. "What they've done to the kids." He stared carefully in the direction of Chris. "They've been squeezed out. People in their forties have the interesting jobs." He indicated the two of us. "People in their thirties have the boring jobs that pay well. There is nothing left for kids. Artists are middle aged; business people guard their preserves. The only thing they like about kids is the way they look. The Sun Bum pose is protective. Love us, we're harmless is what they're saying. Kids are developing physical problems we associate with much older people . . . cancer for instance. They need hope."

The photographer snapped pictures from every angle she could find.

"A legend," Chris said, and the recorder dials jumped. "Something everyone knows is impossible but that they're desperate enough to want to believe in."

Through the walls I saw the peasant Caprii shiver in the chill wind blowing out of Cancer. My pencil fell out of my hands. The last message was a couple of painfully scrawled words. "My place is being watched. Can someone get this to B&T or Joan."

"We can have someone pretend to be delivering groceries."

"Thank you." I turned to Jason and the kids who stood in the shadows. "I've got my game in motion. I could use some assistance from you people."

Jason said, "You understand that these kids have been exploited since the day they were born. I won't do anything that lets them be used as pawns."

"If this place goes bad lots of them will die." Chris looked into Capricorn. A thunderstorm moved over the countryside.

"Is it the anxiety level? Is it the weather that does that to a city?" Jason asked. "I feel something without knowing what it is."

"The Transept grows narrow. Cancer and Capricorn come closer. I don't know if that's cause or effect." Chris stared off as he said that and seemed to fade away.

"What do you need from us tonight?" Jason asked Chris, who looked to me.

"A party will come down the street from my place just before twelve. At twenty minutes to twelve, I want the corner in front of Toys flooded with Sun Bums. I don't want a sign of them before then. My party is going into Toys. I don't want any violence unless there's trouble at the door." Raul and the others nodded. "What kind of coverage can we get?" I asked Jason.

"Fairly good. You have to remember that this is a busy time of year for the media. But I'll spread the right word, and I'll be out front myself. What else do you want?"

"Get the story out."

"Oh, I intend to retire on this one. Where are you going?"

"My place. Chris?"

He was looking out beyond the arrivals gates where if I stared hard I could see Caprii standing guard in the wind and the rain. "They think we ride on storms like that," he said quietly and turned to join me.

"Did you get anything?" Jason asked the photographer as the kids applauded Chris's exit.

Raul and some of the others wanted to escort us, to get us a ride, but I shook them off and started walking east. I was aware that my Skin instead of floating with me had begun clinging to my body like limp tissue. Sickness and exhaustion had started to make themselves felt, but I walked because there were people I wanted to meet. They were waiting around the corner.

"Robert Leal?" the man asked. He had put away the machine gun. The woman stood beside their car, looked at Chris whose hand went to his knife. They were casually dressed, a couple out for a stroll. Only on the second glance would they register as the law. "I wonder if we could have a minute or two of your time," he asked very pleasantly.

"Federales," said the Spanish-looking woman and smiled. "We have some badges we could show you."

"Quite all right," I said.

"We thought you might be going home," said the man. "We wondered if we could give you a lift."

"Would that be wise?" I asked as Chris stared at the car uncertainly.

"Absolutely," said the Spanish fed, moving to open the car door. "We're the good cops."

"This time," said the man. He was unable to see Chris and looked only at me.

Chris hesitated, so I got into the back seat first. The woman gestured politely, and Chris slid in. She shut my door, sat behind the wheel. Chris looked trapped. The man sat beside her and turned toward me. "The police questioned me yesterday," I told them.

"About Jackie Fast," the man said and chuckled.

"Stale," said the woman. "Mangin is our interest."

"A man of the world. In fact a man of two worlds," said the fed as the car eased away from the curb. I had the feeling of being stationary, of being about to rip through the back of the car. Chris's teeth were clenched, his body tense as a trapped animal's. The storm had passed in Capricorn. Beyond the gray winter sun of Cancer, I could see dazzling sunlight. "We'll take it slowly," the woman said, watching him in the rearview mirror.

"I've heard Mangin's running a blood cult," I said, holding onto the seat with both hands.

"We've heard the same about you." The driver accelerated down a block.

Again I had the feeling of falling through the back and into Capricorn. I shut my eyes and offered them something. "Tonight at Toys there will be more than rumors."

"Are you invited?"

"No. Are you?"

"Yes. Are you going?"

"Some friends and I thought we might get in. The floor show should start at midnight." I opened my eyes and saw my own hand, knuckles white, clenching the door rest like I was holding myself in the car and in Cancer.

"The city police might want to interfere with those plans," said the man.

"Sometimes I think they don't want to know as much about Mangin as you and I do," I told him as the car pulled over to the curb a couple of blocks north of my house. "I wonder if you could talk to them."

They exchanged a look and went from being playful to being cops. "Mr. Leal, we know you had said there was some trouble up at Mangin's Roost Saturday," said the woman.

"And my guess is that I wasn't the first."

"Right. But a guess is not enough. We've got some idea of what's happening. When street kids, even when entertainers disappear, we leave that for the police. Even if they don't seem able to focus on the problem."

"When places go bad," said the older fed, "that's espionage. If the locals are dogging it on a case like that, we can take over."

"You think the city's going bad?"

"We don't think it's quite come to that yet," the woman smiled.

"If we thought that, I'd have used the gun this morning," he said getting out. "There are two people watching the back entrance of your place. One of them is ours. I'll block the other one. Give me a minute's head start, then walk down the street casually. Your back door should be clear for about ninety seconds."

He walked toward the back of my house. "One other thing," said the woman and punched a button. Chris Kane sang. "Are you going to be there?" she asked looking right at him.

"That would spoil the surprise," I told her. We listened to Chris on the car stereo.

"Go," said the Federale and opened the back door. When we got out she said, "Hey, your friend there is life and death."

"You play games with everyone," Chris whispered. Toys, the ornate Chemical Exchange Trust, looked forlorn seen from behind in gray noon light, like a Victorian dowager into drugs and on the skids. Walking down the street toward my alley, I touched the bow gun and floated just above the ground in Capricorn. "Those are pigs, man. How far are you going with them?"

"Until they try to stop us. You don't trust them because they're cops. I see them as something we need to keep the other cops off us." As I said that half a dozen horsemen rode past the huge tree that grew in Capricorn where my house stood in Cancer. One of them was a member of the Undying Cabal, and he saw something when we moved.

With each step my feet seemed to plunge through the sidewalk. In a doorway next to my alley a 'drifter' sprawled. The fed stood blocking his view saying, "Buddy, I don't care what you can show me. The owner doesn't want you here."

A short distance away I saw bright tents flying an insignia of two crabs, claws crossed and touching. Chris put his hand on his knife. We were both close to the Transept, halfway between worlds.

"I'm going to bait the Chase. Give you time to work out your plan." Without waiting for me to reply, he drifted into the shade of the tree and climbed it.

I felt eyes searching for me as I hurried to the back of my house. Toys loomed at the end of the block; the buildings between my place and it rose steadily, from two stories to three to four. The windows on the top floor of Toys were only about five feet above the roof next to it. Two goats touched horns on a flag on top of the club.

The back door swung open. As I had asked in my message, Joan was ready to let me in. She blinked several times then saw me, did a double take at my Skin.

"What's new?" I whispered.

"Same old stuff. Sandy Burrell is ready to drop you as a client. The police have been here; a judge is issuing a warrant. Every reporter in the city is looking for you. Dr. Thoreau and the hospital . . ."

"Things of this world," I told her in my ghost whisper. We stood in the heart of the huge oak. "A lot of people are going to show up: Jackie's actors, Vain Video, artists, technicians." I found the stairs, sank through them, pulled myself up one step at a time. I saw the fear in her eyes, but I couldn't stop. "Have you got more Mangin material?"

As I reached the top of the stairs, B&T came in the front door carrying a package. "Is that blood from the butcher?" I asked him. "How many of the dentists are still eager for action? Did anyone follow you?" My hands slid off the doorknob.

"Easy, Pops." B&T gave a tight smile, turned the knob, tried to lead me toward the bed. "Big party tonight?"

"We're going to Toys."

"But, Dad, we haven't been invited." He started to grin.

I turned to Joan. "Very quietly get in touch with the supers on the block. Find ladders. Rent, borrow, steal ladders." She looked at me steadily. "Ladders so we can get from here to the windows up there." I pointed in the direction of Toys.

"Rob, I'm not going to help you kill yourself."

"Kids, that's not what I'm doing. Chris Kane is still alive, and I am going to stay alive the same way." They both looked sad. "This is that one last favor you promised me yesterday." I gave her my bravest, most touching smile. Above, Chris looked down through the roof from where he had blended with the upper tree trunk.

Finally, Joan sighed and asked, "What is it you have in mind?" And I knew they were hooked.

"I call it a media assault. It's going to be in two parts. One of them will be led by you," I told B&T. "Look out through the skylight." B&T went up the iron stairs. "See how you can get from roof to roof right up to Toys. With ladders you and a party of dentists can get from here to there tonight. You're going to be escorting the star of our show."

"I've been watching. Toys now has security like you never dreamed," he said.

"They're going to be too busy to bother with you." As I spoke, a Chase member looked up into the tree and shrugged his red-clad shoulders. The Undying Cabalist peered through the shade right into my bedroom, and I sat very still. Chris made a sudden move and got his attention. "Because as you go in the window, the other part of the assault is going to be going through the front door of Toys."

"Benjy's in for a big surprise?" Joan asked watching me.

"A relative of his and a party of his friends are going to show up."

"You don't say." Joan despite herself was starting to be amused. "Like maybe his late lamented grandfather?" They both knew my mind so well.

"Right. And an entourage of gigolos and flappers."

"You'll be the old man, of course?"

"Yes. We still have those twenties' costumes in the cellar? Good. Could you set up the rec room for fittings? Lay out lots of makeup. Oh, and we need an actress to play Antonia Ferrar, Mangin's mistress. I want someone made up to look just like the pictures."

"I can do that," said Joan.

"You're not tall enough, and not light enough," I said remembering Morgan.

"That's all right. You're not tall enough to be Mangin's grandfather. I want to be near you in case something happens."

She said that with finality. I nodded and asked B&T, "Would you pour the blood into a large bowl and leave it on the table, please?" They both went out, and I fell backward onto my bed and looked up into the leaves. Chris caught my eye. The Chase was all around the tree with nets and spikes. The Cabalist was giving orders.

"Here you go, Drac baby. Sorry they were out of baby's blood," said B&T entering with the bowl and the newspapers. "You only made it onto page 4 of the *Post*. "GAME MASTER MYSTERY: A FATAL FANTASY?" is the headline. Nice pictures, though. The *Times* talked to Sandy Burrell and Dr. Thoreau. But they didn't give it any pizzazz. We got tapes of the TV coverage if you want to see that." I shook my head.

"This is the rest of the Mangin material," Joan said handing me some papers. "It's interesting but kind of morbid."

"Thank you both. I'm going to try and rest until the people arrive." After they went out, I got up and lapped the blood. It tasted sticky and foul. My bones ached. I could feel a longing for drugs creeping up my spine. Sunlight came through the loft windows. I gestured for Chris to come down and drink. He shook his head, touched the small sack around his neck.

The newsprint swam before my eyes. "GAME MASTER DISAPPEARS IN VAMPIRE SLAYINGS TIE-IN," said the *Times*. One photo was of me playing Cobalt. The other was the one from yesterday showing the park and the hospital, this time with my window circled in white.

Morning had passed into afternoon in both worlds. Birds and squirrels darted around the tree; telephones rang downstairs. The Skin clung to me like a fever sheet. I lay on the bed as quietly as I could. Whenever the Cabalist looked my way Chris would move slightly and distract him. I studied the Mangin material. The Chase and Undying Cabal guarding the foot of the tree walked right through the walls.

The door of my room opened, and a work party of the Caprii outfitted with axes and saws arrived under the tree at the same moment.

"You wanted to see the actors?" Joan asked as birds in Capricorn flew through her like elongated streaks of color. I nodded slightly. Chris stood motionless watching the work crew.

Figures in the white clothes of the Caprii bent over their tools, as brightly dressed members of the Chase forced them to work, prodded them on. Chips flew, lower branches of the tree were hacked off. Several more black-clad Eternal Cabalists stood with silver spikes and unfurled nets.

B&T came in to announce. "There's a sound crew setting up downstairs. Did you order them?" I nodded yes as traffic started getting heavy in my loft.

"Some guy dressed as a bum is hanging around the back door. A cable-TV truck has been parked across from next door since nine this morning. A woman I never saw before has washed every window in the building across the way."

I nodded and whispered, "See if you can't let them find

out that all this is just a game you and Joan are running in my absence."

Through the walls I was aware of Chris perched in the oak. Every once in a while he'd move enough to let the Chase know he was there. Long squirrels leaped to safety as saws flashed in the sun.

Jackie's actors came in asking, "Have you seen her?" I said nothing immediately, just got up to drink blood as they watched, fascinated. Capricorn was fading, but I could still see Chris, knife in hand, hanging onto the shaking tree.

"My belief," I told them, "is that the answer to Jackie's disappearance lies down the street at Toys."

They stared at me in my Skin and at the bow gun stuck in my belt. After a long pause, an actress asked, "What do you have planned for tonight?"

"It's the 1920s. You're guests going to a mad party. You're Scott and Zelda and Dorothy Parker. We're going to be doing a little street performance in front of Toys. Inside, too, if all goes well. Anyone who doesn't like it?" I looked around and found them nodding approval. "We have to record some lines first. You're all going to be miked. Are we set up for that?" I asked B&T.

He left to check, and Joan came in. "We've got enough costumes for everyone." I nodded and turned to a black guy I remembered as having a big voice. "I'd like you to read the lines about Mangin from these pages. If you can, I want it Chiller Theater style." A blond actress sat a little apart and aloof. I told her, "There's a dictionary open. I'd like a reading of the underlined definitions. Make it sound like a voice from far away, another world."

The man picked up the pages I had been studying. Joan started the tape. "The origins of the man known to history as Benjamin Mangin are obscure—," he declaimed.

"The First," I interrupted. "Each time you mention his name call him Benjamin Mangin the First and make it sound sinister. You can't be hammy enough here."

"Capricorn," the actress read. "The tenth sign of the Zodiac, which the sun enters about December twenty-second."

"More remote. Like a moon goddess."

B&T appeared. "Vain Video," he said. I gestured for them to come in and signaled the actor to read the next passage as cameras began to hum.

"The death of Benjamin Mangin the First in the fire at Capriole left many questions unanswered."

I signaled for him to stop and cued the actress. "Capriole," she said, "a caper or leap like that made by a goat."

"Good," I told them. "You've both got it. Let's run through the whole thing once." I knew that if the evening went on too long, Cancer was going to envelop me. I had slipped almost all the way over the Transept. Pain lurked just beyond my nerve endings.

I sat at the makeup table staring at a picture of Mangin. B&T and a couple of Spanish supers had just brought some ladders into the loft. The actors were going down for costuming in relays. My dentists and their friends milled around, gawkers backstage.

My eyes ached. I fumbled with a long black mustache like the one in Mangin's photo. Capricorn had faded in the noise and light of my loft. Sitting quietly, though, I could see the sun right through my wall and ceiling. Beyond the axes hacking the trunk of the huge tree were the tents and flags of the Undying Cabal's hunting camp.

"I haven't seen you like this for a while," Joan said softly. She wore a silk dress and cloche. The eyes weren't right. She didn't look haunted enough.

"Joan, watch out," I said. "I think I'm fatal."

"I insist." She began helping me make up.

B&T approached with a bunch of dark scrawny kids in paint-splattered clothes. "The grafitti artists," he said.

"This is what I would like." With an eyebrow pencil I scrawled the words CANCER INTO CAPRICORN INTO CANCER INTO CAPRICORN in an eye-shaped oval. "Will you use those words?" The kids looked at me hard, then nodded.

"There are guests arriving down the street," B&T told me. As he said that, I saw movement in Capricorn, caught a glimpse of nets spread and spikes raised. The oak swayed in the evening sun of the day before the equinox in Capricorn. The tree was falling. The Caprii looked horrified. Chris, shading his eyes, fumbled his bag of blood to his lips and leaped.

Noise died as everyone in the loft stood absolutely still trying to see whatever I was staring at. Everyone heard the thump on the roof. I signaled for B&T, who had been standing on the stairs, to open the skylight. Finding my voice, I said, "Ladies and gentlemen, the star of this evening's presentation." Out of the second-longest night of the year stepped a gray kid with eyes full of death and anger, and I announced, "Chris Kane of the Feral Cell!"

CHAPTER

Eight

A lot of the people in the loft saw Chris. Some of them began to applaud. Something between a wince and a smile passed over his face. That's how I remembered Chris before concerts: stage fright and swagger, both fighting to possess him. Silently he came down the ladder and paused at the bowl.

"Uncanny," an actor murmured.

"Laughter and tears," added another.

"Where did you find him?" someone asked, awestruck.

Before he bent to drink, Chris shot a look around the room like something wild at bay. "Home is where you fucking hang yourself," he said.

"Before we start rehearsal, Chris and I are going to tell you a little story," I said, testing my voice. "You can take it as fact or fantasy as you like. What you can't do is leave once you've heard it. If you wish to leave, now's the moment." I gestured toward the door. No one stirred.

"There are two places: Cancer and Capricorn. And at times the way between them grows very short." I had wondered about how the dentists and their friends would react to all this strangeness. But they were most eager, leaning forward, fascinated. It was a chance for their lives to be like those on television. Maybe they thought it was all part of a game. Or maybe they didn't care. I wondered if this was how places went bad: people's lives became so bitter, or frightening, or boring that they didn't care how they risked them?

"This world where we are standing is called Cancer," I told them. "And we are called the Crabs by those in the world called Capricorn. They call themselves the Caprii. The place where the two worlds overlap is called the Transept. Over the centuries a few of us instead of dying have gone over the Transept from this world to that." I looked at Chris.

We had always been able to trade a story back and forth even when we were making one up on the spot. For a moment he said nothing. Then he began, "Even fewer have returned. In Capricorn, memory of this place fades away to a dream." He looked through the ceiling, toward Toys and the tents of the Cabal. "The Caprii know of this place but have never tried to come here. Because they thought of us as a kind of dream and knew the power of dreams, they fed and clothed those of us they found."

"To reach Capricorn we have to be dying of cancer. We don't know what it takes for one of them to reach us. For a long time it didn't matter because none of them attempted it." Through the walls I could see black-clad figures standing on the huge stump of the tree. Lanterns glittered on silver nets as they peered at Chris and myself, two ghosts floating in their night. "And then there was the Beast," Chris said.

Following his gaze, I flinched at the fires and of the Cabal's camp. A pair of pale eyes stared over the Transept. Standing before a tent, Benjamin Mangin held up Jackie Fast's head by its hair. And I knew for certain where I could find the rest of her body.

Chris stopped speaking. It was my tale. Turning my back on Mangin and my company, I sat at my dressing table and stared at my face. "The Beast was one from that world who found his way to Cancer and back. Somehow in our world he found immortality. When he returned home he founded a cult, the Undying Cabal, to control travel between the worlds."

"Benjamin Mangin is one name by which we know the Beast, but he has had many others. As Benjamin Mangin the First he amassed a fortune in the nineteenth century. He pretended to die in a fire so that he could come back as Benjamin Mangin the Second. When that identity became a liability, he died in a mysterious boating accident off Borneo. That set the stage for his 'son' the Benjamin Mangin we all know to inherit the fortune."

Then we told them of the career of the Beast starting in the nineteenth century, described his obscure origins, his fortune and his bloody trail. As I talked to them, Joan helped me make something like the face of Benjamin Mangin the First appear in the mirror. Then she and B&T dressed me in evening clothes.

I said, "Very conveniently his last wife was supposed to have died in the fire with him in 1927." Standing slowly I turned and said, "This is how he looked then. I have had to disguise myself, just as Mangin now has to disguise himself." My feet and hands began to cramp. Joan took my arm, and together we faced the cameras, struck the pose of Mangin and Antonia in the old photo.

"Is that blood you two are drinking?" one of the dentists asked, still searching for clues.

"Does that have something to do with getting to Capricorn?" one of the artists wanted to know.

"All this was in the past," I told them ignoring the questions. "Here's what we're doing tonight." As I spoke, B&T had put on the Feral Cell tape. A synthesizer played alone at first. Then faintly, from far away, ghost horns began to sound. Chris moved across the floor singing almost to himself:

Just to reach the land of Kane
Where you run until it's light,
and you ditch all human cares
got to hurt with all your might.

Everyone in the room focused on him, cameras turned, eyes followed Chris as he climbed halfway up the ladder. There he crouched and looked at them so intensely that no one could look back. "Mr. Leal acts like this is a game, because he pretends that everything is a game. It isn't. On Capricorn we are as real as hope. Mangin and the Undying Cabal want to destroy us and the place we have in peoples' dreams."

"We have something a little different for you tonight," I told them. Any one of them could have left, I guess, called the police, and had me jugged. No one moved. They all had their reasons. "We're going to visit Toys. They don't expect us. They may act like they're not happy to see us. Chris and I will be going inside. All the rest of you have to do is follow us. Incidentally, my liability insurance is all paid up."

Then I divided them into groups, actors with me, dentists and grafitti artists with Chris and B&T, video people with both parties. "The roof crew is going through a top floor window. They will get down to the first floor and meet the rest of us. We'll be going through the front door. From there we proceed to the dance floor where Chris Kane and I will do a little improvised drama. Then we'll go on to the celebrity lounge where Mr. Mangin will be happy to receive us."

"This is a sequel to the capture the Swedes game, Saturday?" asked a dentist.

"Absolutely," I told him. "People will ask you about tonight's game for a long time." Turning to the video people I said, "What I'm giving you tonight is going to make your reputations. It's a double bill, 'Chris Kane Returns,' and the 'Beast at Bay,'" I saw Chris curl his lip at my spiel, but he was listening hard.

I told the artists, "You get to put your work where it will be seen on network TV." Lastly I turned to the Fast Action Street Theater Company and said very quietly, "This is for Jackie Fast. When this is over, you and everyone else will know what happened to her."

Then I rehearsed everyone as the video crews recorded the whole thing. It made them stop asking questions and made me less aware of how much I hurt. When I tried to look through the walls, Capricorn was almost gone. Out there, I knew, eyes strained to see me, figures stood on the fallen tree and tried to make out what I was doing.

"Half an hour to show time," I heard myself saying. "Let's have a sound check." I sat back and closed my eyes, trying to save energy. Since it was my farewell performance, it didn't matter that I could feel myself dying. They had the sound way up.

"TWO DOZEN WORKMEN DIED CONSTRUCTING CAPRIOLE, HIS ESTATE OUTSIDE NEW YORK. THIS WAS SEIZED ON BY MUCKRAKERS AS A SYMBOL OF THE SELF-INDULGENT CORRUPTION OF THE RICH." The actor on the tape almost slurped his lines.

"CANCER: A ROUGH, HARD SURFACE. THE CONSTELLATION BETWEEN GEMINI AND LEO OUTLINING A CRAB. THE FOURTH SIGN OF THE ZODIAC. A MALIGNANT NEW GROWTH ON THE BODY." The voice of the actress sounded like it came from out of this world.

"Watch it!" Chris was up with his knife out, balancing on the edge of the Transept. Joan pushed me out of the way. A silver spike went through my dressing table mirror without breaking it and disappeared. As I fumbled for the bow gun, a face swam into view, stared at me in amazement. My hand closed on the gun. A man in the hunting clothes of the Chase came into focus. Chris's knife and hand passed right through him. The hunter fell back into Capricorn.

"I caught some kind of flash," said a videoteer.

"There was a face. How did you do that?" an actress wanted to know.

"Is that one of the clues?" asked a dentist.

Chris grimaced as he lapped blood from the bowl. "They sent a hunter because the Cabal were afraid to face us," he told me.

In the silence that followed I spoke in my Benjamin Mangin voice. "I invite you all to my 'grandson's' party. He doesn't expect me. He won't be pleased to see me." I gave a wide and ghastly smile. "But he has no idea how to throw a party. We're what will make the evening for him. I promise you."

Everyone was still for a moment. Then B&T said, "Pops is shooting the works on this one!" and went up the iron stairs and opened the skylight. The grafitti artists ran up after him, and the dentists began hauling ladders while cameras and mikes caught it all. Off to the side Chris stared through the wall.

Eyes stared back from Capricorn, but no one dared approach him.

"Mr. Kane," I said loudly, "you're on." He looked at me, eyes narrow. Then he showed his teeth, turned and slid past people on the stairs like a trail of smoke.

Joan and I went into the next room and down the stairs. "Actors, sound, street video teams: places," I croaked.

"This is your last chance to turn back," she said. I shook my head and suddenly felt very dizzy. I needed her arm on the stairs. A sound tech attached a two-way hook-up to her jacket.

"Now remember the effect that I want here," I told the company assembled in the front hall. "You're my guests. At a dinner party in 1925. I've invited you down to my bank where it's decades later, and someone who claims to be my grandson is having a reception." I felt my voice and manner trailing into old Dr. Cobalt and paused.

"Sound crew," I said in a loud whisper, "cue the first track when we are out the door. Remember to take your cues from Joan after that."

A woman from the sound crew checked speakers on the actors. Another technician opened the door. I glanced outside, a player peeking around a stage curtain. I could just smell the cold, wet air tinged with bums' piss and grass. Above me skyscrapers lighted the night. On Broadway horns honked where the growing crowd in front of Toys blocked traffic. It was opening night, and New York was the scene that I was about to steal.

At that moment the signal from B&T told us the roof

party was on its way. I stepped out the door and was aware of figures closing in.

"Robert Leal?" asked a police voice. I recognized the sergeant from the hospital.

"Mangin's the name," I said and didn't break stride. At that moment, a man who had been leaning over the open hood of his car turned and bowled into the sergeant. He slammed his fist into the throat of another cop and was off down the alley. A woman across the street stopped washing windows and threw a block on someone.

In a rush of wheels, Raul and a dozen skateboarders swept out of the dark and escorted us. Down the street a couple of figures ran out of the shadows and began painting a slogan on the building opposite Toys: *FERAL CELL RULES!* I hadn't even ordered that.

Joan had her arm through mine. Aside from a dying body and a Skin hanging off me like damp Kleenex, I felt wonderful as we set off. Drowning out the sounds of a police-car radio, over all our speakers, Chris Kane sang that old quiet intro to "Stagger Lee."

"Ohhh, jungle music!" said an actor in flapper drag.

"Fierce ragtime," an actress said in a deep voice while waving a glass of champagne.

A hunter ran through parked cars and buildings spreading word to the Chase. A black-hooded figure with a silver spike fell back before me.

"NO TWO SOURCES AGREE ON THE ORIGINS OF THE MAN WHO CAME TO BE KNOWN AS 'BEAST' MANGIN." The recording we had made earlier came blasting out of our speakers and seemed to carry us down the street.

"CAPRICORN," the moon goddess voice cut through the night, "BETWEEN SAGITTARIUS AND AQUARIUS, A CONSTELLATION SHAPED LIKE A GOAT. THE TENTH SIGN OF THE ZODIAC, WHICH THE SUN ENTERS DECEMBER TWENTY-SECOND."

Before us was Toys. Lights played on the goats'-head flags out front. Limos tried to pull up to the curb through a large crowd. Mangin may have intended it to be a quiet affair. But Jason had summoned the press. And with them had come a crowd of the curious, the idle, the ones for whom an appearance on television was a validation of existence.

Glancing up I saw dark figures planting ladders, scrambling over roofs. A gray ghost floated ahead of them. For an instant the buildings melted, and Chris was alone striding through the air. The crowd, the cars, the bank also disappeared, and I saw bonfires and tents, figures flickering before me.

"THE TRIAL FOLLOWING THE BLAINE COUNTY MINE CAVE-IN ENDED IN A HUNG JURY. IN THAT INCIDENT TWENTY STRIKERS ARE KNOWN TO HAVE DIED. A DOZEN BODIES WERE NEVER RECOVERED."

Looking back, I saw two cars turn onto the block going the wrong way. They stopped across the street from my house. That meant the law was hot on my trail. Pain almost doubled me up. I quickened my pace. Arrest and death lay behind me. Capricorn lay ahead.

The crowd on the street cleared a way, then closed in around us. TV cameras picked us up as we hit the bottom of the stairs of the Chemical Exchange Trust. At the door stood figures in the bright colors of the Chase. Near them I saw Jason Beautemps with an Art Net camera crew. Microphones were pushed into my face.

"What's your name?" asked a woman with a dead smile.

"Benjamin Mangin the First, young lady." My voice seemed to be running without my help, sounding soft and pre-chewed. "I've come to see if my grandson is worthy of the blood." I felt the hair on my neck rise as I stared up at the members of the Chase.

"CAPRICE: BRISTLING HAIR, GOOSE FLESH," said the moon goddess voice. I looked more closely at the figures in the bright costumes and recognized them as private-security people. My actors not knowing what the door people were supposed to represent had made their way up the steps and attached themselves to the guards.

"And who are all these people?" asked a young man wearing a fashion wig. I was being treated as part of the show. Mangin's people looked edgy. It was my guess that they didn't want the cops either. Mangin had a few things to hide.

"These are my dinner guests," I said, waving my free arm. "The rich and the gifted. We're just down from Capriole, my country estate."

"Did you know that the theme of your grandson's party is encounters with Capricorn?" asked a reporter. "It's his sign. Is it yours?" As I tried to remember, my voice faded. I was waiting for B&T's signal. Until that came I could not look up.

"AS LONG AS HE LIVED, RUMORS OF BLOODY DEEDS AND SECRET MURDERS FOLLOWED 'BEAST' MANGIN," boomed the recorded voice of the big black actor who now, dressed in a spangled silver high-hat and ringmaster's coat, had edged his way almost to the door.

The crowd pushed behind me, desperate to be close to anything important enough to be on TV. For a moment faces swam, lights pulsed, and blue lights shone through Toys.

Jason brought me back by sticking a mike in my face and saying, "Benjamin, may I call you that? Benjamin, weren't there a couple of little, well, rumors?"

"You mean about human sacrifice at Capriole, bodies strung up and drained of blood?" I bared my teeth in a smile that made most of the reporters take a couple of steps back. "People fantasize about the lives we rich lead. Nothing was ever proved."

"AT THE HEIGHT OF THE FIRE THAT CONSUMED HIM AND HIS ESTATE OUTSIDE NEW YORK, GUESTS SWORE THEY SAW MANGIN AND HIS MISTRESS WALK NAKED THROUGH THE FLAMES, LAUGHING TOGETHER."

"It's somewhat before I was presented socially, Benjamin," Jason persisted, "but weren't you presumed dead a while back?" Behind me I could hear the rush of skates and boards and an occasional loud cry. A siren was coming up fast.

"CANCER: THE CRAB, A MALIGNANT NEW GROWTH ON THE BODY."

I saw Joan's eyes creep upward. She was half supporting me as I tried to get my Benjamin Mangin voice to work. At that moment alarm bells went off overhead. Broken glass and pieces of masonry fell at my feet, and Joan hit my shoulder and at the same time said, "Cut!" into her mike.

The sound system fell silent on cue. I gathered my strength, drew my breath, and screamed, "I have walked through fire and blood to be here tonight! Others have come back from the dead, like Chris Kane!" On the name, I pointed and looked at the party upstairs.

Ladders leaned against the side of Toys; broken windows gaped. Kids hanging on the cornices, leaning on the goat and crab gargoyles, painted *CANCER INTO CAPRICORN INTO CANCER INTO CAPRICORN* in huge elongated blood-red letters. Television lights swept over the façade and picked out a figure in gray poised on a ladder.

Glancing back I saw people jumping out of cars, saw police lights flashing. I started up the stairs. Jason and the cameras followed. Joan cued the sound crew back at my house, and out of the boxes the actors carried came Chris Kane singing:

> *I THOUGHT I HAD THE RAP BEAT,*
> *HE'D NEVER FINGER ME.*
> *BUT WHEN HE'S LEAST EXPECTED*
> *DEATH DROPS IN FOR TEA.*

Toys' security was in confusion. Surrounded by my 'guests,' hearing alarms from inside the building, seeing cops closing in, they wavered. We all moved on them at once, and they stepped back. Through their bodies, I saw pinpoints of blue light in Capricorn.

A couple of them tripped over peoples' feet and fell; the

others went back in front of a wedge of actors. Cameras and reporters followed us through the door. The rush of skates sounded like a flood as Sun Bums closed in behind us blocking the stairs. It would take the police a while to get through all that.

Inside, the psychedelic ornaments still hung. Instead of kids and customers trading favors, a more serious crowd hung out under the Day-Glo chandeliers, people who looked rich enough and old enough to want to make a serious investment in immortality.

Our wedge surged through the lobby, guests cringing away from the cameras, actors calling out to them, "How do you personally feel about Cancer? The place, I mean. Isn't it too mad to visit?" Security people in phony Chase attire blocked our way to the dance floor.

They were in front of the main stairs. As they lined up, B&T and some wild-eyed dentists appeared at the top of the stairs and ran down behind them. Air guns popped, faces and hair turned yellow, a security man gagged on a mouthful of paint. Photographers snapped pictures; videoteers filmed them and were caught in the cameras of the TV crews.

Then Joan killed our sound. The dentists paused, and the actors stood absolutely still looking up as Chris came down the stairs.

"Chris Kane," I said, my Mangin voice full of horror, "you've been dead for thirty years!"

"I've been in Capricorn, Beast Mangin. Just like you." Chris had drunk enough blood, stayed in this world long enough to be rooted here. His voice was raw and hoarse, his eyes were wild, as if he were burning up inside. Cameras caught him as he pulled out his knife and said, "I've come back to destroy the house of Mangin in Cancer." When he plunged down the stairs at me, a couple of people screamed.

I rolled my eyes in terror and began running toward the dance-floor doors, the actors and video following. Joan still beside me, holding me up, said in horror, "He doesn't have long to live."

B&T and half a dozen dentists put their shoulders to the

door, and it gave. Inside, the floor was in motion. Pulsing silver light evoked Capricorn somehow. Guests tried to flee across the undulating floor. The camera crews couldn't function in that light. The momentum of the media assault was lost. "Kill the power in here," I told Joan. A couple of kids with paint cans dashed to a wall. Turning, I saw Chris appear in the door, knife drawn, teeth bared, staring past me.

I followed his look and saw Mangin all the way across the room. Mangin stood in evening clothes with half a dozen members of the Cabal. He smiled right at me and said, "This is very convenient." Joan had disappeared. Mangin sounded, as always, as if he were talking with his mouth full. He made what seemed like a clumsy move. Then he shimmered like a fish and stood right in front of me.

I put my hand on the gun, but he grabbed both my arms. The floor buckled under me, and I rose several feet.

"Oh, Leal, I am going to have your Skin."

Then I understood that in this shifting room with flashing lights, Mangin was at home. He had created a place in Cancer where he could function better than anyone born there.

I saw B&T grab one of the Cabal and throw him to the floor. Chris slashed with his knife. But they were disoriented.

Mangin lifted me by my shoulders. "I will drink your blood for this," he whispered.

Then the flashing lights ceased; the floor went dead. Power in the room had been cut. I stood with Mangin on top of a little peak and knew Joan had found the switch. Mangin let go of me as Chris lunged at him. "Mother fucker," Chris said. "I want to kill you slowly for every single death you've caused." But this wasn't Capricorn, and he missed as Mangin backed toward the VIP lounge. The Cabal also scrambled away as television lights raked the room. Our speakers suddenly blared:

BUT WHEN HE'S LEAST EXPECTED
DEATH DROPS IN FOR TEA.

FERAL CELL/LIFE AND DEATH was being spray painted on a wall. Behind us in the lobby someone screamed, "Police!"

I got the gun out and heard horns, saw blue pinpoints of light through the walls. The Cabal tried to lock the doors of the lounge. But special guests invited for a glimpse of immortality pushed past them trying to escape.

"There's never been a celebrity room they could keep me out of," Jason yelled.

I looked at the figures in black and understood that they wore Skins taken from the people of this world. They made it easy to draw the bow and fire the gun several times. Capsules splattered and someone shrieked. The Cabal broke and ran.

Large bowls rested on either end of a stone table at the back of the room. Between them was a headless corpse. A psychedelic-light display turned the blood yellow, blue, and red. The Cabal bent to drink blood. Mangin tried to pull the body with him. I fired and he stepped away. The corpse fell behind the table.

"Dad, the cops are right behind us," B&T was yelling.

"NO TWO SOURCES AGREE AS TO THE ORIGINS OF THE 'BEAST,'" blared the actors' speakers. Chris went for one of the Cabal with his knife. I recognized Risa, my hostess at Mangin's Roost on Saturday. She faded in front of him like a shadow.

"CAPRICE: A SHIVERING WHIM." Tents and bonfires stood all around me. Through the walls of Toys I saw my next audience: the Cabal and the Chase and behind them horns blowing, blue lights shining, thousands of Caprii.

"Police! Freeze!"

A lot of people caught a hint of that bright light. A lot more saw Mangin dressed in his black tuxedo, slurping Jackie's blood out of one of the bowls. And they could see what looked like a side of meat on the floor next to him.

"Keeping up with the old family traditions, grandson," I said. "Isn't that Jackie Fast?"

"TRANSEPT," said the recorded voice. "A SHORT AISLE THAT CROSSES A CATHEDRAL NAVE."

"Yes. Now explain all this to the police, will you, Leal," said Mangin and tipped over the bowl of Goat's Blood. The mother and father of every pain I'd ever had came back to visit me.

An undignified scramble was occurring near a side door where invited and uninvited guests tried to bolt out of the room. "You did it, man. It worked." I felt a hand like a feather on my back. "We can fade back to Bus Stop," Chris told me.

"I have to show the Caprii my magic," I whispered. "And I want to run in Capricorn. Come with me." He shook his head, gave a look of longing toward the Transept. Then he stuck his bone knife in my belt, and with one graceful move slipped through guests and dentists struggling to escape as police burst in with drawn guns.

"Don't move," a cop shouted. The bowl was empty, but puddles of blood lay on the table. I put my hand down, and it came up covered in Blood of the Goat. "I said don't move." I lapped my fingers.

I saw B&T and Joan surrounded by police. Behind me were the horns of Capricorn. My whole body ached.

One or two cameras were still on me as I put my hand down again and covered it with blood. "Hello, officer."

"Who are you?"

"Robert Leal."

"You're under arrest."

"What about Benjamin Mangin?" I put my hand to my mouth as though to cough. I heard a safety click off. "He killed Jackie Fast." I indicated the form on the floor behind the table. "You'll find her right here." The blood burned and tingled in my mouth, and I felt my clothes, my disguise, falling from me. Someone fired and Joan screamed my name. But I was over the Transept and into Capricorn.

CHAPTER
Nine

Then the dream was my life, and what had been my life was a dream. At the sight of me, Caprii surrounding the hunting camp began to chant and march forward. As they did they doused the ring of fire and torches the Cabal had set up. The Chase members stood stunned. I had counted on my sudden appearance breaking their faith in Mangin's control over Cancer. It would be as if the magician had reached into a hat and brought his hand out with several fingers bitten off.

The Chase backed away from me and the advancing Caprii. Their rockets were clumsy weapons not easily fired by anyone in motion. They pointed them to keep us at a respectful distance, but they and their servants got onto their horses as quickly as they could.

The Cabal snarled at me and brandished their nets, but I drew the bow again, and they, too, went for their horses before the Caprii closed in. Mangin was too far away for me to hit as he grabbed the stake with Jackie's head. He said in a quiet voice that echoed, "We will meet again at Capriole Castle, Leal," I smiled and shrugged, convinced the whole thing was over.

Then I watched the Cabal and their servants led by Mangin ride into the center of a mass of horsemen: gentry of the Chase, liveried retainers. A few horsemen deserted and rode away alone, but for most Mangin was their god, and faith doesn't die all at once.

The blue lights parted as they galloped away from the camp and headed north. Some of them could have been pulled from their horses and cut off. But the Caprii did no more than herd them on their way. Large parties of Caprii each led by a member of the Cell trailed the Chase into the night.

"We crushed them!" I told Morgan when she appeared. She was followed by half a dozen of the Cell and by Caprii holding blue lights and bowls.

"You have hurt Mangin's pride in Capricorn," she said. "But you haven't broken him. He still has resources."

"Mangin can't go back to New York."

"Can you?"

I thought about that. "Maybe. If I keep a low profile."

She crouched on the ground, panting, looked north in the path of the Chase, then turned to me. "We will follow Mangin to Capriole Castle. You must stay here to guard Chris."

The rest of the Cell members on the scene crouched with us. Lurch and Garbo and one or two others remained a little distant, watching but removed, smoke silhouettes in the night. They smiled and blinked when Morgan nodded at them and told me, "Those lived in these hills like lone ghosts when I first came to Capriole Castle."

Ruby and Speedo looked at me closely as Morgan said, "They were brought over the Transept by Chris. He would have brought hundreds if the land could support them. These are the Cell members who always stay in this country. They will remain here to assist you and guard our rear. As you hold the bow gun you must protect Chris. He is now our main operative in Cancer."

One more game was taking shape. I nodded my understanding, and she went on. "The rest of us are going north. We will let as many of the Chase as wish to get to Capriole

Castle. There Mangin will try to prove to them that he has power over Cancer and this world."

"You're going to storm the castle?"

"No. This will be a contest of religion, of magic. An attack on the castle might succeed, but it would certainly cost lives. The Caprii are poor people; just for them to have mustered in the middle of the growing season is a grave enough burden."

"You plan to overawe the Chase?"

"They are Mangin colonists. He brought them here from the coast and from overseas and gave them Caprii land at gunpoint. The Caprii had never seen anything like those rockets. Members of the Cabal knew how to tame natural gas and fortify strong points with it. Their magic is the science of Cancer.

"Mangin is using that to prove that he and the Cabal are mightier than the Cell. He's trying to break us without the help of soldiers. We are trying either to force the Chase to surrender him to us, or to make him abandon them and flee to Cancer. Without him the Chase is nothing but a back-woods vigilante force. They will fade away."

Knowing him as I did, I said, "And Chris got tired of all the maneuvering."

"It angered him that while we are elusive, children of the dark, our Caprii are not. He feels that Mangin has done more for his people than we have for ours."

"He wants to bring the war to Cancer."

"Capricorn is not as volatile as our world, not as adventurous. People do not abandon the old ways as readily. Mangin is trying to change that, to introduce technology. He has offended kings and their priests. Some of them are very strong, but none of them has his magic. He amassed a fortune in our world to make himself a messiah in this one."

"And Chris is trying to do the same thing for the Feral Cell in New York."

"Yes. We are trying to crush Mangin between the two worlds. Tell Chris that we are raising the mountain Caprii. When I first came to this world, the people rose up and destroyed the outer defenses of the Capriole Castle. Recently they were hastily rebuilt and ringed with light, the symbol of Mangin's power."

"What I did tonight barely dented his prestige." It seemed that immortality was a full-time job.

"It will take more, much more. Mangin will not yield while there is ground for maneuver. That is why it is vital for you to protect Chris."

The rest of the Cell nodded, licked their teeth as Caprii approached, put down bowls, and poured the Blood.

While they did, I asked a question that occured to me since realizing who Morgan was. "What happened that last night at the Roost? Did Mangin set fire to the room?"

She drew her lips back in a smile. "And offered a choice of the flames or the blood." The Cell listened breathing quickly.

"Why did Chris change your name from Antonia to Morgan?"

"I had lost my old name. I didn't think of myself as that any longer. Chris named all of us who had forgotten their names. Mine is short for Morgan le Fay."

"He named me Ruby Tuesday," Ruby whispered.

"You and the Beast had a stormy affair?" I asked Morgan.

"The Beast was well-named. He found me in Paris where I was dancing and said that I had haunted his dreams." She pointed at a bag woman on a street in New York who stopped talking to herself long enough to back away, staring at us horrified.

"One understands the fascination Cancer must have for him. I believe that Mangin was an outcast here, diseased, perhaps, or mad. It is one of his oldest secrets, and all who knew him then are dead. Long before he saw me he had found his way over the Transept.

"He never told me what in Cancer gave him his immortality. That is the Cabal's strongest secret. It is said here that anyone who once drinks or eats in the world of the Crab will live forever in that world or this."

She shrugged. "When I first met him, I didn't know that

the one who called himself Benjamin Mangin was ancient. But he was old and disgusting enough not to interest me. The choice was not mine. I realized something was very wrong with me, and a man so rich who knew I was dying and said he could save me was not to be dismissed."

"What is he like?"

"For Caprii in our world it is different than for us here. We bound; they feel heavy, stolid. This sun blinds us, but what we can see is magic. Our world was always cloudy and unreal to him."

"But with the fountain of youth."

"And riches beyond gold or gems. Mangin told me once that Cancer was like an immense sunken ship that he explored. The machines and inventions are like miracles to him. And stealing them has made him a great man in both worlds. If one lives for hundreds of years, even if one lives like a slug at the bottom of the sea, one accumulates knowledge and wealth."

"You got away from him?"

"I had never loved him. He was strange and disturbing. But instead of brilliance he had the ruthlessness and patience that come with centuries of life. He had fallen in love with the sight of me dancing at twilight in Capricorn. He assured me that in his homeland all would be different, and I would be cured. He taught me how to see more and more of this place."

"When you got here you found out he was the scourge of the earth."

"This is a beautiful country, and it captured me so that at first I didn't understand anything else. There was Blood of the Goat in abundance, brought to me in silver dishes. And Mangin looked differently, moved differently. If we gorge on blood we can become far more solid. In Cancer I became his wife. Here I became his lover, but I did not love him.

"I knew that there had been other women, ghost lovers like myself at Capriole Castle. He had built the castle and at the same time built Capriole in New York as a mirror of it."

"What happened to the other wives?"

"It is my guess that he grew tired of them." She shrugged. "That he would see something or someone that he wanted in Cancer. When that happened it was convenient to have Blood of the Crab so close at hand.

"I thought about none of this until I saw another Crab in Capricorn. She was young, in her teens, being bled into a silver bowl by the Cabal. It took a while before I understood, before I wanted to understand, but . . ."

"You escaped?"

"My father was English, but my mother's family is from Piedmonte, between France and Italy. My mother's father was a smuggler. I understood the border and its uses. I had discovered the Caprii and their worship of us. They hid me from Mangin when I ran away. He searched for me at first, tried to terrorize them into giving me up. Then something called him away or distracted him, and he and the Cabal went elsewhere to hunt for Blood of the Crab."

The Cell stirred, and I saw the blue lights ripple and a gray form lope through the dark. It was one of the Feral Cell I didn't recognize. He crouched before a bowl and drank between pants. Then he said, "They are in place. Their work is going well."

She gave a short laugh. "I was not religious until I became a god. It is easy here to forget our home, to let the years slip away. Since the Caprii saved me I have tried to stay half-Cancer and half-Capricorn." Morgan stood, and the Cell stirred from where they had been sitting, rapt, listening to her. She whispered. "It is important to do as little harm as possible here, to take no more blood than will keep us alive."

I wanted to know more, but Morgan was on her feet assigning the Cell to their posts. She stood in the night, held me for a moment, and whispered in my ear, "Tell Chris that the mountain Caprii are at Mangin's castle. Tell him their magic will work the evening of the solstice at the full rising of the moon." Before she turned away, she repeated, "Remember that, the evening after tonight at the full rising of the moon."

When she was gone, the rest of the Cell dispersed. Ruby went to keep watch on the House of Usher. Speedo was to stay in the grove outside the crossroads village. Others disappeared to watch the roads from the south or to mount guard at other strong points of the Chase.

When they left me alone, I went back to the ruins of the hunting camp and looked at where my house stood in another world. It seemed I was still curious even though that house and that world were no longer mine.

Since I was of Cancer, I would have floated back to my own world unless I drank the blood of someone or something born in Capricorn. That would always be so. Although my illness and my anxiety could bring me over the Transept, I would never be wholly part of that world and would remain at odds with its laws of physics, vulnerable to its sunlight.

The bow gun, Chris's knife, my Skin—all created in Caprii out of material that had crossed the Transept—drew me toward Capricorn. Blood from Cancer would anchor me more firmly to the world of my birth. What Morgan had done when she guarded me was to balance on the edge of the Transept, becoming a shadow in both worlds. That—I understood, only when I tried it—was a skill like learning to swim or to fly.

At the Cabal's camp site, the tents had been torn down and burned. Sparks and ashes flashed as I walked back across the field. A Caprii who had been ridden down and injured during the Chase's escape cried out in pain. Looters searched the wreckage for valuables. Once the problem of Mangin had been dealt with, I could enjoy the life I had been given.

I kept reminding myself of that as I went to the place where the tree had been cut down the day before. I hadn't drunk Blood of the Goat, and I kept my hand off the gun so as to bob between worlds in the Transept.

Floating above me were familiar faces: B&T and Joan looking scared, the hack detective sergeant and his partner from the D.A.'s office, the ones who had questioned me at the hospital. The furniture, the walls, and the floor came into view. My desk was spread with a white cloth. On it were things the police had found. One of them was the bowl of blood. Another was Dr. Cobalt's outfit. The last was Desmond Dupree's license.

The last seemed to interest the police most at that moment.

"What do you know about this?" the sergeant asked pointing at it. Mangin's people had meant to taunt me with it, to show me that they could kill anyone who came near me. Through my stupidity it had gotten turned into the kind of evidence with which even the dullest cops could hang me.

"The blood is from a butcher shop in the Village," B&T said.

"I mean the license. Have you ever seen the guy in the picture?"

"It wasn't here when we left." Joan told him staring straight ahead, wearing a wilted-looking twenties' costume, and smudged makeup.

"You're awfully sure about that," the partner said. "We found it in his desk drawer. All covered with blood. Were you familiar with the contents of his drawer?"

Joan shook her head.

"You recognize the face?" the sergeant asked. Joan just shook her head again. "That man was a cab driver who was found with his neck broken and his wrists slashed."

"Under the Williamsburg Bridge Sunday morning," said the other detective. "It didn't make the news. But we paid more attention after the skaters died in the park the next night, right across from the hospital where your boss was staying."

"A pattern emerged. Did anyone besides Leal have access to the drawer?"

"There were dozens of people in here last night."

"They're all being questioned. Does anyone else stay here?"

B&T started to shake his head then remembered. "There are a couple of house guests. They'll be back this afternoon, but they haven't been here since Saturday."

The cops shrugged that off, and the sergeant asked. "Your boss, Mr. Leal, could help us a lot with this. Where is he?"

"You were at Toys." Joan choked as she said it.

"People say he's taken the identity of Chris Kane."

"They're wrong."

"You're awful sure about some things. You're also in a lot of trouble. Unless you cooperate you could be charged with aiding and abetting," said the partner who was going to play the bad cop.

"We want to talk to a lawyer."

"Listen, we don't want to charge you. Not if Mr. Leal can explain this." The sergeant gestured at the table. He was the good cop and wore a phoney little smile. The I.D. was covered with blood smudges that I knew would show my fingerprints. "We would be more than happy to listen to his story."

"We don't know where he went."

"You're awful unsure about other things," said the bad cop. "You have no idea at all where he went?"

Joan just shook her head, eyes down, crying.

B&T held her and told them, "Capricorn. Something about Capricorn. And I don't know what that means."

"A code?" The two cops looked at each other. "Do you have a record of the telephone calls in and out of this place yesterday?" the sergeant asked Joan, lobbing a soft question at her, smiling encouragement.

"Downstairs," she said. "I'll get it." She went to the door. The two detectives and B&T followed.

As they reached the stairs, Bridge and Tunnel turned and looked right at me. The others kept on walking while he stopped and whispered, "Dad, you have done it this time." There was no smile on his face. "You fucked it up for me, and I guess those are the breaks. But look what you've done to Joanie. Do us a favor. Either come back and talk to these guys or disappear. Anything in-between is killing us."

"What's that?" asked the sergeant, and B&T looked away from me. I fell back from Cancer as if I had been slugged. On the other side of the Transept, a Caprii appeared and knelt with a bowl. I sipped just enough to keep me hovering between worlds. It also removed me from the pain B&T had just caused. I thought of Chris's line, "And you ditch all human care," and remembered that I was supposed to guard him.

The Caprii offered me a bag and thong of gray leather. I bent my head, and he put it around my neck. I nodded to dismiss him and turned to face the night, which was alive in both worlds. Bands of Caprii moved north; looters ran home with their spoils. Headlights in Cancer shone right through them as I floated on the Transept.

Sometimes I went through walls. Sometimes cars went through me. For a while I was below the street, down with the wiring and pipes. A subway train screeched out of darkness as I stood on a hillside. Its cars were almost empty. A couple of the passengers, a drunk and a crazy girl, made eye contact with me, then were gone.

Passing the shallow cave where Chris and I had gone over the Transept, I saw that the Supermarket was in business. Figures moved under street lamps, and the emaciated woman we had seen the morning before was still there. Again she stood at the end of the pier and talked to herself. A good distance away, near the overpass, skaters cruised, one of them talking to himself. I realized that they were in radio communication with each other.

She squinted into Capricorn, a sentry on watch. To avoid being seen, I pressed into a corner of the cave and waited. It didn't take long for the ones she expected to come out of the night: two of the Undying Cabal—one a native of Cancer, the other of Capricorn—traveled fast before the dawn, looking at nothing but the woman standing like a beacon.

They stopped at the hollowed rock, and one of them poured blood onto it. Both threw back their hoods, and I saw that the one from Capricorn was Risa, the woman who had judged the game at Mangin's Roost. As they crouched, gray and flickering, I realized that the one from Cancer was a guy I had seen around parties in New York for years. I didn't know his name.

"She sees us," he whispered.

"What is important," said Risa chewing her words carefully, "is their finding us a prize to make this worthwhile."

As they lapped blood, the woman on the pier spoke very quickly into the mike inside her collar. The two Cabalists rose, reached out their hands to her, and went over the Transept as I drew back my bow. Then I noticed there was only one capsule left and that the sun was coming up behind me.

That gave me pause as did the skaters who rolled over to the Cabalists and hurried them away. I bent down and licked up the Blood of the Crab they had left. It tasted like rusty water, and I wondered if it was Jackie's as I gagged it down. Then my heart beat more slowly and my eyes adjusted to a mundane world as I went over the Transept.

The woman on the pier saw me, and we both froze. In my acting career I had killed in cold blood many times. On the last season of "Hill Street Blues" I recited nursery rhymes as I strangled six nurses. In the film *Somewhere in the Night,* I had a bit where I shot two cops during a liquor-store holdup. As Dr. Cobalt I had condemned clients to mock extermination at the hands of dwarfs. In the last few days I had fired the bow gun in anger quite a bit. But to empty it into a face two feet in front of me gave me pause.

Then she made the mistake of trying to talk into her mike. Automatically I put one hand up to cover her mouth and pulled out Chris's knife. I could feel it begin to draw me to Capricorn, and for a moment it seemed that my hand and the knife were going to pass right through her. Then my palm stopped her mouth, and my knife slid through her jacket and shirt, sliced between two of her ribs.

Fire and ice,
Yours for a price.

A dealer chanted as he walked under a street lamp and didn't look at us at all. The woman, I noticed when she hit the ground, was young and so thin her bones stood out. She had been dying and would have called death down on me if I hadn't killed her. My immediate feeling was regret at wasting so much Blood of the Crab when all I needed was a mouthful from her wound.

That was enough to enable me to float across the overpass again and through the predawn streets. I caught sight of bright red "BLOOD CULT: BLOOD FEUD" headlines on a copy of the *Post* at an all-night newsstand. There was no sign of the Undying Cabal or their phoney Sun Bum escort. As I hurried toward Bus Stop I thought the prize they had referred to was Chris. It never occurred to me that I would do just as well.

Passing down old streets that dated from the time when Mangin was only beginning to assemble his fortune, I was startled a couple of times by how fast cars went and how bright the ads were. One or two people out on the predawn streets, mostly those going home stoned, looked hard enough to see something skitter past the corner of their eyes.

A block or so away from Bus Stop, I looked into Capricorn and saw the sun shine on a rock outcropping. On and around it I could see the white blur that were the clothes of the Caprii shepherds. A couple of sleepy Sun Bums who were supposed to be watching the street leaned against a car and didn't see me.

I went to the front door and knocked but made almost no sound. I tried jiggling the door and couldn't grab the knob. I circled the outside of the building and saw the sun go behind a cloud in Capricorn. There young shepherds stared in awe. Following their gaze I saw Chris floating above me, asleep on a mattress.

Then I was aware of eyes looking through a peephole. After a delay, the door swung open and a boy and girl in their late teens stood in fighting stances. They saw no more of me than a gray blur, a ghost walking.

In between them was a short, fat black kid who looked totally wired. She stared right at me and said, "Heaven and hell, Feral Cell," and gave a high quavery laugh. The other two peered, unsure of what they saw but impressed.

"You want to see Chris Kane." That was not a question. The black kid turned as she said it and immediately started rolling toward the stairs. She wasn't four ten and must have weighed two hundred pounds. The others went back to watching the front door.

"No one wanted even to talk to me, cause they say I'm only fifteen and I'm crazy," the kid told me as I glided up the stairs. "Then they found out I could see the Cell." The Club took up the first two floors. The floor above was a huge open area, raw space. Islands of sleeping bags and futons lay scattered around. On most of them kids lay asleep, though one group at the far end watched television screens and wore headsets.

"They all call me Cannonball," said my guide with a high-pitched laugh. "We gave Chris Kane the best place." She led me to where a hard-looking young guy leaned against a door. "They made me in charge of night security because I don't ever sleep," Cannonball said as the guard gaped at me.

They let me into the room, and I nodded my thanks. Unless I spoke most people wouldn't know I was there. The two windows in the room looked out onto an alley and fire escape. By first dawn and the light from a TV with its sound off, I saw that I was inside what had been an office. In the middle of the floor was a large mattress. On it under covers were Chris and the girl who I had seen visiting Gary at the hospital.

She lay very still in deep sleep. He turned over a couple of times. I squatted with my back against the wall in a corner from which I could see the window and the door. I could also see the television set, but its images were just a shifting pattern of colors to me. Sitting like that I was reminded of Billy Gee waiting to kill me and of Morgan guarding Jackie and myself.

Chris lay still for a while, and I realized that his eyes were open and he was looking right at me. "You were great last night, man," he said, and I nodded. Those skills were no longer important to me if they ever really had been.

In the growing light I saw a gray puddle next to the futon. It took me a second to realize it was his Skin.

"It doesn't stay on so well," Chris said, sitting up slowly and drawing it on, then wrapping a blanket around himself. "Hey, I'm back in New York!" His voice sounded hoarse; his hair was matted and hung in his eyes. He rubbed his chin. "My beard is starting to grow," he said, then asked, "What's up?"

"Morgan will follow the Cabal up to Capriole Castle. She said the mountain Caprii would do some very strong magic tomorrow night at the rising of the full moon."

"Thursday night, the solstice. Got it." Chris nodded. "What I have to do is make sure they can't escape here in Cancer." He gave something between a laugh and a shudder and pulled the blanket around himself more tightly.

"There's pain?" I asked.

"Yeah, but mainly there's fear." He had to look carefully to see me. At that point he stopped trying and stared off in the direction of the flickering screen.

"You don't have to stay," I whispered.

He ignored that, indicated the sleeping girl, the kids outside. "This whole scene is like a crash pad on a peace march." He smiled at that.

"They're much more polite."

"More scared than we were." Chris was silent for a moment. "I understand that better now," he said quietly. "I looked for you after I went to Capricorn. A couple of times I found you. By then I was far enough into Capricorn that I couldn't understand the disguises and the drugs and how scared you were."

"It gets to be a habit."

"I'm doing a performance here tonight. They'll put out the story that it'll be here tomorrow. That's to throw off anyone trying to stop me. I'm going to try something like you did last night." He looked more closely at the television and said, "Hey, we're on." He fumbled with a control box and turned the sound up a little.

". . . described by police sources as a rival cult leader also disappeared last night. Two of Leal's associates in last night's incident will appear later this morning in court for arraignment." A camera caught a few seconds of Joan and B&T leaving Toys under police escort the night before.

Shots of my media assault on Toys appeared on the screen. I spotted myself chewing the scenery as Benjamin Mangin. Then came shots of what I recognized as the stone bowl on the floor of the Toys VIP room and of Jackie's torso being carried out in a body bag while a female voice said, "Tests will determine whether these are, in fact, the remains of Jackie Fast, missing since last Friday, as police continue the search for club owner Benjamin Mangin, who is wanted for questioning. Now this."

Chris managed to turn down the sound. The girl on the bed was awake and pulling on a shirt. "Good morning," he said. "Sorry to wake you up. Ada, this is my invisible friend, Rob."

She shook her head. Unable to see me, she smiled sleepily. It reminded me of the old days back on East Seventh Street. "I'm getting coffee," she said. "Do you want anything?"

"Yeah." He hesitated, then said almost embarrassed, "Something to eat." I touched the bow gun, looked into Capricorn, and spotted one of the shepherds on guard in a shadowed part of the rocks. Security on that end was taken care of.

"How does this thing do what it does?" I asked indicating the gun.

"I'm gonna talk about the bow gun tonight, man. I want you to hear that. Basically Crabs can't die in Capricorn. They can cut us up, drain our blood, turn us into weapons, but something in us goes on living. Hasn't it begun to know you, to come to you?" I nodded.

An announcer's face, looking very serious was on the screen. Chris turned up the sound. ". . . just in. Police announced that another victim, a woman in her twenties, has been found dead on the West Side Esplanade. Sources say the circumstances of her death seem to tie in with the so-called Vampire Murders, including the two skaters in Central Park Sunday night. Police are also linking these to a taxi driver discovered under the Williamsburg Bridge Sunday morning and the victim at Toys last night."

Chris looked at me. "I did that," I told him. "She tipped them off about us yesterday. She was going to do it again." I remembered the Cabalists I'd seen enter the city and wondered where they were.

"I found out it's a lot easier to kill than it is to die," Chris said almost apologetically.

I was about to tell him that he didn't have to do either, but just then a figure appeared on the fire escape and smashed a window. Another one aimed a pistol at Chris's head.

CHAPTER

Ten

"Freeze! You're coming with us," one of them said to Chris. Both of them watched him; neither of them was aware of me. Before I even thought about it the bow gun was in my hand, and I fired the last capsule. It hit the edge of the window frame and burst. One of the gunmen yelled, grabbed his hand, and dropped his weapon.

The room had no cover. Chris tried to roll into a corner. The one who had broken the window aimed a pistol. His eyes narrowed, and I jumped between him and Chris. Several shots sounded. His whole body jerked, and a bullet went past my head. Then the one whose hand I'd burned was looking above him and making surrender moves. The one who got off the shot had fallen from the fire escape.

Kids outside the door had heard the gunfire and had run into the room. Several more armed figures had appeared on the fire escape. Chris stood absolutely still, but one guy outside looked right at him and said, "Your security's kind of what they call laughter and tears."

I recognized him and whispered, "Federales."

"You were right," the man said to his partner. "It isn't Leal." He couldn't see me, but the Latin woman could. She gestured in my direction; he blinked and nodded. They still had their guns out. "Any idea who these guys are?" the fed asked Chris, who stared at them defiantly.

"If they'd wanted you dead, you would be," I murmured. "They were useful before."

"Servants of the Undying Cabal." Chris spat that out.

The feds nodded that it seemed likely to them also. They put away their guns, and their friends removed the one I had burned with acid. The intruder they had shot was dead in the alley. I knew none of this would get reported. My friend the fed said, "We'd like to talk," and gestured toward the window.

"Could you let them in?" Chris asked a couple of the Sun Bums. They got the window open but didn't look very happy about seeing the cops. "I'm going to have to talk to these people alone," he told the kids who filed reluctantly out of the room.

As the fed climbed through the window, he said, "I don't know much about theater, but that was quite a production Mr. Leal put together last night. You're the one who was Chris Kane. Do we get to find out your real name?"

"Do I get to find out who you are?" Chris asked.

"We could give you names. Credentials. Leal didn't seem to care about that when we talked to him."

"Let's just leave it that names get in the way," said Chris.

"We wanted to talk to your friend Robert Leal," said the Latin agent. She looked my way and said, "If he should happen to overhear, that's all right."

"Back when Jackie Fast was just a missing person, he was cooperative," said the fed. "He initiated that action at Toys, which was satisfactory."

"Up to a point. He exposed Mangin and embarrassed the city police. But he got incriminated himself." The Latin looked in my direction while the fed watched Chris who sat on the bed with a blanket wrapped around him like an Indian.

The fed told Chris, "People are afraid the city is going bad. We think that they're wrong. This time. But that concern plus the locals' booting it gives us the case. These kids probably mean well, but they can't give you security."

"Which you could."

"Of course. But now that we have the case, we need results," said the woman. "That corpse has been I.D.'d as Jackie Fast. It'll be announced this afternoon. We might be able to hang that one pretty solidly on Mangin if we could talk to Leal. It seems we don't have any witnesses whose testimony makes a lot of sense."

"Lots of talk about drinking blood and seeing lights. But no one saw Mangin do anything. And Mangin has places where we can't reach him."

"And we need an arrest. Not an absentia thing."

"And you wanted to talk to Robert Leal about that?"

"He was our strongest contact. Unfortunately, last night he got set up very badly," the fed told Chris. "The NYPD is leaking information linking him to Dupree, those two skaters in the park, and this thing near the West Side Highway today. It's a smoke screen to cover their mistakes. But the media likes it and has played it up."

"Frankly, even if he did kill them we don't care," the woman said to me. "Mangin is the one we want. We are now in the position, though, of having to come up with some answers or getting taken off the case ourselves."

The affairs of Cancer were Chris's concern. I watched a stray cloud pass over the sun in Capricorn.

"You want Mangin?" Chris asked.

"It's gotten beyond that. We need Leal, too."

"What if he turned up dead?" Chris asked and got my attention.

"It would leave us with a lot of unanswered questions."

"What if you got Mangin alive as the murderer?"

The friendly fed said nothing for a while. The woman stared at me. I caught curiosity in her eyes and wonder, maybe a little bit of fear. After all, she had to have some kind of problem to see me as well as she could.

"It would solve quite a few things," her partner said thoughtfully.

"Does that mean you might not I.D. the body too closely?"

"We'd do an autopsy. And there would be next of kin identification." He shrugged.

"But if you had Mangin alive at the same time?"

"That would shift public attention."

"Can I trust you with a time and place?" I wondered what Chris was doing. The trick I had pulled the night before had taken years of practice.

"We're discreet. Ask Robert Leal."

"Tomorrow night at like . . ." Chris did some kind of calculation, "say nine P.M. at Mangin's Roost." Chris looked tired. "Surround the place, because Mangin is going to be trying to escape. A little after nine you'll see a light at the top of the hill. Close in then, and you'll get Mangin, a murder weapon, and someone that those closest to him in the world will swear is Robert Leal."

"Obviously we can't make promises. But that's an attractive scenario. What are you planning to do?"

"Tonight, I'll be here giving a performance. That's a secret, understand. Tomorrow night I'll be out of town. That's an even bigger secret."

"We know there are places we can't reach," said the fed. "Are they . . . secured?" Chris indicated me with his thumb and managed a smile. The Latin nodded.

After the Federales disappeared down the fire escape, Chris looked toward me. "I want to protect Joan and B&T. Both because I'm going to need them for what I have planned, and because I saw what they mean to you. Can you get in touch with them?"

I thought about the pain I still felt at B&T's telling me to get lost that morning. "It would be better if you did it," I told him. "What's this about my corpse?" I asked to change the subject.

"I plan a couple of solo performances, one here tonight,

one at Mangin's place tomorrow. If you can keep me alive till then, we'll have Mangin in deep shit and your disappearance all covered. Then you can run in Capricorn as long as you want. You deserve it, man."

"But you don't, huh?"

"Maybe some time you'll understand my doing this, the way I finally understand you."

Then there was a knock on the door; it opened, and Sun Bums started coming in. They brought him food and coffee, which Chris sniffed at but didn't eat. He sat in the blanket shivering while the kids walked around in shorts.

Raul appeared at one point, and Chris asked him, "Have we staked out Rob Leal's house?"

"Yes, the two people who worked with him left this morning and went downtown with a lawyer. We have someone following them."

"Could you tell me when they get back?" Raul nodded and was gone.

Ada came back wearing a gray suit in which she was obviously not comfortable and told Chris, "I'm going out to do business. What do you need for tonight."

"Someone who worked on the album is coming in to help with the music. Jason is taking care of publicity. All I need is some lights and a stage."

"Her father holds the lease to this place," Chris told me. "When his club flopped, he let her take over. She moved a couple of her friends in."

"Quite a few," Ada said, looking where he looked, straining for sight of me as I hovered on the Transept. "The idea was that we could be a commune with a policy. Like the sixties. Then we started to hear about the Feral Cell." The way she said that made me understand that the sixties and Capricorn were both mythical lands.

When she left, Chris told me, "Dig it. People think the kids are just cute and stupid. It's more than that."

Raul came to the door. "Leal's people made it back home. There's some other stakeouts, reporters, cops."

As Chris nodded, Jason stuck his head in and said, "Come out of your cave and hear what they're saying about you." Chris stood up slowly, dropping the blanket, and walked into the open area. He didn't glide. He put a half smile on his face, but for a moment I saw pain and fear in his eyes.

Outside half a dozen Sun Bums sat watching themselves or kids who looked just like them on several large TVs. It was hard for me to focus on the screens.

"Big mystery for the police," a wise-ass deejay voice said. "All centers around Toys, what we might call a déclassé nightclub. It seems Chris Kane came back from the dead to put in an appearance, which proves that someone is trying very hard to promo this next selection."

"Death Drops in for Tea" played along with shots of Sun Bums on skateboards in front of Toys the night before.

"With the right visuals, this thing is ready to take off," said Jason.

In Cancer it was the cloudy afternoon of the second-shortest day of the year. The sun was already dimming. By touching my knife and gun I could see it blaze in Capricorn. I did that as Chris and Jason talked and saw one of the shepherds blowing a horn in my direction. A lean-to had been set up in the shade of the rocks.

"Right back," I told Chris and descended stairs that melted under me, crossed the waiting room/dance floor, which was being washed, entered the arrivals area. Holding the bone knife and gun I saw Bus Stop turn into a heat mirage as I stepped into the shade on the rock outcropping.

An elongated figure knelt with a bowl from which I wet my lips, another gestured to the north. Beyond the shade the light poured down like molten steel. All that I could make out were dark forms, the shapes perhaps of trees or boulders or sheep standing stationary in the heat. One form moved through the light, but the runner was up the rocks and standing in front of me before I understood that's what it was.

The runner circled his fingers around his eyes and pointed first to me, then to the northwest. I remembered that Ruby was in that direction, watching the walled manor Chris called the House of Usher. The runner pulled a piece of red cloth out of his belt, put it across his chest: the Chase. He made a house shape with both hands and showed me ten fingers, then two more.

Twelve hunters had sheltered at the fortified house instead of riding north. That meant there was a mobile force loose in the area. Putting my hand on my head to indicate a hood, I pointed to myself. He shook his head. No Cabalists were with them. That made them a lot less dangerous. I had forgotten about the two I saw come to New York that morning.

Sitting in the shadows, I wondered if the hunters were just tired of Mangin. Even if they were still loyal to the Cabal, we had them under observation. I couldn't see them as a threat to Chris in Cancer. The shadow shifted slightly, and I moved with it. Ruby would know what to do about the Chase.

Time passed so easily away from Cancer that going back was like coming out of a deep pleasant dream. Bus Stop had an evening-before-the-performance feel to it. A video crew shot footage of the stage being set up. The half-light, the kids' excitement, the sound of drilling as carpenters worked on the stage brought back memories thirty years gone.

"Some of the Cabal are from here. Some of them are like the Beast himself: maniacs out of Capricorn," Chris was telling Jason. He wore a heavy coat over his shoulders as he would a cape and looked relieved at catching sight of me. Over a couple of days we had exchanged places, and now I was his link to Capricorn.

"And why hasn't anyone seen this world?" On a table were the remains of a meal and a small bowl of blood.

"Everyone's seen it, man." Chris sounded tired. "You saw it. But you called it something else. Did you ever wake up dreaming you were drowning or flying? That's what you were doing in Capricorn."

Raul appeared and said, "The ones watching Leal's place

got these." He handed something to Chris, who looked at it and gestured me over. I had to taste blood from the bowl before I could focus on the photos he put on the table. I saw Erika embracing Joan at the front door of the house. Joan looked very shaky and teary eyed. There was also a shot of Erik and Erika toting their bags inside. "They got there about ten minutes ago."

Chris gave me a questioning look. "House guests," I whispered and nodded that they were all right.

"OK, these are people who are staying there. Try again to get word to Joan or B&T that I'd like to talk to them?" Raul left, and Chris turned to a synthesizer musician who had just started to set up. "Glad you could make it, man. I remember Drew saying he used you on some backing tracks for *the Feral Cell* album."

For the rest of the afternoon and into the evening, Chris threw himself into preparations for the show. Sometimes he had to sit down and huddle in the coat. I recognized the nervous energy that he had always had before a performance. But this time it was more intense. He was being consumed as he sat there. Every once in a while his eyes would dart around until he found me. Then he'd relax a little and get back to work.

During one break, Ada came in looking strained. She sat down near Chris. "Can you get in touch with Rob Leal?" Chris nodded without looking my way. "Tell him I was just up at Cedars hospital. There's a kid up there, Gary, who was Rob's roommate."

"I remember him."

"Well, we were just visiting him and he started getting real upset. He said it was life and death, that there were people in black around the park. He said the . . . the dying kids all saw them and that you and Robert Leal had fought them, that they killed Jackie Fast. We thought it was drugs and pain but he sees Capricorn sometimes. His nurse said we should tell Rob."

"You just told him," Chris said very quietly and looked toward me for my reaction. I shrugged indicating that a couple of Cabalists up in Central Park were no danger to us. The truth was that I could see nothing that could be done about it. Speedo was watching the crossroads village and would know if the Cabal crossed into Capricorn. Everything should have felt right. Instead I began to have the suspicion that someone was stealing moves on me in a game I didn't know about.

"Tell Gary to keep in touch if he sees anything more." Chris sounded worried, but a costume-fitting distracted him. The Skin had started to sag and wrinkle against his body and had begun to look dead instead of alive. A couple of Sun Bum fashion designers pinned an imitation together backstage. Under the lights it would look the way it was supposed to.

Chris was starting to fidget as techs did a sound check. The pain was beginning to get to him, I could tell, also his nerves. I remembered his tension as the hip kid from Long Island in the city, looking for a hit, desperate for the spark of recognition, even if it killed him. Now he had a world and a cause riding on his performance and a death that was more than just a possibility.

Selections from the *Memorial Album* played on the club sound system. A small audience was filing into the former waiting room, carefully watched by Ada and the kids. "Now, you musn't expect something as elaborate as what Leal pulled last night," Jason told a woman I recognized as a *Village Voice* culture monger.

"What was that all about, anyway?"

"That was the war, buttercup. This is what they're fighting for." No cameras were allowed backstage, but the performance itself was going to be taped and filmed. I had no idea what Chris was planning. I could feel myself pulling away from Cancer, already losing my feel for what was happening.

Then I realized someone was staring right at me. "Hey, aren't they calling you?" said Cannonball, the kid who'd spotted me that morning. Looking where she pointed, I saw Ruby and Speedo standing in the Capricorn twilight.

Chris's rendition of "Up in the World" was coming to an end, and the show was about to start.

"Be right back," I whispered to Chris as I touched gun and knife and felt them draw me over the Transept. Live synthesizer playing the opening bars of "Lonely Is the Wind" was drowned out by a shepherd blowing a goat's horn.

On the other side I touched blood to my lips and heard Ruby's whisper. "The Chase got out. We knocked some off their horses. At least seven got away, so I alerted everyone."

"We were told to guard Chris," Speedo added. "Seven armed riders could off the few shepherds that are still here. So we decided to concentrate."

I nodded as if everything was going according to plan. Again I felt that someone was playing rings around me. Mangin and the Cabal knew where Chris was but also knew they couldn't get at him. They also knew the Feral Cell would guard him with everything we had. I remembered the Cabalists uptown and realized that no one was watching at the crossroads village. But I didn't understand what that could mean.

Chris was still the important thing. I returned to Bus Stop on the other side of the Transept and was caught in his performance. "The way her hands moved, the way her hair flowed was like smoke from a joint," he told the audience, and I knew he was talking about Morgan.

"Every night in that hospital I dreamed of her. She stood under a tree looking up, her eyes reflecting the light, and this song kept running through me. One day they told me I could leave the next morning. I was torn between hoping that was good and knowing that was bad.

"That night I saw her again, and this time she came right into my room, and we made love. At the end of that I was with her in a place where there was no pain, and I looked like smoke and felt like it too." It seemed that no one in the audience breathed as music came up and Chris did "Moon Dance" very softly.

I'd taken up a position backstage where I could see Chris and be seen by him. Raul suddenly appeared holding what I recognized as more photos. He stood in the wings watching Chris and looking worried.

Chris finished the song and said, "There was someone else who was interested in my dying. It surprised me at first because I didn't know him that well. He was a rich guy, so I despised him. What's more he seemed as old as death and had no idea what it meant to be cool. At the time I had no idea that my dream from Capricorn was his ex-old lady." Chris smiled a little, and the audience started to smile with him.

"Laughter and tears," someone said aloud. The audience was divided between young contemporaries of the Sun Bums for whom Chris had been a secret rumor, and ones my age for whom he was a very faded memory. He had all of them caught up in a weave of idealism and nostalgia on that stage. All of *us*, I should say, because he had trapped me also. Nothing else can explain the extraordinarily stupid thing I was about to do.

"And the sicker I got the more interested in me he became. I started calling him Mr. Death. And I wrote this song for him. He wasn't amused." As Chris started to sing "Death Drops in for Tea," I saw Cannonball gesturing to me. Reluctantly, I went backstage and saw they had laid out the latest photos. Staring hard, I made out a photo of Joan, B&T, Erik and Erika leaving the house by the back alley. I told myself it was nothing to be concerned about, that they were probably sneaking out for a quiet supper. Chris sang:

If I hadn't dreamed enough
I'd have acted like a fool,
Tripping off to far Nepal
Or trying to live piously.

Instead I left as farewell,
A fond note for him to see:

"Action shifts to Capricorn
When Death drops in for tea."

All I wanted to do was listen to the song, which I now understood was about Mangin. "I see a knife in this shot," said Raul. When he put his finger on it, I saw it too: Erika held it at Joan's neck.

The last photo showed the four of them and a few others driving off in a car. Whoever took the picture made sure it included the license number. They didn't have to; I recognized the blue Buick four-door, the anonymous company car that was parked on Saturday up at Mangin's Roost.

On stage, Chris said, "The millionaire, let's call him the Beast, had people to do his dirty work here and in Capricorn. Some of them he hired, and some he tricked with magic, and a few he bribed with immortality. One of the last group was a guy a little older than I, who had been dying of leukemia until the Beast showed him Capricorn. In return this guy showed them how to make a silver net with which he could catch people like myself. Let's call him the Crab Fisher."

"They headed uptown," Raul told me. That kid was smart enough to handle any revolution, but I already knew where the car was headed.

After drinking from the bowl of blood on the table, I said, "Central Park East. How fast can you get me up there?" In the face of all this strangeness, they didn't hesitate.

It had taken me too long to understand that Chris wasn't the prize. He was so well-guarded in both worlds that Mangin knew he couldn't reach him. The phone call would be coming soon, telling where to deliver the ransom. I was what the Beast would demand. My only chance of breaking up his game was to get to the designated spot before they expected me.

The Sun Bums got ready fast. Something, probably sheer hammyness, made me exit through the auditorium. Some people in the audience saw me and nudged others. Chris, standing on the tiny stage lighted with a couple of spots, saw me too. I don't know how much he guessed, but without back up he suddenly screamed:

Just to reach the land of Kane
Where you run until it's light,
And you ditch all human cares
Got to hurt with all your might.

CHAPTER Eleven

That sent me out the door on a rush. Sun Bums rode uptown spinning around corners on their skateboards. I rode with them as they grabbed the bumpers of cars bombing north. Horns blared; lights smeared against my eyes. In Capricorn we sailed over a pond, silver with moonlight, and I told myself that surprise was on my side.

We rolled across Central Park South past the horse carriages and the street lights into the night of Central Park and Capricorn. Racing toward Cedars of Lebanon I was also approaching the crossroads village. It was about then that I remembered that the bow gun was empty.

They were all waiting when I arrived. The only surprise was mine at my own stupidity. Above us, floating in the air, seven horsemen of the Chase waited on a hill just south of the village. Most of the men and many of the women had gone north. Once Speedo had gone to guard Chris, the few who were left could only watch from their houses, intimidated by hunters armed with rockets.

The Chase served two purposes in Mangin's plan. First they tricked the Cell into thinking Chris was the target. Then they rode to a spot just beyond the crossroads to make sure there was no escape into Capricorn for me. They held their silver nets and spikes ready, while in Cancer skaters spun under the street lamps. Both worlds were secured against us. I had exactly no chance of reaching my goal.

Standing perfectly still in the shadow of some trees were Erik and Erika, who watched everything carefully, and the two Cabalists I had seen that morning. Those two held knives against the throats of B&T and Joan. The skaters spotted us and began to close in. Erika pointed me out to the Cabal.

"Stop where you are," whispered the man from Cancer. "If you don't, these two die."

"You're going to kill them anyway," I breathed. But I stopped because I had no choice.

"It is you that we want, Leal," said the Cabalist who had called herself Risa, and I knew that Mangin had played me perfectly. My escort was a bunch of out-of-breath kids who were just going to get themselves killed. "If you surrender, I assure you we have orders to deliver you alive if at all possible."

Motioning for them to stay where they were, I stepped away from the Sun Bums, drew the bow gun, and began to circle the group on the lawn. They couldn't tell that it wasn't loaded. The man nicked B&T's cheek. He and Joan were both crying.

"Stand still and throw down the gun," the Cabalist said. Knowing how desperate the thought of losing Capricorn made me, I understood how desperate a man he must have been.

"If I do that, you have all of us," I said, circling the group on the lawn, aware that the Chase were watching and ready to net me if I went over the Transept. Erika and Erik observed these negotiations with great professional interest. "A bother if all you want is me."

"A trade-off," Risa said in a voice that was hauntingly like Mangin's. "They go free. Your Sun Bums get to leave peacefully. In return you will come with us."

I heard sirens. "Even the dumbest cops are going to have some questions about this," I told them. When I said that, though, they cut Joan, so I stopped moving and lowered the bow gun. I felt myself nod agreement and heard myself say, "Release them first and I'll back my people off." It didn't seem possible that I was doing this. But a part of me must have known at Bus Stop that this was the only way I was going to free Joan and B&T.

It was a delicate business, executed in fast intricate steps. The Sun Bums retreated very reluctantly. The Cabal let go of Joan and B&T. "Chris Kane knows what has to be done," I told them. "Those kids will take you to him."

Joan kept looking back, not wanting to leave me. B&T edged her away, out of the circle of light, over grass where skates couldn't go, toward the stone wall and the lights of Fifth Avenue, telling her no doubt that they could get help for me that way. As he did that, the Cabal and the skaters closed in on me in Cancer while the Chase held their nets in Capricorn.

Bow gun in hand, I straddled the Transept, one foot in Cancer and another in Capricorn.

"Let's have the gun, Leal," said the male Cabalist. I raised my arm and saw the children of Cedars of Lebanon look down. I thought I could pick out Gary standing at his window. Turning toward him, I hurled the bow gun as hard as I could. Risa gave a cry like a strangling sea gull as it seemed to fly. I watched it disappear into the dark as the silver net fell through me and hands in Cancer took away my knife, grabbed my arms and legs.

"They were right, Leal," a voice whispered. "The twins said those two would draw you." From the moment I felt myself caught, I was too numb to resist. All I could think was that if Mangin wanted me alive there was at least one round more to play. They tied my hands and forced a blood-soaked rag into my mouth. They wrapped me in a sheet and hauled me through the night.

I felt them lift me over a wall and shove me onto the floor in the rear seat of the car. I could tell that Erik and Erika sat up front with a driver. The Cabalists sat in back with me. Risa pressed the knife Chris had given me to my throat.

"Don't waste a drop," the man said, giggling nervously with the release of tension. They had me face up so they could keep the rag in my mouth wet with Blood of the Crab. The car did a few turns on city streets, then headed north. We were under the ground in Capricorn.

As the car picked up speed, I had a sensation of not being able to keep up, of hurtling through the rear window. I would smash my body on the pavement in Cancer or smother under the dirt in Capricorn. It bothered the Cabal, too. They made the driver slow down.

As we went up-country we rose above the ground in the other world, and I saw the moon and stars over Capricorn. Were they the same ones that I could see through the windows? It was the safest thing to think about as I rode to meet Benjamin Mangin.

I wondered about the twins also. "Erik and Erika?"

"Yes?"

"Why did you do this?"

She said a word to him in Swedish, then told me, "Capricorn was the most important part of your knowledge and you didn't share it with us."

"Even after we let those disgusting clients of yours do those things," Erik added.

"I didn't know about it."

"How could that be?" she asked with a little laugh. "You had the look on you." She repeated the word that I supposed meant elves stealing babies on nights when the sun and the moon stood together in the sky at the stroke of twelve.

"It was an opportunity," Erik said. "Much more than game-mastering. Fire and ice," he added.

"And if you didn't know about Capricorn," Erika said. "You would have died very soon anyway."

The simplicity of that shut me up, and I yielded myself to terror. I had been dying slowly and had been given a chance at immortality. For reasons still not entirely clear to me, I surrendered that for a chance to die fast and badly. I remembered Billy Gee's headless corpse, Jackie's head on a stake.

Several times they forced blood into me. Feeling began to

return to my body in the form of pain. My arms and legs hurt, and my guts started to ache. My only comfort was when I looked at the Cabal and saw this trip causing them terror and misery too.

Because of them we drove slowly and stayed off the main roads. It grew darker as the night went on, and we got farther out of the city. The car passed through a river in Capricorn. The water seemed ready to pour over the Transept and drown us all. Then the land rose in both worlds. We rolled past trees and the shadows of trees.

Sometimes I felt myself almost able to fall through the back of the car and out of Cancer. Sometimes I wanted to scream in fear and rage. For years I hadn't dared to care or hope. Now the only ones I cared about had led me to my death. All I hoped was that the attention I drew away from Chris and Morgan would let them crush Mangin before he drank my blood.

The hills got steeper in both worlds. We made several sharp turns and stopped. Above the sleeping suburb, lights burned on castle walls. In Cancer the car had stopped blocks from the entrance to Mangin's Roost. But through the suburban houses I could see the outer walls of Capriole Castle and a camp of the Caprii who surrounded the place.

The driver got out of the car and opened the door near my head. I tried to shout, but the sound turned into a low moan inside my throat. A few house lights shone on the quiet street: insomniacs and early risers. No faces came to windows as cold hands pulled me off the floor.

But the Caprii saw me and raised an alarm. Goat horns sounded and hands reached out to grab at me as the Cabal snarled and gestured at my throat with the knife. The Caprii couldn't save me; I was nailed to the Cancer side of the Transept. As they slid me out the door I tried to twist free and could do no more than feebly twitch.

"He doesn't weigh anything," the driver muttered throwing me over his shoulder as if I were an overcoat. He was huge, but something like despair caught at his throat when he touched me. I wondered what terrors had driven him to deal with demons.

They carried me into a garage and from there down a few stairs to an ordinary finished basement. I realized that the gatehouse must be under observation and that this was a secret entrance to the estate. I saw castle walls blaze with gaslight as they brought me out into a dark backyard. The yard ran right up to the overgrown hill. An iron fence separated it from Mangin's Roost. Going through a gate in that fence in Westchester, we walked right through the walls of Capriole Castle.

Inside those walls, shadows hurried to us with bowls and nets. The driver put me down and took a few steps back. He and the twins stood peering around carefully. Maybe they half glimpsed a ring of lights and flickering figures reaching out to seize me. Or maybe all they glimpsed was me fading into nothing, as unseen Cabalists poured Blood of the Goat down my throat.

No one had to force me to drink. I wanted to be in Capricorn even if it meant being on the wrong side of prison walls, getting blinded by the gaslights Mangin had placed around the walls of Capriole Castle, or eventually getting strung up and drained of my blood.

The two Cabalists gulped blood also, and the three of us stood in the outer yard of the castle. A silver net had been thrown over me. I heard a stir and guessed what was coming. Peering away from the lights, I saw Cabalist hoods and hunter red. Then I saw the Beast looking at me with his greedy child eyes and heard his preposterous and chilling whisper.

"Mr. Leal, I have the gift of prophecy. I told you I would drink your blood."

"That hasn't happened yet," I said knowing that I was in the midst of Mangin's game and that the people around us were his clients. His eyes narrowed, and the Beast looked half-pig and half-cat. I was a prop in his act, a symbol of his power. He planned to kill me. All I knew was that somehow

I had to prevent that from happening until the full rising of the solstice moon.

"Not yet. But my magic is very strong." The Cabalists around Mangin watched him with expressions of wonder and horror.

Trying not to imagine what things they had witnessed, I whispered, "There's a difference, Mr. Mangin, between making prophecies and making death threats. You're a murderer on the run." That was one of the reasons he frightened me and the main reason I could never let him know how much he frightened me.

"Oh, well, let me tell you what is going to happen today," he said, keeping his voice low and soft so that I could hear. "You will spend today strung up outside my highest tower where all the Caprii can see you screaming for them to go home so that you can die. Believe me when I tell you that's what you will do.

"The sight and sound of the holder of the bow gun in my power and pleading for death, will disperse them back to their farms. And this evening your blood will carry the Chase into another world. That is magic enough I think." He turned to the Cabalists who had brought me. "Where is the bow gun?"

The lights on the walls made it hard for me to see, and faces in Capricorn were difficult to read. Maybe my own intense fear made me more sensitive to theirs when one whispered, "Lost." And the other said, "Thrown into the Transept between Capricorn and Cancer."

I could make out Mangin's frown. Again in spite of everything, he reminded me of Saturday morning television. He said something aloud to the Chase, who murmured. To me he whispered. "I told them I would have a new one made from your muscles and bones when you have dried out."

"I don't think the prison authorities will let you do that, Benjy." I talked, but with those eyes, flat and dead looking even in Capricorn, staring at me, I trembled. The greatest fool and clod who ever lived is a figure commanding respect when he holds your life in his hands.

They took me up the hill, women and children in flowing nightclothes coming to castle windows to watch in wonder. Torches blinded me if I didn't look straight ahead. We passed through an arch framed by two giant crabs touching claws, went down a passage, and crossed the diamond-patterned killing floor.

There they took my Skin off and used it to tie my arms and legs. They made me drink more blood and wrapped me in a silver net hung with small bones. Then they carried me up the circling stairs outside a tower. I recognized the top of the stairs as the spot where Billy Gee's headless corpse had hung in that long ago time, the Saturday afternoon before.

They strung me up facing west. The gaslighted walls made me close my eyes.

Mangin spoke aloud, then said in a high whisper, "Since you seem a bit slow to grasp things, let me explain what will happen. The sight of you will shake the Caprii. The morning sun will blind you and burn off your skin. You will worship me and plead for your own death. I will show you how to form the words that will make the Caprii disperse."

"So that the Chase can have their way with them?"

"Only the ringleaders, the demon worshippers."

"As an old game player, I can tell that you're putting a lot of hope on one roll of the dice," I replied, but it seemed at least possible that the Caprii would be shaken by the holder of the bow gun begging to be put out of his misery. And it was a sure thing that once I begged for death I was going to receive it. As an old game player I knew I had to resist doing that until whatever came with the rising of the moon.

Mangin made no response. I heard the roar that I knew was voices and a rhythm like tamed thunder that I later identified as drums.

"Leal, open your eyes," a voice whispered in my ear. Doing so I found the flames on the walls out and the landscape lighted by the first dawn. From just above me on top of the tower came the noise of a voice shouting. "He is telling them that before the sun sets you will beg him to drink your blood," the Cabalist from Cancer told me.

Below us were the towers and windows of Capriole Castle. These appeared to sway in the advancing dawn like coral reefs seen through moving water. On the outer wall were men of the Chase and their servants holding silver spears and aiming rocket guns. Those walls looked new and perfunctory compared to the rest of the castle.

I could make out metal goats' heads, which I knew were the gas jets. Beyond the walls were the Caprii, camped on the open ground, looking up and pointing at me. Behind them, flitting in the shade of trees, were the gray outlines of the Feral Cell.

The land around the castle was almost parklike, lawns dotted with clusters of trees. The Caprii camps also didn't look serious, nothing more than campfires and the blankets on which the people slept. Caprii were thick on the ground; there appeared to be thousands of them. I knew they couldn't all be fed and would have to go home in a day or two. After the excitement at the rising of the moon, they would be gone.

At that moment, they were all staring up at me and glancing back toward the trees where the Cell was sheltered from the light. All at once a couple of hundred Caprii on a spontaneous impulse rushed the walls shouting. The Chase was thin on the defenses. But they had rockets and didn't hesitate to fire one into the crowd. The bolt exploded in the front rank of the charge; several Caprii were burned and went down wailing. Another rocket went right over their heads, burning some more of them. Dragging their fallen, they ran back toward the trees.

A noise came out of the defenders that I realized had to be a cheer. I could hear what I knew were the cries of the Caprii even after the rising sun began to blot out the landscape. They had been injured trying to help me, which was bad enough. And their attack was completely useless, which meant I could expect no rescue from that direction.

The growing light drove the Cabalist away. The lightest colors evaporated first: the Caprii, clouds. Then the grass, the hunters' outfits, the castle walls disappeared. Finally all that I could see were the outlines of trees and boulders. At that point I shut my eyes.

And Mangin spoke just behind me. "I told them to go away. They wouldn't listen. In a short while you will ask them the same thing."

"Seems unlikely." That speech to the Caprii was my first sliver of hope. He had promised them something that only I could deliver.

"Oh, you will. Because only then will we open your leg arteries and let you die."

I clamped my mouth and eyes shut as the light grew. At first it wasn't so bad. Morning light didn't hit my side of the tower. I could squint down and make out the pattern of the marble killing floor. Then the sky darkened. I felt the chains and the ropes around my arms. Ruins rose up all around me. I could feel my body. The clouds were in Cancer.

Blood of the Goat was forced into me before I could slip over the Transept. My old world receded. Hours passed that I knew were only minutes. The sun shone right through my clenched eye lids. The image that occurred to me was of silver spikes being driven into my head.

Several times that morning the light receded, and when I opened my eyes I saw a cloudy day over Mangin's Roost in Westchester. Then, trapped between slow death and fast death, I would gag down more Blood of the Goat and be dragged back into Capricorn.

There the spikes of sunlight returned. The light burned an outline of the net into my body. I felt my bones exposed, felt them silhouetted against the wall like a graffito X ray. My brain burned like paper under a magnifying glass.

"Leal, you were moaning." Mangin chewed words carefully next to my ear. "Call out to the Caprii. I will show you how to form the sounds in your throat."

"What's in it for me?"

"An end to your misery here and in Cancer." He waited. "I know it sounds much better to you now than it did a very short while ago. That is what happened when I won control of Central Steel. Eventually, surrender was a relief for the other shareholders. Of course, I could offer them their lives. Once they were impoverished in that world they couldn't harm me. You would be trouble, I'm afraid."

Maybe it was the circumstances, but talking to Mangin was more interesting that I could ever have imagined. "What happens after I make the Caprii go home?"

"Your blood will drain out of you. The sun will cease to bother you. You Crabs die hard in Capricorn. Some say the pieces of them here never fully die. But by this evening you will be empty of blood. Your head will be displayed in the local towns. Your body will dry out here and be formed into a weapon, a bow gun, for my own use."

I could feel that, could feel myself cut into parts that tingled with faint life, as the bow gun did. "And the Chase gets a view of the promised land? But you can't take them anywhere. You're a marked man, Beasty."

"What they will see will be wonder enough." I felt in Mangin's voice a trace of resentment at the wonder he still felt. "Your world is an endless surprise. Who would have guessed that a man like Mangin would be tolerated let alone welcomed and respected?"

"Standing bare-ass on a hill in Westchester County watching rush-hour headlights on the parkway?" As I said that, nostalgia tore at my heart. "Sounds boring."

I got no response. Mangin was gone. The sun burned down from directly above. I was a bug, a roach trapped under a relentless light. I was the most worthless being in two worlds. Once or twice blessed gray Cancer drifted into my sight, and I wanted to crawl there and die. My mind burned away. To stop that I recited poems I had learned in school, parts I had played in summer stock twenty-five years before, old rock lyrics.

"You are screaming, Leal."

"Pardon me, I was singing."

"I suppose," he said thoughtfully, "that I could let you die in Cancer, leave you alive enough to slip over the Transept. After you disperse the rabble."

I continued singing. Silence followed. I drowned in boiling gold. Darkness and death were my friends. The sun shone directly into my bowels. My eyes were gone, my ears were useless. Only my mouth worked. "I guess my race is run," I remember screaming to the accompaniment of goat-horn blasts. "I fought the law and the law won."

Then I felt shadows and looked for the winter afternoon. I saw it but only outlined against Capricorn where a cloud had passed over the sun. It only lasted for a few moments before my eyes got burned shut again. But I thought I saw more clouds, and they were hope.

Once as two Cabalists forced blood into me, I opened my eyes, and they shrank back. Clouds played games with the sun letting it in and out. Then a dark cloud covered it entirely. A wind sprang up, and horns out beyond the walls sounded a welcome.

"We have recaptured your two young friends." I could see the outline of the Beast in his dark clothes. Then the sun came out brighter than before, and he disappeared.

He was lying and he was insane. But at that moment I was far crazier. They had trapped B&T and Joan once, why not again.

"Let me far enough into Cancer to see them."

"We can't move them around the city under present circumstances. But we do have them I assure you."

"Ask them what we call our clients." I got no response. More clouds passed in front of the sun. The trees bent. Mangin returned.

"Your clients are called the American Dental Association."

For an instant I wanted to scream. Then I remembered the twins. "You got that from Erika and Erik." Rain drops fell, and the Caprii cheered and rushed at the walls. Rocket fire drove them back.

The storm passed before the afternoon was over. Evening sun shot out from behind clouds. It seemed that the Caprii were drifting away from the castle, retreating behind the trees far beyond rocket range. Just before the light blinded me, I saw black-clad figures using a bone knife on my ankle. One of them bore a bowl.

"Your friends are giving up. They will run away rather than see what we are doing to you." Mangin told me.

For a moment I saw thousands of lights spinning in darkness. They had made a tourniquet out of my belt and were slowly draining my blood. Dying ounce by ounce I looked into Cancer where Cabalists who had drunk my blood walked on the grass grown marble floor.

When I looked back into Capricorn I found the light dimming. The Caprii were gone. The watchers on the walls fired rockets into the twilight, raised their long arms in triumphant salute toward Mangin, who stood beside me. In the distance one horn blew long sad notes, and a familiar gray face appeared in the sky.

"At the full rising of the moon," I said.

"What?" Mangin asked. I saw him look far away, perhaps into Cancer. Or maybe he heard something. I was aware of some kind of commotion below. I could see my blood drip steadily into the bowl. I noticed that the two Cabalists who had brought me were standing on Mangin's Roost and looking downhill into the dark.

"At the rising of the moon," I told him and was blinded all over again as the gaslights came on. "The mountain Caprii," I heard myself babbling. If he had just asked me, I'd probably have told him hours before I did.

As it was, just as he began to understand, I was deafened by a roar, and a huge section of the wall collapsed. Pieces of stone fell into an enormous hole. About half of one side of the outer wall collapsed. People inside the castle wailed like sirens and started to run as the gas jets along the walls began exploding.

The metal goats' heads flew like missiles, and all the lights went out. Members of the Chase were on the ground dead and injured. When the explosions stopped, I saw Caprii advance through the twilight. As they reached the trees, gray figures dropped down and joined them.

They came halfway to the ruined wall and stopped. Two

Caprii stepped forward accompanied by one of the Feral Cell. It seemed I could recognize Morgan. One of the Caprii raised a trumpet. I could hear the blast of sound, then the voice of the other Caprii shouting a message at the walls.

"My beloved," Mangin hissed. "It seems she used the mountain Caprii to undermine the outer walls." He stood on the stairs next to me, listening. "She offers terms to the Chase. They are to give up their hunting horses and guns and tear down their walls." I realized he was cutting me down. "Oh, and they are to surrender both the Undying Cabal and you. They especially want you and me."

Two Cabalists carried me down the stairs and onto the killing floor. Mangin went first.

"It will go badly for the Chase if they don't surrender us both alive," he said. "Sad for them, but they have served their purpose."

I caught sight of men of the Chase, hands on their swords, kept out of the courtyard by an iron gate decorated with crabs and goats. Frightened and angry, they were shaking the bars trying to get in, calling out to Mangin and the Cabal.

Right through them I saw a million lights and the dark outlines of ruins.

"Cancer and Capricorn are so close tonight," said Mangin, "and you are so close to death that little holds you here." Cabalists drank my blood from bowls while threatening the Chase with silver spikes. Hands pulled the nets off me. Metallic-tasting blood was smeared into my nose.

"You are a valuable asset, a prize hostage in both worlds," Mangin whispered. Burning pain tore my body, and I began to scream as I passed back into Cancer. Something was stuffed into my mouth. "With you to turn over to the authorities my passage through New York will be eased."

The Cabal, about a dozen of them, stood in Cancer waiting for Mangin's instructions. Right beside them members of the Chase broke down the metal gates and stood on the killing floor in Capricorn with drawn swords and loaded guns searching, wild eyed, for something they could trade for their own lives.

Every nerve in me twisted in pain. I could feel myself dying as they started to carry me downhill. Mangin led the way. I was heavier here, and the Cabal were clumsier. They panted and stumbled as I writhed. Headlights moved on the parkway; Christmas decorations and lighted picture windows circled out from around the foot of Mangin's Roost. But on the hill itself, all was still and dark.

Mangin stepped between the first of the goats' head pillars that lined the road. As he did so, someone just ahead of him on the road struck a match and lighted a cigarette. For an instant we all saw Dr. Cobalt in his slouch hat and phony nose.

"Benjy, baby," said a voice that sounded just like mine, "the game's afucking foot. Now put my friend down and let's fight." From beneath his cloak, Cobalt produced a gun. For a moment I thought it was a hallucination, a trick by my mind to take me away from my pain.

But the Beast and the Cabal knew better. Their knives were out. I saw a few of them look over their shoulders, assessing their lines of retreat.

"Chris Kane is it?" Mangin asked. As he spoke, two of the Cabal rushed forward. There were two dull pops, and they staggered, blinded by facefuls of nontoxic yellow dye.

Mangin made a noise in his throat like a truck starting. He took one long step, and the white shirt front on Cobalt's evening clothes was right in front of him. Mangin was direct and brutal. He grabbed Cobalt's arm to stop him from getting off another shot, then put his bone knife between two ribs and twisted it.

As he did, a voice I recognized said, "You'll never buy your way out of this one, Benjy." Chris was inside the Cobalt outfit. Mangin hit him, and Chris fell against a pillar and slumped to the ground. As if on signal, lights went on all around the hill: spotlights, cherry tops, flashlights bobbing up the slope.

Mangin looked at me and at his knife. Then he caught

sight of something and hesitated for the first time all day. The Cabal looked, too, and began to dither. The ones carrying me let go. Across the killing floor the Feral Cell was advancing. Some of the Cabal ran toward them, others started down the hill.

Mangin said to me, "There will be other days in Capricorn," tossed aside his knife, and went toward the lights.

"He knows the cops will give him a better deal than he would have gotten from the Cell," I heard Chris say.

"Chris, come back to Capricorn," I whispered.

"No, man. It's all set up. We got Mangin's big gooey fingerprints on that knife. B&T and Joanie will identify me as you. The feds will make everyone go along. Mangin isn't out, but he's down for a while. The Cell's coming for you. Capricorn will heal everything. It's up to you to watch out for things here. Understand?" I said nothing. He repeated. "Understand?"

"Yes."

I heard shouts from below and a gunshot. Chris lit another match, and in the flare I saw him look off. "Fifty million Christmas lights. What a way to go." He wiped his face, smearing the makeup. "I like what the kids say."

"Life and death?"

"That, too." He made a sound that could have been a cough or a sob. "But I meant laughter and tears." I called out to him after that but got no answer. I was still calling when long hands reached out and carried me over the Transept.

CHAPTER Twelve

My burns and wounds healed themselves as I rested in a tower at Capriole Castle. One dawn I saw the departure of the mountain Caprii to their homes up-country. They were the ones whose tunnel had collapsed the outer walls and whose fires caused the gas explosions at the rising of the moon. Tough-gnarled miners, they bowed when they spotted me. By then, all of the walls surrounding the castle had been torn down, their gas piping destroyed.

The Chase were forced to execute the members of the Cabal who had returned to Capricorn. Then their hunting clothes and horses were taken, and they were let go. The walls around their manor houses were torn down, and the gas pipes smashed all through the hill country.

"This will break their spirit without causing a bloodbath," Morgan told me. "They won't be able to live here as ordinary farmers."

During my recovery, I tried not to think about the promise I had made to Chris before he died. Caprii brought me the blood of my enemies to drink. The Cell came by to sit with me in my dark tower. One evening, toward the end of summer, the one called Ruby told me, "Bow gun has appeared among the dying children."

I prepared to leave the tower for the first time and travel to the village at the crossroads. Before that happened, however, Morgan summoned the Feral Cell to Capriole Castle. All the members that I knew plus ones I had never seen before, some forty of us, gathered on a moonless night in the tile-floored courtyard. Wildflowers already grew on the ruins of the outer wall. All gates and doors, everything that could hinder the Feral Cell, had been destroyed, but the gateway with its arch of interlocking horns and claws remained.

Morgan spoke while standing before it. "Word has come from over the mountains," she gestured toward some Cell members I had never seen. "Our Caprii there face persecution. The Cell members believe it necessary to make our presence felt before winter. Do we agree to that?" Most of the members licked their lips, smiled and nodded.

"Some must stay behind here in the hill country," she said. "When I first came to Capricorn this castle had just been built. After I escaped and went among the Caprii, after Mangin was done hunting for me and killing those who hid me, he went away. Then the Caprii rose up and tore down the walls that guarded Capriole Castle." Lurch and Garbo and a few of the others flashed their teeth in memory.

Everyone watched her curl like smoke under the arch, stars in Cancer visible through her hair as she whispered, "Then I myself left to see more of this world. When I returned it was to find Mangin's presence again. He had installed one called the Crab Fisher to catch us. The faith of the Caprii was shaken.

"At that time I brought Chris Kane over the Transept, and together with a few of you we caught the Crab Fisher." She paused, then said, "We found a better use for him." The Cell laughed, and Morgan stood silent before continuing. "Again I left to travel this world with Chris and with what he called the Feral Cell. When we returned it was to find that Mangin had colonized this land with the Chase, had rebuilt the castle walls and ringed them with fire."

She looked toward me. "We must not leave this place

unguarded again. I ask that Leal, the bearer of the bow gun, remain here." The eyes of the Cell glowed in the dark night. It had never occurred to me that I would have to leave, so it took little for me to nod assent. Lurch and Garbo, Ruby and Speedo, and a few others who always lived in the hill country would remain with me.

The rest all left on a road of lights. Thousands of Caprii had gathered around the castle; more lined the route. All carried the pinpoint lanterns. As the late-summer evening darkened, I could see blue flickers rising for miles into the foothills. Each member of the Cell who was leaving came to touch those who stayed.

"You must keep these Caprii prepared," said Morgan, who went last. "The Undying Cabal will try to return," she whispered as she held me. "Mangin wants to live again at Capriole." With that she turned and became one of the elongated shapes that moved uphill through the chanting peasants.

The next night I started south and reached the crossroads before dawn of the second day. Cancer and Capricorn had drawn farther apart, but I spotted Gary floating over the trees. The next night I stood from midnight to dawn watching him, but he was so drugged that he slept. His hair was all gone; his face no wider than a hand. When his eyes opened he saw me.

I gestured for him to come down to the hallway outside Children's Oncology. He indicated very weakly that he couldn't, that he was hooked up. He held out the bow gun with a look in his eyes that was hopeless and yet full of hope.

For three evenings I refused the blood the Caprii offered, had them pour it into a pouch that I wore on my belt. Each night with Gary watching, I tried to step from under the trees into the hospital corridor. Twice I walked through it as if it were a mirage. The second time, though, I felt and smelled its metal sharpness. On the third night, my feet found the floor, my lungs panted the heavy air of Cancer.

Finding my way to Gary was like treading through a

nightmare, one in which I could see through walls but couldn't open doors. It took me the better part of the night to get to his room. He was dozing when I found him. Tubes ran out of his stomach and his arms into various machines. I said his name aloud. It came out as a soft whisper, but his eyes sprang open.

"Chris!" He reached under the covers and pulled out the battered bow gun.

"Robert . . . Leal." It had been months since I had spoken in Cancer. The gun moved to my hand reluctantly. It had grown used to Gary.

"They said you had died. I found the gun that night you threw it. People looked for it but not the right ones. You'll take me? Please, I'm going to die. They don't even pretend." The other patient in the room, face lost in shadows, groaned in his sleep.

The world of Cancer closed in around me, horrible and deadly. It was hard for me to breathe. The life-sustaining equipment pinned Gary to the spot where they expected him to die. "You must get downstairs. Third floor. Children's Oncology."

"But I can't move."

I put the sack to his lips. He tasted it and gasped. "Montoya," I told him. Out the window it was night. Through the walls an early fall dawn was due. The world of Cancer was a trap, a maze of complications. "Tomorrow night," I whispered.

"He's on another floor," Gary began. But the taste of blood was in his system. He held the edges of his bed as though he could feel himself falling into Capricorn.

"Montoya," I breathed. It was something I could hold onto, something I could remember from that world. Then a security guard walked down the hall. "On the Children's Oncology landing," I said and followed the guard until she opened a stairwell door. She shivered as I stepped around her.

Dawn was starting to shine through the walls, as I found the upper branches of the trees. Grasping the bow gun, wetting my lips on blood, I jumped into the wide-eyed topiary faces now turning copper colored and found shade.

The next night was easy. Gary was slumped in the stairwell. The places where tubes had been removed were hastily bandaged. His eyes were closed. As I pressed the sack of blood to his lips, I saw movement on the stairs above and recognized Montoya.

"He saved me," Gary said.

Returning even briefly to Cancer reminded me of many things about it. "You ran risks to bring Gary here," I breathed.

"I know the signs, Leal," he said. "Things are going to go bad. Think of this as a good work and remember all of us in places that have started to go bad." That reminded me so much of a prayer that I was chilled, but I saluted him silently and brought Gary over the Transept. Montoya had given a dying kid his only chance. The rest was up to me.

One leg and all, the villagers accepted Gary. They fed him on the first night, dressed him on the second in the Skin of a dead Cabalist. I taught him what I could teach, brought the Cell to meet him. His hair grew back but not his leg. He could swim in Capricorn but not as quickly as the rest of us.

Gary told me about New York and that other world, more than I wanted to know.

"Mangin has disappeared," he said the first night. My heart jumped but my face, I knew, remained impassive. I smiled. "I didn't understand it all, but he was supposed to have killed you. His lawyers wanted him declared insane. They got him put in a hospital outside the city. They insisted on that. It was a maximum security place, but after a few days there, he was gone. He's got to stay in hiding, but he's loose."

Mangin was free somewhere in that world or this. Had the Federales screwed things up or had they struck a deal?

Gary told me, "People in New York have been in touch with places all over the world where they have Feral Cell groups. They play that video Chris made. It's a big cult thing. He talks about you on it, you know. Kids from all over say that they've seen him walking at night." Again I knew from my own first experiences with the Cell that my face registered nothing.

Again the bow gun was taken by the people of the crossroads village, restrung and reloaded. This time I met the man who had created it, a traveler from a land far to the west. He had crossed the mountains and settled in this hill village. He explained all that to me in pantomime.

He didn't explain why he had made the trip or where he had learned his art. I wondered if he may have been on the run, if making weapons from the bones of spirits wasn't regarded there as witchcraft. The Cell never tried to speak the language of Capricorn. It was too difficult, and not being able to talk to us made us more remote and mysterious to our worshippers.

And in Capricorn it was easy to dream and hard to concentrate. As I continued my recovery in the crossroads village, dying children floated in air above the faces of the trees. They grew farther away and dimmer as the nights in Capricorn grew longer.

Cancer and New York were not much on my mind as the seasons came around. That first winter Blood of the Goat was in short supply. The Caprii were generous, but they were not rich. The troubles that summer had destroyed property and interfered with farm work. The blood the Cell drank had come largely from these people and their farm animals. They were weak, and the winter was a hard one for them.

Those of the Feral Cell who stayed in the area split up and lived in widely separated villages where we each had our own cult. I roamed the territory around the crossroads in the long nights, and even on the gray snowy days. Where my domain touched that of another Cancii, we would meet sometimes, exchange a few words, leap like foxes in a mating dance, join in the air, roll in the snow, and part before dawn. Gary and some of the others slipped back to Cancer from time to time and found partners and pleasure. But I wanted to avoid that world for as long as possible.

Once on my travels I found a party of small children who

had gone out sledding and had gotten caught in a late-afternoon blizzard. They could see me through the swirling snow, and I led them back to their town. Toward the end of winter the Caprii could bring me only a little blood, and I didn't want to know how they had gotten it. So I rested for days and nights in the hollows of great skeleton trees, the shadows of caves, hibernating until spring.

Then my hold on Capricorn weakened, and even when grasping the bow gun I could feel myself sliding over the Transept. First the lost and mad and dying appeared, then the streets and buildings of New York. I heard cars and voices, and once I thought I heard Chris singing.

That reminded me of his last request, "Watch out for things." I tried to make a point of thinking of him every day. And that would remind me of all the others. Sometimes I would sing his old songs softly to myself and understand how hard a thing he had done in not forgetting me and the world where we had been born.

When the weather got better, Caprii from other villages brought blood offerings to the altar near the crossroads. When I was firmly bound to Capricorn again, I made a circuit of the settlements in my territory. As Cancer receded, my concern with that world faded. It wasn't so much that I came to understand how the rest had lost touch with our world, rather, loss of interest came gradually and seemed so natural that I didn't even notice it.

Gary went over the Transept often and persisted in bringing it up. "These people in New York who are in touch with groups around the country say that the Cell was out in the midwest. They have a message they wanted me to memorize in case I ever saw you again: 'Morgan sends greetings to Leal and says that the Cabal and Chase are riding in the southern islands. The Cell is going after them.'"

As he told me all this, Gary's face and eyes, elongated in this alien world, looked at me expecting some kind of answers. "Because of the weather being so freaky, a lot of places don't have enough food. They say the news isn't covering it, but that Mexico City is going bad."

That summer a few of the Feral Cell traveled with me through the countryside we were supposed to protect, showing ourselves in the villages and towns. Gary was left behind because of his leg and because he kept reminding me of home.

Caprii traveled with us, holding their blue lights aloft in the night. In the dawns and twilights they would mime the story of the rout of the Chase, the defeat of the Undying Cabal. We played ourselves, moving through the gray light, smiling and magical, carrying all before us.

Our audiences, wide-eyed, chanted songs as they watched, offered Blood of the Goat. Their altars sometimes had to be uncovered from where they had been hidden. In some places the Caprii had obviously forgotten us. I could see memories of the old ways stir in adult eyes, and find wonder in young ones.

We bore east as we traveled and found that the land fell, the woods thinned, towns grew more frequent, and the Caprii grew more surprised to see us. There for the first time I saw temples. They were large marble buildings with pillars in front and huge gold eagles on their roofs.

"The eagle is the sign of the state religion," Ruby told me. "Even here it hasn't much hold on people. The priests and local rulers are afraid to cross Mangin and the Cabal. They don't think the Feral Cell is anything more than a superstition."

Away from the hill country, the houses of the rich were sprawling and lightly defended. Some displayed the sign of the crab discreetly on their gateways. These people thought it wise to render some homage to Mangin. I wondered if their relatives were among the colonists who had gone upcountry to form the Chase.

Guard towers with uniformed troops stood along the roads and represented the civil authority. Despite their presence this did not seem a warlike land or people. So far down country, though, our Caprii escort traveled by stealth and had to buy the blood with which they fed us.

As we traveled down from the hill country, I detected

more and more signs of the sea. Gulls flew over the sparse shelter the Caprii found for us during the day; morning dew smelled of salt. One evening we came to a large town where they would not admit our Caprii, and I knew it was time to turn back. From a hill outside that place I saw infinite water, heard the distant rush of waves.

Far down the coast, the sky glowed.

"Sanctana," whispered Speedo, standing with me. "That's the biggest city around. We never got any kind of welcome there, and it looks like they got gaslight now."

"And because of miracles like that they tolerate Mangin," I said to myself. "And on Cancer they tolerate him because he made millions." Then I listened to the waves and squinted at the sky glow, feeling this world I barely knew changing in ways that threatened me. On our way back we cut northeast passing through different towns, finding a welcome as we went back upland.

I did certain things to make us more secure. Caprii scouts were sent down to the border of the hill country to watch for any moves toward us from the coast. The Cell patrolled our territory. The man who had made the bow gun was growing feeble. I had him instruct young Caprii from the village. From the treated sinews and dried bones of the Cabal they made more guns. They mixed acids preserved from those bodies, combined them with poisons from Capricorn, and made pellets. By that winter all of the Cell were armed as I was.

About other things I could do nothing. There is, I believe, no cancer in Capricorn. But something I thought might be polio ran through the hill villages in late summer. The Caprii as I saw them were beautiful and lived in an enchanted world. But the lives they led were hard and short. I would live as long as my wits let me. The wisest of them were all too mortal. In a way, Chris had died because they had to.

Gary wanted to bring more kids to Capricorn. I tried to explain that this was a subsistence economy, but I knew that wasn't why I resisted. That autumn I let him remain in the crossroads village, and I moved up to Capriole Castle. Offerings of blood were brought to me; Gary and the others of the Cell visited from time to time. But the ones for whom I could do nothing—the suffering Caprii and the doomed children floating in their hospital beds—I didn't have to see.

My most frequent visitors were Crabs bobbing on the edge of the Transept. I saw them especially at early dusks and late dawns, and they saw me. I learned enough to know that Mangin's Roost was both a shrine and a scandal. Only the most devout or desperate—assuming there was a difference—could see and be seen. Once I caught sight of Jason's friend Raul. Once I thought I saw B&T.

That was on an evening in late fall that reminded me of the Saturday when I had climbed Mangin's Roost and wrestled with the Beast. Looking out at lights coming on in the Caprii villages, I saw a ghost figure stumbling in Cancer. The face was grimy and the clothes unfamiliar, but as he looked up, eyes glazed, he saw me and half-smiled. I said the name B&T aloud, but at that moment he disappeared back into Cancer.

I searched for him that night. But I was full of blood and tightly bound to Capricorn. Telling myself it had been my imagination did no good; seeing him disturbed me. Other things I had suppressed welled up: the Beast was loose, and I had lost touch with Morgan and the Cell.

That made me range farther up-country in those last weeks before winter, following Morgan's route. I might have thought I was searching for trouble; in truth I was avoiding it. In the mountains where Caprii were tough but thin on the ground, I found the pass through which she had gone. They had no word of her there, and I sat under the stars, drank the blood offering of a tiny fur-trading settlement.

Then I knew the information I wanted could only be found in Cancer and that I had to return to New York. With great reluctance I went downhill in front of the first huge blizzard, traveling at night and on the overcast days. It was a useless trip unless, perhaps, it saved my life. Caprii met me just outside the castle. They covered their eyes with their fingers, imitating the masks of the Beast and the Undying Cabal; they moved their feet in march time to show me that soldiers had been there. The rest was too awful to be described. They led me back to the crossroads.

The flames were visible for miles in the dark. They were doused before I got there, but the grove was gone, the trees turned to charcoal, the piles of dry leaves to ashes. All of the houses in the village were looted and empty. The stone altar had been smashed. And on what had been the biggest tree, a long silver spike nailed Gary's corpse to Capricorn.

His head was gone, and they had taken his skin and the gun I'd given him. No doubt his blood had been drained as well. From what I learned from those Caprii who crept back to their homes, Gary had distracted the Cabal so that everyone else could escape. Even with his one leg he could have escaped, too, if he hadn't turned in front of the grove to get off one shot at the Beast: Mangin himself. The ones who had seen his death kept pointing to the spike and miming the firing of a rocket gun.

None of the kids from Cedars of Lebanon floated in the air that night. I wondered how much they had seen. Had Mangin murdered Gary and used his blood to go over the Transept right under their eyes?

The rest of the Cell assembled, and we set off after the raiding party. That's what it was, a raid from down the seacoast and a successful one. They had needed Blood of the Crab to get Mangin back into New York. They had found it, but they had no intention of holding the place just then. Those Cabalists who hadn't crossed the Transept into Cancer fled down country with their soldiers before bad weather and the Feral Cell could catch them.

Their luck didn't hold out. A blizzard had followed me down from the mountains, and light came late on that December morning. We caught them as they were breaking camp and led the chanting Caprii through swirling snow. That was where I saw demonstrated what the Caprii tried to show me. The Beast had provided the soldiers with guns that shot silver rods. One went over my shoulder as I leaped a fallen log to burn the face off the one who fired it.

We killed a lot of them, but all of the Cabalists escaped, so we captured no Blood of the Crab. The site of the battle was near the place the Cabal and Mangin once pitched their hunting pavilions and tried to show the Chase the wonders of Toys. Back in my old neighborhood, nothing stood between me and what I knew had to be done. The rest of the Cell continued the pursuit while I searched that area of Capricorn by night and refused all offerings of blood.

At first I saw very little. From the cave with the hollowed rock, I looked into Cancer and picked out only a solitary runner on the Esplanade and occasionally someone watching the water off the pier. The Supermarket had moved elsewhere. Though I had lost track of time, I knew New York was in the third millennium and wondered what else had changed about the city.

EPILOGUE

On the second night, I saw two whom I recognized: Mangin and Joan. Neither of them saw me. Mangin floated in a car traveling quickly away from Toys. His hair was dyed, and he wore dark glasses and what looked like a uniform, but I recognized him. Joan walked a few feet above the ground in a late evening. She wore dark glasses and a summer dress and stood out so clearly that I knew she was now desperate and sick enough to cross the Transept. Keeping an eye out for Mangin, I stayed close to her.

Shoots had grown around the stump of the tree that had been cut down the night of my attack on Toys. As I watched through that night, the world around Joan filled itself in. As it did, first my heart and then my body started to ache. And I wanted to turn and run away in Capricorn.

My house, hers now, was the same, and Toys still stood at the end of the street. But all the buildings between them, those roofs over which Chris and B&T and the dentists had climbed, were gone. Bulldozers were flattening an expanse of broken bricks and glass that glittered under the blazing sun. Those were the only two buildings on the block.

In all the time I watched, B&T never appeared. The image of a hunted figure climbing Mangin's Roost kept making me writhe. Joan only left the house to shop. A couple of times a package or letter was hand-delivered, and she had to answer the door. I noticed she carried a pistol when she did that. She rarely spoke on the phone, and no one came to visit.

Up on the second floor, the front room had been changed around, but the loft, my place, was exactly the same. In the evening Joan would go up there and play music. I found myself unable to leave the spot. I watched Joan until light made me seek shelter. Once or twice it seemed that she saw me. She would stare hard, shake her head, and cry. When that happened, I thought my chest would tear open.

As Cancer drew me closer, I felt the warmth of scorching summer, heard the noise of bulldozers at work. Caprii who brought a pouch of Blood of the Goat had trouble seeing me. On the third evening I stood on the tree stump, put my foot on the floor of the house, and was walking in Cancer.

The doors upstairs were open, and I felt myself trembling all over. Chris sang:

Instead I left as farewell
A fond note for him to see,
"Action shifts to Capricorn
When death drops in for tea."

I moved silently on the steps and through the front room. But Joan knew. She stood looking at the door as I came into the room. The last rays of the summer sun fell on her through the skylight. She tried to speak and couldn't. She tried to walk toward me and was unable to.

The ghost suitor had come to take her away. It had been Joan who had knocked the bow gun out of the hand of Billy Gee that first night how long ago. I felt the warmth of her body as I touched her. That night we would drink the Blood of the Goat. Caprii would dress her, and we would dance on the silver snow.

"Rob. We had to tell everyone it was you who died. People think Chris is going to come back and save us. It's all going bad. They round people up without warrants, without saying where they are. They took B&T, and Sandy can't do anything. They closed Bus Stop last year and arrested a lot of those kids. Raul got killed and nobody can find Jason." She gasped it all out as I nodded, knowing I would have to hear it all.

"Mangin is back. They say it's a cousin from South America who inherited the estate, but everyone knows. He bought all the buildings on the block. They threatened me if I don't sell this place. I can't even pay the taxes." She stopped talking and just cried. As she did, I looked over her shoulder and saw Chris. He stood on the stage of Bus Stop dressed in his Skin, proud and defiant. "They've been seizing all the copies of that video that they can find."

As I watched, I saw something move over the screen like a shadow, a pale form floating out of the club. And Chris on stage screamed out some lyrics, then pointed and said, "Robert Leal, my oldest friend in either world. We learned from each other when we were kids. I'm learning from him still. One way or another we will never forsake you."

I knew that I would have to be heard and to be seen in Cancer. And as a result I might have to die. But that night I would pass on to Joan what Morgan and Chris had given me: life long enough to know what life meant. I took Joan's hand and led her to the door as Chris sang of laughter and tears:

Betrayed and saved
By the Feral Cell
Killed and cured
By the Feral Cell.

Richard Bowes' first novel, *Warchild*, published by Questar in April, 1986, introduced the character Garvin, a teenage telepath who, after being kidnapped from his home in an alternate New York, was sold as a slave in Goblin Market to serve the dreaded riders. The riders used telepaths as their hosts to move across the timelines of time and space, enslaving as they went. However, Garvin will never be anyone's slave. . . .

The story of Garvin's revolt is continued in *Goblin Market*, to be published by Questar in Spring, 1988. The following is a preview excerpt of it.

The image of a boy with a Mohawk, looking into her mind and telling her *rise up!*, caught Alexis between a nightmare and a memory. The nightmare was one she'd had so often that it was wearing out. In it she came home from school on a soft spring evening, saw her whole family out back on the sun deck, went to the screen door and called to them so they could turn and show the gaping pits where eyes, noses and mouths should have been. Her flash of memory as the dream woke her was just as familiar, but it still went through her like a cold blade. Alexis again felt the anger and fear in the minds of the family that remained with her on the day she left home.

Awake, staring at the ceiling, Alexis tried to concentrate on the boy, to connect the ridge of blond hair and the slightly flattened nose to something in her life. Somehow she knew he was neither dream nor memory and that he was a powerful telepath about sixteen, her age.

Before telling her to rise up, he had called himself something but that had faded as Alexis, half asleep and trying to find an explanation, decided he was a member of some new band. What stayed with her longest was a trace of hope, of purpose, which she didn't know how much she needed.

Then Vasa the Keeper's mind scanned hers and Alexis was fully awake. Facing the blank bedroom wall, she remembered that there were no more new bands. And since Time and the Goblins had found her world, there was not an awful lot of hope. Automatically, the girl noted the way Vasa probed the mind of each apprentice in the Bates Motel, then the way she blocked all of their minds from her own before starting to scan the neighborhood. Alexis understood that Vasa had looked into the minds of the kids of the Breakfast Club for traces of the message. Now she was looking for the telepath who had sent it.

What? She could feel the others first ask the ones sleeping in their rooms, then the Club in general. *What is she looking for?* Stretching under a down comforter, she concentrated on the feel of it, the noise of the furnace coming on in the cellar and the sight of her breath puffing out into the cold November light, filling her mind with them. That was how she blocked the other apprentice telepaths from asking her, *Lex, what is it? What is she doing?*

Lex, as they called Alexis, knew that she could block any one of her fellow apprentices in the Breakfast Club or even most of them together. But that was not polite, nor wise, nor politically correct for those who served the Riders and the Goblins. But she also suspected what she had seen was treason and some of the kids would try to use that against her.

So Lex let them feel the cold as she threw off the covers and put her bare feet on the icy floor of the motel bedroom. She heard Johnny and Sandy next door give little screeches as they withdrew from her mind. From rooms further away she felt resentment, even hate. *Bitch thinks she is so fucking chill* Brent told Amy, forming the thought carefully.

Their feelings and the morning cold brought Lex unwelcome memories of her family on the day she had left home. That had been a morning in March just after the Goblins and Riders arrived in her world. Remembering that wasn't wise or politic either. But even a hint of thoughts like those was enough to keep the rest of the Breakfast Club at bay. Besides, as she shivered in a thick robe and waited for the shower water to heat up, Lex couldn't stop remembering.

She had found her mother, brother and sister squatting in front of the electric stove warming their hands. Mandy, her little sister, had been the easiest to take. Her mind was fully occupied with remembering the path of obedience. Lex caught the litany taught to quiet kids with no telepathic potential. "The child obeys the teacher, the teacher obeys the soldier, the soldier obeys the Keeper, the Keeper obeys the Rider, the Rider obeys the Goblin, the Goblin serves the Gods of the City." If Mandy could say that aloud for her teacher she would get a candy bar at lunchtime. Being seven had advantages: the capsizing world made less of an impact on you.

The minds of her brother Bobby and her mother brought pure pain. In moments like that when they first woke up, they felt their losses like wounds. So did Lex remembering them. She could again feel Bobby's alteration. Some surgery, some implants, some drugs and he was half-lobotomized and totally neutered. Lex recalled him shivering, not so much with cold as with delayed shock, pressing his hands against his chest to see if at the age of fourteen he had begun sprouting tits.

Her mother was the hardest memory. All she ever thought about was her family and what had happened to them. That morning she looked at her children, Mandy mumbling her lesson, Bobby cringing into himself, Lex standing in the doorway, staring at them with what seemed very much like horror. As always, she also thought of her husband. The image of her father tore through Lex's mind.

Or rather she caught a kaleidoscope of her mother's memories of him over twenty-three years, images old and recent, tender and profane, which Lex had learned to see but against which she couldn't yet close her mind. Lex, feeling the first steam of the shower water, stepping into the warm spray, realized now that six months later she would know how to block a non-telepathic mind from her own. But her training couldn't stop memories of the man who had gone into the city on the morning of the day when everything changed and never returned.

Lex felt Johnny wanting to tell her something. His mind brushed hers and withdrew when he realized she was thinking of her father. She remembered not so much the way he looked or sounded, as the calm way his presence felt. She remembered how they would both *know* something at the same moment, how ideas would crackle in the air between them.

Lex tried to get her broken family back into a corner of her mind. Her brother and sister had mumbled, "Bye," without looking at her and gone off to labor and school. Her mother worked as a truck driver, a position of trust. "You need a lift?" she had asked. Lex found herself unable to speak aloud and had formed an image of the brightly colored jitney that was going to take her away. Her mother hugged and kissed her and said, "All we can do is survive however we can. Remember that." Since then she had seen each of them and found that for her family she had become like a Keeper, a figure against whom there were no secrets and no trust.

Her family had just about faded in the steam when Vasa overrode Lex's defenses, entered her mind and told her, *Enough. Such introspection is useless indulgence.* Alexis toweled herself off, looking in the mirror, facing the big fashion question here at Bates Motel: what to wear in a conquered world? The answer was: anything you had ever seen anyone else wear and wanted to have.

Lex combed her hair in the mirror. At one time she had hated the nothing, dark-brown color her mother wouldn't let her change. Now she noticed how it stood out against a face that had gotten very pale and thin. Before Time and the Goblins, the mirror had brought her news, both good and bad, depending on her mood.

In the months at Keeper's School, days passed in which she didn't think of her looks. During that time, she had turned sixteen and her body began rearranging itself, trading baby fat for curves. At moments, Alexis could actually see herself becoming beautiful. Ironic, since those she would have wanted to impress were either gone or terrified of her.

Pulling her hair into a ponytail, she turned away from the mirror and got dressed. Now when she drew clothes out of supply she was mostly interested in fit. The night before she had found a blouse and remembered seeing it or one like it in a specialty shop. It was a handmade import and she thought briefly of ways to get someone to buy it for her as a present. Her mood had been sentimental when she saw it the night before. Putting it on that morning, Lex found it did nothing for her.

As Lex opened the door of her room, Vasa the Keeper entered her mind from quite a distance and exhibited the image of the boy with the Mohawk. *You recognize?* she asked. As a loyal servant of the Goblins, Lex didn't resist the Keeper looking into her memory of waking to the same image. She did notice, though, that the message troubled the older woman deeply.

Suddenly, the welter of erratic and half-trained minds of the Breakfast Club vied for Vasa's attention. *Hey Teach, I did it!*

What do you mean you did it? I did it.

Enough! Vasa seemed distracted. Lex almost thought she detected worry. *I am sure the Goblins and Riders congratulate Amy and hope for a healthy baby. Do your morning exercises. I will return shortly.* And Vasa broke contact.

Lex cast her mind after Vasa's in a probe. Her last six months had been spent learning to turn flashes of intuition and fragments of insight into disciplined telepathy. Probing Vasa was still like grabbing smoke. Once contact was broken, Lex couldn't find her teacher.

As she stepped into the hall, a tiny kid in an oversize sweater looked out of a door down the way. *Lex, I did it,* the girl told her, happy but apprehensive, patting the nonexistent bulge on her belly. *One of the servants just brought the test results.*

Congratulations, Amy. Lex put as much light and warmth into her thoughts as she could. *I hope the baby makes you happy,* she added. A woman in a grey coverall hurried down the hall past them carrying a pile of towels. The other kids took it more casually, but the servants embarrassed Lex.

A big, pudgy kid with acne wearing only a cowboy hat and jockey shorts appeared in the doorway behind Amy. #3 *for me,* Brent told her. *That leaves only you, bitch.* He formed the thought slowly, projected it crudely for all of the Breakfast Club to share. Groans came from other rooms.

The woman with the towels suddenly dropped them and began clapping her hands, doing a shuffle dance and saying "Congratulations!" over and over. The look of despair in her eyes made her celebration grotesque. Lex reached out and broke Brent's connection with the woman's mind. As she did, she caught fragments of the woman's memories: her name was Dee, she had been a paralegal before everything changed.

I am just trying to celebrate. You got something against happiness? came from Brent. The woman Dee, finding their attention diverted, grabbed the towels and scuttled away. Brent projected his image of himself: big, heroic, a harem behind him, the last jock in the last high school on Long Island.

Brent was a fool, too extreme to deal with. Lex turned her back and went down the hall. Brent probed after her, but she evaded his thoughts. He called out, "You don't let me do it, teacher will knock you up herself." He showed her a crude caricature of Vasa doing just that and gave a phony laugh. Brent really didn't understand that it was his stupidity not his joke that made her cringe and that Vasa was going to see the cartoon on every mind including his own.

Downstairs in the motel restaurant, now the dining hall, Culture Club played. Dinah and Samantha, Brent's first two conquests, two and three months into pregnancy, sat near the door and barely nodded to Lex. Johnny and Sandy sat toward the back. They had gotten their hair to the same shade and wore identical outfits of jackets with shirts hanging out and leg warmers over their pants. They watched quietly as she got coffee and orange juice from the counter. *Killer stud get to you Lex?* Johnny asked and motioned for her to sit with them.

Lex and Johnny had gone to high school right in that town, back when there was a town. That and both losing their friends during the Change had made Johnny her closest friend. When it turned out that making telepathic babies was a sure way of pleasing the Riders and Goblins, he suggested they try it. When Lex wasn't interested, it turned out that Johnny and Sandy thought and even looked so much alike that they made a cute couple. Sandy had gotten pregnant a month before.

Johnny stared into his bowl of cereal. Making sure no one else was probing them, he showed Lex an image of the boy with the Mohawk. *I was awake this morning and saw this. Vasa did too and took off after the one who sent that thought.*

And is still out looking, Lex added. She and Johnny were the two strongest telepaths in the group. By concentrating hard, they could communicate with each other and at the same time block other students' minds. The exercise was Inhale and Block; Exhale and Send. As they did, Sandy reached for a cigarette. Johnny took it out of her hand and crumpled it. *Who is he?*

"What are you two showing each other?" Sandy wanted to know.

Warchild. Johnny formed the image of the face. It fascinated him too. *The mind that sent that image said this is the warchild,* he told her. *Vasa interrupted before I caught the rest.* They broke contact with the same treasonous thought: whoever had shown that image wasn't a servant of the Goblins.